Unsinkable

ALSO BY NICOLE BRADSHAW
A Bond Broken (an original ebook)

Unsinkable

Nicole Bradshaw

SBI

STREBOR BOOKS

NEW YORK LONDON TORONTO SYDNEY

Strebor Books
P.O. Box 6505
Largo, MD 20792
http://www.streborbooks.com

This book is a work of fiction. Names, characters, places and incidents are products of the author's imagination or are used fictitiously. Any resemblance to actual events or locales or persons, living or dead, is entirely coincidental.

ISBN 978-1-59309-483-6
ISBN 978-1-4767-0391-6 (ebook)
LCCN 2012951572

First Strebor Books trade paperback edition May 2013

Cover design: www.mariondesigns.com
Cover photograph: © Keith Saunders/Marion Designs

10 9 8 7 6 5 4 3 2 1

Manufactured in the United States of America

For information regarding special discounts for bulk purchases, please contact Simon & Schuster Special Sales at 1-866-506-1949 or business@simonandschuster.com

The Simon & Schuster Speakers Bureau can bring authors to your live event. For more information or to book an event, contact the Simon & Schuster Speakers Bureau at 1-866-248-3049 or visit our website at www.simonspeakers.com.

Dedicated to my wonderful and supportive family, Neal, Savannah, Brandon and Dylan. They encourage me every single day. Also dedicated to the Laroche family, who inspired this novel, and to my mother, whom I miss very much.

Acknowledgments

Thank you to all who have supported me in my writing career. Some days I just wanted to throw my hands in the air and give up.

Thanks to my dad who held on to all my work and proudly passed it on to others. Thanks to Alicia for giving me some juicy single girl material to write about. Thank you, Sharon for passing my work to co-workers (even if it wasn't your taste in material.) Thank you Dawn for copying those manuscripts and sending them out, even way out in no-man's-land Texas. Steve, I'm counting on you to hook me up with some good sales! (There's a shiny quarter in it for ya!) Thank you to my publisher, Zane, for continuing to produce great work while still supporting new authors. Thank you Charmaine and all those at Strebor Books for your hard work. Most importantly, thank you to God for giving me a gift that has taken me a loooong time to realize. I still need work, but I'm gettin' there.

I'd also like to acknowledge the only black family on the Titanic. It was the Laroche family that inspired me to write this work of fiction in the first place.

"Sébastien, stop." I giggled. "My parents are in the house this time."

He grinned. His cold, chapped lips connected with my chin and then lingered on my forehead. "You so beautiful, Corinne," he whispered in broken English.

"Stop!" I commanded, this time more sternly. "We'll get into big trouble."

An hour-and-a-half ago, I had snuck out of the house and raced down to the barn to meet an overly eager Sébastien stretched out on a mounting haystack with a single strand of hay dangling between his lips. My parents thought I was secured in my twin bed, tucked away and fast asleep under the covers. If they found out, I would be in more trouble. This would make the second time Sébastien and I were caught together. The first time I had skipped history class to meet him behind the schoolyard, but when Mistress Gaielle spotted us, she immediately notified my parents and I was banished to scooping horse excrement for three weeks.

"What do you expect me to do?" Sébastien whispered. He blew tiny puffs of smoke in the frosty night air. "You've been my girl-friend for eight months, no? I thought you loved me."

"Of course I love you. I thought I proved that before."

"I need more."

Sébastien LeFevre was the most popular boy in our colored school. His fútbol ability outmatched any of those white boys in the bigger schools. They knew it, too. His superior athleticism was met with many enemies as well as admirers, one of them being Claudette Beauchamp. At the white schoolhouse, Claudette was one of the prettiest girls with her sun-kissed hair and naturally rosy cheekbones. She also had a corseted waist that was smaller than any girl's I had ever seen. I thought it a crime for a girl to be that petite. All women in my family, with the exception of Momma, had the same features—full bosom, thick waist and an even larger backside.

"I don't know," I told him. "But—" *But what?* I had no reason aside from the fact that I was scared, the same way I was scared to stand in front of my intermediate French class and not speak my native English, even though as a child, my French mother had taught me the language. As Momma had said, *"La confiance d'une fille vient de ne pas la façon dont elle regarde, mais par la façon dont elle parle"*—"A girl's confidence comes from not how well she looks, but by how well she speaks."

"You know I care so much for you, so please—" he begged, this time locking his fingers behind my waist and pulling me closer to him.

I didn't want to lose Sébastien the same way I had lost Arnaud six months ago or even Frédéric the year before that. Those were just boys. Now, at fifteen, I understood that I had to do more in order to keep Sébastien. If I didn't, plenty of girls waited for the smallest opportunity to be the one to keep his body warm in some cold, dank barn well after daylight.

We had only lived in Cherbourg, a tiny city just outside of Paris, for four years. Daddy had brought the family over from Canada in search of better job opportunities. Leaving Winnipeg and Emma, my best friend since grade three, was the hardest thing I had ever done. I had cried for three days straight. That was the last time I had shed a tear for anyone.

"Come on," Sébastien pleaded, suddenly serious. "We're both fifteen, Corinne. We need to be together as often as possible or else..." He pulled me closer. His dry lips lightly brushed against my cheek and his large hands fumbled around, finally resting on my shoulders. Slowly, he pushed me downward onto the haystack. The sharp edges of the hay poked me in the back.

"*Une belle femme*, you are, with your long hair and light-brown skin. Do you know how beautiful you are?" His voice was barely above a whisper.

My arms held my body upright as his strong hands pushed against my shoulders, trying to force me onto my back.

"Sébastien, wait. *Please.*"

Frustrated, he threw his hands in the air. His narrowed eyes seared right through me and I felt a cold chill travel down my spine. He was almost unrecognizable, but then he took a deep breath and softened his expression. He hesitated a moment, then calmly stood up and brushed the hay from his trousers. "I must leave."

"Don't leave just yet," I begged. "My parents are still in the house. They don't even know I'm out here. I can stay for a little while longer. There are other things we can do."

"I don't understand you, Corinne," he said, pulling up one suspender. "One minute you want me to leave and the next, you want me to stay. Which is it?"

"I just want..." I began, not sure of what I wanted. "I..."

He stood there staring at me, waiting for an answer. I had none.

"I understand."

"You do?"

He shook his head. "No, not really, but if you do not want to be with me tonight, then yes, I will wait for another time. I had only assumed you would take no issue considering last time, but if you say no, then no it shall be." He reached into his trouser pocket and pulled out a tiny leaf. He pinched the stem and held it up to my face, only inches from my nose. "This is for you, *ma belle femme.*"

"What is it?" I gently took it from his hand.

"It's a leaf from the tree we sat under," he said. "Remember? The first time we met?"

My heart sank. He actually remembered. I reached for the precious memento and held it close to my heart. It was so beautiful, not so much the crumpled-up dried leaf, but rather the symbol of our togetherness. I looked up to thank him, but he was already headed toward the barnyard doors.

"Where are you going?" I asked, pulling away loose strands of hay from my hair. "Please don't leave."

There was a very quick but uneasy hesitation before he responded, "I have to go to the market for *ma mère* before it gets too dark. I'll see you at the schoolhouse tomorrow, yes?"

"But—" Before I could protest, he passed through the barn doors and headed down the dirt drive.

I looked down at the leaf in my hand. I pulled myself up from the haystack and followed. I peeked out of the double wooden barnyard doors and when he was far enough down the road, I followed, making certain to remain at least ten paces behind as he strolled along the dusty path and toward the market. The strong winds carried his soft whistle and his strides picked up pace. Dark clouds partially concealed the half moon as thunder roared off in the distance.

It was about a quarter of a mile before he turned down a side dirt road and made his way through Fresca Fields, clomping down on every flower in his path. Without a care, he glided into the grocery store like a drink of cool water would down your throat on a steaming, hot, sunny day.

A feeling of relief washed over me immediately followed by a feeling of guilt. How could I have ever doubted his fidelity? Sébastien LeFevre was probably going to be my husband and the father of my children some day. It didn't feel right not trusting him. If I wanted to be with him, I had to believe he was faithful.

Before I turned to make the trek back up the dirt path and to my house, the tiny bell fastened to the store handle chimed. A shadowy figure entered the store. As the person entered the market, she turned. That was when I clearly saw the heavily made-up blue eyes.

It was Claudette Beauchamp.

Her blonde hair was tied in a ponytail and she wore a full, poufy skirt that somehow managed to add curves to her otherwise emaciated figure.

As Claudette disappeared further into the dimly lit store, I crouched behind a bush and patiently waited.

This has to be a coincidence, this has to be a coincidence, I kept repeating to myself. It had to be. Tears stung my eyes as I squatted in the dirt, brushing away the ants and bugs making their way up my skirt. Tiny droplets of rain started to sprinkle down.

I took the back of my hand and swiped at the falling tears. No way was I going to cry over the likes of Claudette Beauchamp, but the tears kept rolling and that frustrated me even more. The more I watched and waited, the angrier I became to the point where I wished I could snatch out every single strand of her hair and shove it down her boyfriend-stealing throat. And no way was that two-timing Sébastien going to get away with this either. I was going to make sure of that.

I glanced down at the bald dirt holes and realized I was yanking out patches of grass. The tiny droplets fell harder and faster and soon my hair was matted to my forehead. Tears continued to roll down my cheeks as I slowly stood up, preparing to gather up what dignity I had left and return home.

Before I had the chance, the store bell chimed once again and Claudette emerged. She wasn't alone. Her arm was locked in Sébastien's. Outside the store, they embraced passionately, with him giving her a long, wistful kiss as he had me only minutes ago. With the back of my hand I wiped my lips and then leaned over and spat out any lingering germs of his betrayal. *That cheat!*

The mixture of rain and tears trickled down my cheeks as I stomped up to both of them. They were so engrossed in their embrace they didn't even notice me. When Sébastien's gaze finally lifted, he saw me—fuming and with balled fists—standing in front of him. My heart pounded in my chest and I struggled to keep focus on the disloyalty in front of me without getting sick right there in front of the store.

He pulled away, practically shoving Claudette into the bushes. "What are you...I mean, I thought you—"

I lunged at a stunned Claudette, knocking her to the ground, which by this time had turned into a cold pile of mud. I smashed her face into the sludge. She reached around and grabbed my hair. With my left hand, I tugged at her blonde ponytail while with my right, I jerked at the sleeve of her white blouse. *Riiiiiip!* I pulled away, but I was still clutching the sleeve of her mud-stained blouse. I attacked again, this time preparing to strangle her with her own sleeve.

"*L'arrêter!*" Sébastien shouted. "Stop it!"

I felt his hand on my shoulder, but I shook it off. I bent down, reached for a handful of the cold, dirty mud and smeared it into his face.

"*Descendre de moi vous le gros cochon!*" Claudette screamed.

"I'll get off you after I make you choke on this!" With my extra twenty pounds, I could have strangled her with my bare hands. Instead I took her dirty, torn sleeve and shoved it into her mouth. We rolled around for a few minutes until Sébastien finally pulled me off her.

"*Prostituée sale!*" I screamed.

Claudette, still on the ground, sobbed as she brushed herself off and picked pebbles from her blonde mane.

"And you!" I whirled around to face Sébastien. "*Je vous déteste.*" With the same ferocious tenacity, I lunged toward him. My fingers were inches from his broad neck.

I felt warm palms pressed against my shoulder, holding me back.

"*Quittez s'il vous plaît mon magasin!*" Mr. Brousseau, the shop's owner, commanded. In heavily accented English, he repeated very slowly, "You. Kids. Leave. My. Store. Or. I. Will. Call. The. Police."

I turned and sprinted down the dark road, each step angrier than the last. As I ran, I listened for a second set of footsteps behind me.

There were none.

I continued racing through the fields and toward home. With each choppy step, I thought of revenge. *She* was not my concern anymore. Watching her squirm in the mud like the sneaky worm she was was enough. Like others, I had entrusted Sébastien with my heart, only for him to stomp all over it as if he was squishing a bug. I never asked for much from him, only loyalty.

"Lord, please get me away from here, *s'il vous plaît!*" I yelled, running faster and harder.

Tired, my fast run had turned into a jog and then into a hasty walk. Heated tears stung my eyes, making it even more visually difficult in the darkened night. I tripped on a stone, fell to the ground, got right back up and continued. Each infuriated step brought on a painful sting in my right knee. I looked down and saw a tiny trickle of blood.

When I reached the edge of my driveway, I hunched over and caught my breath. Each deep breath brought the cold evening air into my lungs. When I looked up, I saw two police cars at the top of the drive, parked side by side. Inside, I heard loud muffled voices. When I heard the sound of crashing glass, I pushed open the door.

Two brash-looking police officers in full uniform stood over Daddy, who was lying on the floor, bleeding from his mouth. One of the officers stepped on Daddy's neck while the other repeatedly jabbed at Daddy's leg with his large, shiny black shoe.

"Daddy!" I screamed.

"It's all right, Corinne!" Momma yelled from the corner of the room. She was crying hysterically while a police officer held her back.

"You live here?" one of the officers asked. He had an English accent and was fat. Not just a few pounds overweight, but extremely obese. He smelled like cologne and cigar smoke.

I wanted to shout, *Why else would I be here?* But instead, I nodded. "Yes, sir."

The two officers holding down Daddy folded their arms across their chests and glanced at each other. The one securing Momma in the corner released his grip and in French, he commanded her to leave the room. She did not comply immediately, so the irate officer grabbed her arm and forcefully removed her from the room. When they disappeared into the kitchen, the portly officer turned back to me.

"You a Negro, too?" His neck fat jiggled when he spoke. "Well?" He turned to the officer in the corner and mumbled something in a language I did not recognize. The other officers laughed.

Scared, I looked down at Daddy.

"What are you doing here?" the officer asked. "You don't look like a Negro."

My heart pumped faster. I glanced around at each one of the angry-looking officers. The one with his foot on Daddy's neck eased his hand toward the black, shiny gun in his holster. The other glared down at me with such hate, I thought he would have killed me right there if he had the opportunity.

"Does this man speak French?" the officer asked, motioning his head toward Daddy on the ground. "And if you lie, girl, I will see to it that both of you are punished severely."

I swallowed hard while glancing at Daddy. He blinked twice. "Yes," I mumbled to the officer.

"*Speak up, girl!*" his voice boomed.

"Y-y-yes, sir."

The officer narrowed his eyes. "He is a citizen then?"

Slowly, I nodded. In my mind I pictured the officer asking for proof of citizenship, which we did not have.

To my surprise, the burly officer did no such thing. Instead, he turned toward the men holding Daddy down and in his English accent said, "*Permettez-lui d'aller.*"

The men removed their feet. Daddy slowly stood up.

The first officer called back to the man in the kitchen holding Momma. One-by-one they shuffled out of the house, with the last officer slamming the door behind them. As soon as they were gone, Momma burst out of the kitchen. "Joseph, are you all right?"

"What happened?" I asked. "Why were the police here?"

"Corinne," Daddy said. "Please go to bed. I need to speak with your mother."

"Daddy—"

"Now, Corinne!"

I turned and headed toward my bedroom. Daddy escorted Momma into the kitchen. I could hear Daddy's voice whispering, "Those policemen will be back and next time, I don't think they are going to be as polite."

·❧·2·❧·

"They're all racist. Every last one of those officers," my older sister, Astrid, whispered to me from her twin bed on the other side of our tiny bedroom. "They still treat us like we're slaves. You should have seen the way those bastards barged in here like they owned the place." Her words were so angry, they scared me.

I tried hard to focus on her accusations, but in the darkness I could only spotlight the hatred in her eyes. Astrid was eighteen years old, only three years more than me, but she had seen and experienced plenty. Right before I was born, she told me she had been placed in short-term care with strangers under the claims that Momma was not fit and Daddy was unable to properly support his family. She believed the authorities were only called because Daddy was a Negro man married to a white woman. Although only three at the time, that was Astrid's first taste of racism and even at such a young age, she claimed she remembered every single detail.

Aside from Momma, of course, Astrid didn't care much for white people and kept them at a safe distance. Often she would say she was going to America to find a good Negro man and have babies so black, they wouldn't be able to be seen in the night. She stayed out in the sun all day, tending to the animals so she could gain more color to her skin. Astrid was lighter than I was and sometimes it felt as though she was jealous of my tanned skin. I would never tell her that I thought she could darn near pass for white if she wanted to. The only tell-tale sign of any black in her was her full lips, which she made sure everyone noticed. Last Christmas she rubbed on lipstick so bright, it blinded everyone within a ten-mile radius. In case anyone missed it—although I didn't see how that was possible—she made sure to pucker up like she was kissing a frog.

The door to our bedroom was shut, but we could still hear Momma sobbing and Daddy yelling those words he told us to never use or we'd be punished by God.

"I hate this place," Astrid whispered, staring up at the ceiling. "They treat Daddy like he's some dog begging for their leftover scraps." She leaned up on her elbows and turned toward me. "They must not realize that he is an educated Black man. He's probably smarter than those white police officers that held him down on the ground like some soiled rat." She flopped down onto her pillow and blew out a long, exasperated sigh. "I want to kill them all, just take a gun and shoot those pigs right between the eyes."

For another few minutes, she repeated, over and over, those forbidden words Daddy had warned us about. I closed my eyes and begged the Lord's forgiveness for both Daddy and Astrid. Eventually, I dozed off somewhere between Astrid's reference of those *porcs sales* and *bâtards de police*.

I wondered how long I had been asleep. It was still night because the sun was not shining through Momma's homemade, white translucent curtains hanging from our bedroom window.

"Astrid," I whispered.

There was no answer.

"Astrid," I whispered again, slightly louder.

Still no answer.

I hopped up and tiptoed over to her bed. Her mattress was tattered and dropped in the middle—just the way she liked it. I looked down at a hump in the bed that was completely covered from head to toe. "Astrid," I whispered, jabbing a finger into her.

Something was strange. Before getting fired, Astrid had helped out at Jor'dan's bakery in downtown Cherbourg, constantly binging on treats of puff pastries or hot buttered croissants. The mound lying before me was not fleshy enough to be her.

I flipped off the covers. As expected, the mound was a pile of pillows. Astrid was gone. That explained the cool draft coming from the window. She had left it open after sneaking out again.

In a panic, I ran to the bedroom door, careful not to step on the squeaky board right in the center of the room. I pulled the door open just enough for a one-eyed peek. I heard Daddy's footsteps trudging against the wooden floorboards, so I quickly, but quietly, shut the door and headed back to my bed. In my haste, I stepped on the squeaky board. *Crreeeeeeeekkkkk!* Daddy's footsteps stopped. So did mine.

In my nightgown, I stood frozen in the middle of the floor, quieter than a tiny church mouse, and listened. If I made the slightest move, Daddy would be in the room faster than a rooster at a cockfight, and he was definitely not in the best of moods tonight.

"What are you doing?" Astrid whispered as she squeezed herself through the half-opened bedroom window.

I lifted my finger to my lips. "Shhhhhhh." The cold air rushing in from the opened bedroom window quickly dried the beads of sweat forming around my hairline. Realizing what happened, Astrid stopped in her tracks. She listened for Daddy's heavy-laden steps. We stood frozen, wondering who would get the hide first if caught. The last time Astrid snuck out of the house, she had asked me to lie for her. "Tell Daddy I went to bed early," she had told me. Well, I did and when Daddy found out, we both got the hide so hard we could not sit down for two weeks.

I turned back toward the door. The footsteps had stopped. No sooner than we had taken a deep breath did the footsteps begin again, this time much more quickly.

Seeing no way out of this, I raced toward Astrid who was stuck with one leg in and one out of the window.

"Come on," I whispered in a panic. "He's coming."

"I can't," she told me, jerking back and forth. "I'm stuck."

Desperate, I grabbed her by the elbow and pulled hard. "Have you gained more weight?" I asked between gasps of air.

"You're one to talk."

The footsteps were still coming. Any minute, Daddy would be at the bedroom door with a large switch in his hand, ready to make our worst nightmares come true.

"Come on." I gave one last tug.

She dislodged and we both fell to the ground.

Kaathuddd!

Quickly, she hopped up and jumped into her bed, clothes on and all. I jumped into mine. As soon as both of us were safe, our bedroom door flung open. The hallway light shone through my tightly closed eyes.

Surely, he had to have heard the squeaky floorboard and if by chance he fell deaf for ten minutes and missed it, he had to have heard the struggle and the thud of his two not-so-tiny daughters.

There was an uneasy silence. I listened to Daddy's deep, belabored breathing and in that time, it crossed my mind to open my eyes and confess everything in the hopes that he would go easy on us. Instead, Daddy took another deep breath and then said, "Girls, get up. You've got to start packing. We're going back to Canada."

❧ 3 ❧

Momma looked so peaceful as she quietly rinsed a tomato under the running faucet. She had a habit of softly humming to herself, which I liked. With her long, sinewy fingers, she gently scrubbed away the garden dirt, placed the tomato back into the basket situated on the kitchen counter, and then grabbed another. She glanced back at me sitting at the kitchen table, watching her, and gave a gentle smile.

"Do we have to go back to Canada?" I asked.

She handed me a tomato. I diced it up and placed the pieces into a container of water for her to boil.

"*Mon petit chérie,*" she wiped her hands on the apron fastened to her waist. "You'll miss this farm, won't you? And then there's that young man."

"Who?"

"That lovely boy who plays *fútbol* I see you talking to." She handed me another tomato.

I wanted to shout, *That lovely boy is a monster who supposedly cares for your daughter and, it would seem, every other girl he lays his eyes upon.* In fact, I had never even heard him utter the word "love" before, especially when it came to me. It was always, "I care for you" and "I think you're special" but never the word, "love."

I shook my head. "I don't think we're destined to be together, Momma." I felt a lump forming in my throat as I blinked back tears.

Momma's eyes softened. "Oh, what happened?"

I shrugged. "I tried, Momma, but being with Sébastien is so difficult. It shouldn't be that way, should it?"

"Ahhh," Momma said, "*le garçon trichant*."

"The cheating boy?"

Momma nodded as she dried her hands with a towel and sat down next to me. "Every young woman encounters the boy who cannot commit. Looks like you found yours."

"Why do they do that?"

Momma peered over her shoulder. When she was sure we were alone, she whispered, "I'll let you in on a little secret. The man before your father was the same way—a cheat."

"Really?"

"Yes. Adrien was a true ladies man, so good-looking and desirable any girl was fortunate to be with him. But I was the lucky one he chose to deflower."

"Really?" I asked again. Momma had always told me stories of when she was a young girl. This was the first I had heard about a boy named Adrien.

Momma nodded. "Yes. And then as soon as our love affair began, it was over. Two days later I caught him with an older, more experienced married woman who lived only a few blocks down the road."

"How did you catch him?" I asked.

"Very simple. I followed him one evening and watched as he met her in the field. Then, on my bike, I followed them back to her house. Her husband was a fisherman and frequently out of town. There they spent the evening. With a broken heart, I left and went to the store to get a kerchief. That's when I met your father. He had seen me crying and offered to walk me home."

When she saw my confused expression, she smiled and explained, "Corinne, dear, it simply means that the next man you encounter will be your soul mate. You will be attached to him forever—even through death—like your father and me."

I laughed at how silly she sounded.

Her face suddenly turned serious. "Oh, no, no, no, *ma chère fille*. Never mock fate. It's true." She went back over to the kitchen sink, grabbed another tomato and began rinsing. "You'll see."

"Do we have to go back to Canada?" I asked again. "I don't want to have to start over at another school." I paused, deciding on how much I wanted to divulge. Finally, I said, "I won't know anyone and all the Negro kids will say I'm white and all the white kids will say I'm black."

Personal experience says this is so. Three-and-a-half years ago, before becoming affluent in the French language, another colored classmate of mine, Louise Laurent, called me *une fille blanche* in front of the entire class. For days, everyone snickered behind my back. With my French still being a little rusty, it took me a day or so to figure out what the name meant and that was only because Nicholas Bertrand shouted, "Look, it's the white girl!"

The very next day I had felt very much justified in reaching into Louise's sack and ripping out the page in her book that contained our housework. She received a zero for that day and every time I thought about it, it made me smile.

"Corinne, why are you smiling so wickedly?" Momma asked.

"No reason."

"I know it's *très difficile*," Momma said with sympathy in her eyes. "But you cannot let people tell you who you are. You have and will always be strong, Corinne. Never doubt that." It was sometimes hard to believe Momma had been living in English-speaking countries for so many years. Her French accent was as pronounced as it had been the day she met Daddy—at least that's what he tells us.

"That's just it," I complained. "I'm not strong…compared to Astrid anyway."

Momma laughed. "Astrid? Your older sister has always been made of *le béton*, but trust me when I tell you that underneath all of that stone, there is a soft, warm heart. Now you, you're different. You have the strength of an army, but your emotions are more delicate than the petals of a flower. There's nothing wrong with that, my dear, it shows your humanity. Listen to me, no one is going to treat you differently because of your mixed race. And if they do—" She rolled up a dishtowel and snapped it into the air. "If they do, I'll burn their little hides," she said, pronouncing the word *hides* like *heeds*.

Her beautiful, infectious smile made me grin. Momma's heart was so pure and I was jealous I wasn't born that way. She had never walked to the schoolyard with the vicious taunts from white classmates because of skin color. I didn't necessarily want to be the one to let Momma in on the secret that these things still happen. The days of whipping enslaved Negroes may have been over, but the mentality was still there, lingering in the atmosphere like the foul stench of rotting fish.

"You're stronger than you think," she said, wrapping her tiny arms around my broad chest. "I wish you understood that. You just haven't had that chance to prove your strength because you've been under our wings for so long. But that time will come soon, dear Corinne. You'll see."

I pulled back from Momma's bear hug. Being at least two inches taller, I looked down at her. "*Je vous aime*," I told her.

She gently pecked the side of my face with her lips. They were dryer than usual. Her tiny hands were extra thin and pale and shook quite noticeably. Softly, she whispered, "I love you, too. Please never forget that."

❧{ 4 }❧

"What do you want, Sébastien?" My arms were folded across my heaving chest like a drill sergeant.

Earlier during class when he had begged to meet in the barn that evening, I was disgusted with myself for being secretly happy at his request. I wanted to be angry, but whenever he smiled, all thoughts of Claudette and his infidelity dissipated into thin air. Together with him now, my words remained harsh, but my heart melted inside with every word he spoke.

"I love you, Corinne. You have to believe me."

"What did you say?" I asked.

"You have to believe me."

"No," I said, shaking my head. "Before that."

"I love you?"

My heart fluttered, but I pushed away, pretending his words meant nothing. It was my false anger that meant nothing. The truth was, I was shaking. This was the first time he had told me he loved me. *What was I supposed to do now?*

"What about Claudette?" I asked.

"What about her? You are the one I want to be with...forever." He bent down and kissed me. His kiss was so soft, so gentle. It felt like someone tickling my lips with a sparrow's feather.

"There's something I need to tell you," I said. Before I could, he reached around and locked his fingers behind my back, pulling me closer—so close I could detect the faint smell of mint leaves on his warm breath.

"You really love me?" I asked.

"Of course and I want to show you how much I love you right here." He started pushing me down toward the ground.

"Wait!" I shouted. "I need to tell you something first."

The barnyard doors swung open with hurricane force. My entire life flashed before my eyes. It had been months since the last time I had been caught with Sébastien. This must have been God's way of punishing me for sneaking out to be with him again.

"I thought I saw you creep in here." Standing at the door, Astrid grinned with a smile so broad, I thought it would crack her face wide open.

"Get out!" I yelled. Then I remembered our parents were only a few feet away inside the house. I lowered my voice. "Leave us alone."

"Hello, Sébastien." Still grinning, Astrid crept into the barn, not once taking her eyes off him. "I'm surprised you've gotten this far with the little prude. I have to hand it to you, it takes a special boy to get my sister in the barn after daylight." She shifted her attention back to me. "What was that other boy's name you used to meet in the barn? You know, the tall, skinny one with the big ears."

"Get out, Astrid, or else," I warned.

"Or else what, dear sister? Or else you're going to yell and tell Daddy that I followed you? Go ahead. I'd love to see you do it.

I'm sure Daddy would love to catch you in the barn with a boy."

She was right. "Just get out, please," I whispered.

Her gaze remained fixated on Sébastien, who stood in the hay, shifting nervously back and forth. "Did my sister tell you she's leaving tomorrow?"

Sébastien raised his brow. "Leaving? Where are you going?"

"I tried to tell you," I stammered. "You kissed me and—"

"You *didn't* tell him?" Astrid said with faux surprise. "How could you not tell your boyfriend you're going back to Canada and never going to see him again?"

He frowned. "What is she talking about, Corinne?"

"I don't have to stay in Canada," I told him. "I'm just going back for a little while."

"And how do you plan on getting back here?" Astrid asked. "Is there something you're not telling me?"

"Shut up!" I yelled, not caring if Daddy heard or not.

I wanted to tell Sébastien this could only be a temporary thing... if I had something to come back for. The words wouldn't come. The warmth rose up into my cheeks as feelings of confusion took over. I was upset about Sébastien, but at the same time, I wanted to squeeze the life out of my sister with my bare hands. I imagined my fingers wrapped around Astrid's fleshy neck and her turning even paler than she already was. I had saved her from Daddy's wrath several times when she snuck out of the house. *Why was she doing this to me now?* She was the evilest person to walk this earth.

"I guess you both keep secrets, don't you?" Astrid asked. Like the cat that devoured the canary, she had a secret. Her eyes narrowed and the corners of her mouth turned upward.

I looked at Sébastien, waiting for his response. He kicked at the hay and kept his mouth shut.

"What are you talking about, Astrid?" I finally asked.

"I'm surprised he didn't tell you, but then again, this isn't something you'd want to tell your girlfriend."

"What are you talking about?" I was becoming impatient.

"Moments ago, your devoted boyfriend came from the bushes with the one and only Claudette Beauchamp." With her narrowed eyes, Astrid stared him up and down. "Now, I'd be inclined to think that perhaps they were only bird watching, but when she hopped up from the bush and her blouse was undone and he was buttoning up his trousers, I said to myself, 'Something is not right here.'" She turned to me. "Hmmm, now what do you suppose they were doing in those prickly little bushes all alone?"

"I, I can explain." He didn't need to say a word. His expression told all.

"I'd like to see you try," Astrid said. "Go ahead, explain it. Were you sewing a button on her blouse or maybe Claudette is the trouser inspector and she—"

"Shut up, Astrid!" I exclaimed, still staring into Sébastien's cheating face. He couldn't even get a word of explanation out before I reached down, picked up the first thing within my grasp and tossed it at him. The handful of hay landed right in his face.

"You have to do better than that," Astrid said, disappearing behind the barnyard door. When she returned, she pitched a medium-sized rock that landed at my feet. "Try that."

I reached down and picked it up, preparing to crack open Sébastien's head with it. As I drew back, Sébastien sprinted toward the door. Astrid stuck out her foot and he went crashing to the dirt. He pulled himself up and dashed out the barnyard doors and down the driveway. He tripped again but this time over a sticky bush. It ripped a piece of material from his suspendered trousers and left a gaping hole. He hopped up and continued his sprint without even a glance back.

"Sorry about that," Astrid said, still looking after him. "But I thought you should know before you get all upset about having to leave that cheat."

With much skepticism, I glared at her, hoping words weren't necessary.

"What?" she asked. "I know I was cruel, but—" She shrugged and then tiptoed toward our bedroom window. I followed. "Go in this way," she commanded. "Daddy's still up." She raised the window and I climbed through.

4 days until…

·❧[5]❦·

*T*he next morning had started nippy but then warmed up a few degrees by mid-afternoon. By the evening the temperature had dropped several degrees, creating an unpleasant chill. From the docks, I stared up at the ship in total disbelief that something so big could float on water. From the tip of the bow all the way down to the stern, it had to have been as big as the city of Cherbourg itself. Even the ship's name printed boldly on the side, *Titanic*, gave way to indestructible images. The ship resembled those colossal iron tankers in Daddy's old engineering manuals, only this one was more decorative. To those already on the ship, we must have looked like tiny ants climbing aboard.

The evening of April 10, 1912 was a melancholy one. Wrapped in a shawl, I stepped onto the large gangway and glanced back at the onlookers waving good-bye to their families. It saddened me to leave, seeing as I had come to love the town, especially in the spring when the fresh scent of honeysuckles floated through the air or during the cold winter months when Cherbourg came alive with the lightest coating of snow. Cherbourg had been my home for over four years and I was going to miss it.

"Have you seen Sébastien?" Astrid asked.

"Was I supposed to?" I replied curtly. "The only way I would want to see him is only to spit in his face."

Astrid smirked. "Good. I was afraid he'd show up and beg you to stay behind. Knowing you and your incredible sense of gullibility, you probably would. Then you, he and Claudette would live happily ever after."

I fought hard to ignore her, but she made that feat nearly impossible. Every time we took another step aboard, she'd giggle and whisper Sébastien's name, adding what a fool I had been for trusting him in the first place. Her attitude was precisely the reason I was going to carry what had happened at the store the other night with Claudette and Sébastien to my grave.

"You sure do know how to pick 'em," she said smugly.

That's how Astrid was; one minute she called herself helping like last night in the barn, but then it always seemed as if there was an evil motive behind her actions. She would hold open a side window for me to sneak through but would then threaten to tell Daddy about it the next day. Last night's motive is taunting ammunition today.

"Keep them in close proximity. That's what I do," she said. "That way you always know what they're doing. Believe me, boys are always guilty of something."

Tired of listening to her incessant taunting, I blurted out, "Too bad we're going back to Canada. Now you'll never be able to marry an American boy and have those black-as-night children you're always rambling on about. You'll be stuck in Canada forever with twelve little yellow kids and a husband who drinks so much he'll pass out every night, leaving you to tend to your insufferable brats."

She drew back her fist and slugged me hard in the shoulder. "I will not." She glanced back over her shoulder. When she thought it safe, she whispered, "For your busybody information, when the boat docks in New York City, I'm getting off."

"You are not."

A sneaky smile formed across her brightly painted lips. "I am. As soon as the ship stops in America, I'll get off."

"You are not," I repeated.

"Am to."

"Are not."

"Am to."

"Are not!" I yelled.

"Girls," Daddy said as we continued up the gangway. "I will not hear this bickering during the entire trip."

With a satisfied grin on her face, Astrid passed through the ship's entrance. I stared hard at the bun fastened tightly at the nape of her annoying neck and secretly wished I could rip it out.

My thoughts drifted to this morning before we left. I had hugged Momma good-bye. As she always did when I left for school, she kissed my forehead and then gently whispered that she loved her little butterfly. "*Je vous aime mon petit papillon.*"

"When did you say Momma was coming to join us?" I asked Daddy.

Daddy scratched his head. "Shortly," was his curt reply.

"Will she come in a few months after you find a job?" I asked, remembering last evening's conversation.

"Sure, I suppose," he answered. "Now hurry along. We're holding up these good folks."

I had cried all morning long. My heart ached thinking about being without Momma for months. Astrid, as usual, was only worried about herself, thinking what *she* was going to do back in Canada or how *she* had to cope with this new change. The funny thing was, she complained the entire four years in Cherbourg.

"I hate it here," she would whine every day on the farm. "It's boring and I'm getting fat because there's nothing to do besides eat." After hearing one too many complaints about her weight, I told her maybe it was the overeating of Jor'dan's pastries that was making her backside spread, not the boredom.

Astrid was a selfish girl and I didn't much like her for that.

"Girls, come on," Daddy said, "you're lagging behind."

An instrumental rendition of the tune "Lead Kindly Light" played softly in the background as passengers, one by one, filed onto the ship. At the very top of the gangway, gentlemen in seamen's uniforms greeted men with a firm, welcoming handshake. Women and children received a brief peck on the cheek.

Halfway up the steep slope, the ship's horn blew. I wanted so badly to run back down onto the docks and stay with Momma. When the gangway pulled back, I knew it was too late. I was here on the Titanic and there was nothing I could do about it.

When we reached the top, my father was greeted with the handshake, and Astrid and I were both met with a peck from a uniformed seaman—only he was much younger than the others that stood about him.

"Welcome, ladies," he said. He bowed his head and gave a gracious, warm smile.

"Welcome yourself," Astrid said with an embarrassing hint of inappropriate suggestion.

I blushed. My gaze fell to the ship's plush entranceway carpeting.

Upon first inspection, the ship was beautiful. A crystal chandelier with tiny pieces that glistened like diamonds in a midnight sky hung directly above our heads. Everything about this ship was extravagant. To the left were two glass double doors that looked to be ten feet tall with the words, *First Class Dining Area*, engraved in gold on the front. To the right, narrow, never-ending corridors led toward the staterooms. According to the signs, the first hall was for first-class, the second, for second-class. The narrowest of the three halls further off to the right led down a second flight of stairs. I gathered that to be third-class.

"Where is our room?" Astrid asked. "It's been a long day and I want to lie down."

Daddy looked down at the ticket in his hand and then nodded toward the three corridors. "I think the rooms are down that way. Why don't you go find your stateroom and we'll meet up for dinner."

Astrid and I looked at each other. I assumed she was thinking the same thing I was. "Find our stateroom?" she finally asked. "We're not staying together?"

Daddy reached into his pocket and pulled out two sets of tickets. "The surprise is, we sold the farm!" he exclaimed. "We're going back to Canada with the money from the sale."

Thinking it was some sort of joke, Astrid and I stared at him, waiting for the punch line. But Daddy insisted it was true. The farm had been sold and according to him, at a great price. Astrid jumped and squealed with excitement right there in the hall. "Oh, Daddy, that's great! Can I go shopping when we get back to Canada? I saw a lovely dress downtown that would look so good on me, but since we didn't have the money, I couldn't buy it. If they have the same one in Canada, can I please buy it, Daddy, *please*?"

My perception of the situation was slightly different. "But, Daddy, what happened to Momma? I thought that was why she was staying in Cherbourg? If you sold the farm, where will she stay?"

"Oh, honey." With one arm, Daddy pulled me close while securing the other around Astrid. "Let's not talk about that yet.

Let's enjoy ourselves. We're on the Titanic—the greatest ship ever built. This is her maiden voyage. Do you know we're making history as we speak?"

When he saw the look of concern still on my face, his excitement softened. "Corinne, your mother is fine. She can stay with her family for a while."

"But she hasn't talked to her family in years."

Daddy sighed. "Once we're further into the trip, I'll explain it all to you. I promise."

The wearisome calmness of his voice did nothing to ease my questions. "I don't get it," I challenged. "Why wouldn't she be here with us, on this trip?"

Daddy's lips tightened. He cocked his head to the side and with his most serious expression, he slowly said, "I told you everything will be explained at the proper time. This is not that time."

On several occasions, I coaxed information out of Daddy with one or two sugary sweet, *Please, Daddys*. If he was real stubborn I could give him the wide eyes, but apparently, now was not the time to push. Taking heed to his warning, I kept my mouth shut, but this conversation was definitely not over.

"Are we going to sit at the Captain's table for dinner tonight, Daddy?" Astrid asked.

"That's only for first-class passengers. We have second-class tickets."

"Second-class?" Astrid sulked. "But the sale of the farm should have given us enough money for first-class. Why are we stuck in disgusting second-class? We don't have enough money from the sale?"

"Would you prefer third?" I asked, disgusted with her behavior.

Astrid glared in my direction. "Would you prefer a swift kick in the—"

"Girls, please," Daddy groaned. "That's just how things work around here. Don't worry, we have enough money." He handed Astrid one ticket and me the other. "Now go find your stateroom and enjoy yourselves, girls. This is a once-in-a-lifetime opportunity." He grabbed his bags and headed down the hall.

Astrid rolled her eyes. "It's only a great opportunity if you're rich and white, otherwise, we might as well be stuck in the steam room rowing with the rest of the slaves." With that, she snatched her bags and trudged down the hall in the opposite direction. I picked up my bag and followed.

As soon as we reached the cabin and opened the door, Astrid began complaining. It took all of ten seconds before she said, "This room is ridiculously small. I bet the staff has bigger quarters than this."

I looked around. The room was small, but to me, more in a cozy-type way. The carpeting was sturdy and rather industrial-looking, but the fabric patterns and furniture styles were up-to-date and clean. The small single beds were situated so that one was harnessed over the other.

"There is no way I am at the top," Astrid said as she flopped her suitcase on the lower bed.

"I think it's rather quaint," I admitted.

"You would." She went over to the closed bathroom door and opened it up. "And this bathroom is so small."

"I had heard some second-class cabins didn't even have private bathrooms," I told her. "Consider us lucky."

She plopped down on the edge of the bottom bed and flipped off her shoes. "You see a bright side to everything, don't you?"

"I try."

She laughed. "Well, I don't know about you, but I'm tired. I can't seem to keep my eyes open."

"Don't you want to see the ship?" I asked. "How can you be tired? It's not even nine o'clock.."

"Why don't you see the ship and tell me all about it in the morning?" She pulled up the bed sheet and closed her eyes. "If there's anything interesting, it'll be there tomorrow."

I picked up my suitcase and rested it on the upper bed, deciding like Astrid, to rest for the evening. Tomorrow was a brand-new day.

3 days until…

···❦❘ 6 ❘❦···

"*I*'m bored." Astrid bit her fingernail down to the nub, spat it out on the ship's deck and then went on to the next nail. "Who suggested we tour this ridiculously oversized ship? Who cares?"

Shhhhhhh.

The uniformed man stood at the front of a crowd of about thirty passengers, giving details on the ship, which apparently Astrid had no interest in. Others, including Daddy and I, seemed to be quite fascinated.

"The Titanic is constructed by the shipbuilding firm of Harland and Wolff at their Queen's Island Works in Belfast. This glorious ship is eighty-two feet, eight inches long, ninety-two feet, six inches wide and one-hundred-four feet high with nine decks and boiler rooms and weighs forty-six thousand, two-hundred thirty-eight tons. This is the only ship that is boasted as being 'unsinkable.'"

"Did you hear that, girls?" Daddy asked. "This ship is unsinkable."

"I'm not feeling well," Astrid complained. "I think I'm seasick. I spent the entire morning stooped over the sink. "

"Daddy," I whispered, "make her be quiet. I'm trying to listen."

"A few years ago the Construction of the Olympic and Titanic began in Belfast, Ireland at the Harland and Wolff shipyards. The Olympic successfully launched October twentieth in nineteen-ten. In June of last year, the Olympic made her maiden voyage."

"Daddy," Astrid whined, "I'm bored, and this rocking motion is upsetting my stomach again. Can we please go back to the state-room?"

One of the tour-goers shot us a look. "Shhhhhhhh."

"Oh, be quiet yourself!" Astrid shot back.

"Astrid, if you want to go back to the room, that's fine," Daddy finally said. "I'll check in on you later."

"Fine." Astrid turned on her heels and stomped off.

My attention turned back to the uniformed seaman. He wasn't alone anymore. In a fully pressed uniform, the boy that had greeted us on the gangway yesterday evening stood beside him. He stood atop a small platform and from the back of the crowd, I was able to see him quite clearly. He spoke in a pronounced British accent as he explained details of the ship.

"An ocean liner is usually a ship designed to transport people from one seaport to another along regular long-distance maritime routes according to a schedule. Liners may also carry cargo, and may sometimes be used for other purposes like pleasure cruises or as troopships. Cargo vessels running to a schedule are sometimes referred to as liners. The category does not include ferries or other vessels engaged in short-sea trading, nor dedicated cruise ships where the voyage itself, and not transportation, is the prime purpose of the trip."

"This young man seems to know plenty about this ship," Daddy said. "I wonder who he is."

I nodded, barely hearing anything Daddy said. I was intrigued by the boy's confident mannerisms. When he spoke to the crowd, he made eye contact and occasionally smiled while delivering his rehearsed speech.

"Later this afternoon," the boy said, "we dock in Roche's Point in Queenstown, Ireland. Photos of this grand ship will be taken and I would be honored if all of you could attend the ceremony." He glanced in my direction.

"Now if you'll follow Mr. Richards, he will continue the tour," the boy said.

Eager, Daddy walked up ahead. Being an engineer, he found this fascinating. I did as well, but the glaring sun slowed me down until I found myself at the end of the pack, walking alongside two older ladies and a heavyset gentleman.

"I hope I didn't bore you."

I whipped around. It was the boy who was aiding the tour.

"I've given this spiel so many times in front of schoolchildren, however, this is my first time in front of actual passengers. I hope it wasn't boring for you."

"Not really," I told him. "I'm only lagging behind because of the sun. The tour is quite fascinating," I reassured.

"Good, then." He winked. I blushed. He lowered his voice and then said, "If my uncle hadn't insisted that I give this dreary tour, I suppose I could be doing something more interesting…like spending time with someone whose company I'm sure I would enjoy. However, I do have some free time later. Would you care to join me?"

"For what?"

"What would you fancy?"

"Mr. Smith," Mr. Richards, the older gentleman, called from the front of the group. "Will you please do us the honor of detailing the bridge?"

"Of course," he called back. He turned his attention back to me. "Pardon me." With his chin held high and chest poked out, he headed toward the front of the growing crowd. He hopped up onto the platform and began his explanation of the ship's bridge.

"Such a knowledgeable young man," the lady next to me whispered. "He'd be perfect for my granddaughter."

Feeling more effects of the sun, I decided to find Astrid. I stepped out of the group and headed back to the stateroom.

"Pardon me," the young man called from the head of the crowd.

Was he speaking to me?

"You there, young lady."

"Me?"

Like a tennis volley, the onlookers watched the back-and-forth dialogue with interest.

He nodded. "Yes, you. Will you be joining us this afternoon when we dock at Roche's Point? I would love to see you there. We can go for a quick dip, that is, if you enjoy the cold."

The passengers laughed.

With a face I imagined as red as a cherry tomato, I said, "I, uh, I don't know. Besides, I'm not a great swimmer."

"Not a great swimmer" was an overstatement. The last time I had even attempted to swim was years ago as a child. Momma had tried to teach me, but I had kicked and screamed for hours until, sick of the noise, she finally gave up. I knew my tantrum would someday snap me on the rear like a rattlesnake in heat and I would regret not learning.

He smiled. "I hope to see you there." His attention turned back to the crowd. "I hope to see all of you there."

I quickly turned and darted off before he had the opportunity to score match point. Further down the ship, I took a seat on a lounge chair, where the sun's beams warmed my skin.

"Do you mind if I have a seat next to you?" a woman asked. She reached down and pulled up her bustle a few inches before plopping into the seat next to me. "The name's Brown, Margaret Brown."

"Corinne LaRoche."

She grabbed my hand with the force of a man and shook hard. "Glad to meet you, Miss LaRoche. Everyone calls me Molly and personally I prefer that, seeing as Margaret is an old lady's name. I don't look old, do I?"

"Uh, no."

"Ms. Brown, how nice to see you again." The uniformed boy had come back.

"Mr. Smith!" Molly stood and gave him a firm embrace. "Haven't seen you since our wonderful voyage on the Olympic. You have grown so much. And this ship…" With the back of her hand, she swatted the side of my arm. "This ship is gorgeous, don'tcha think?" She tilted her oversized hat to the side., "I guess I'll get back to the tour now, seeing as this may be my last voyage for a while. I have bunions the size of Bismarck so the doctor is going to slice those things off. That'll lay me up a good few months." She turned to the uniformed boy. "I'll see you later." She gave a quick nod and scurried off to catch up to the rest of the tour.

"So the tour isn't boring, eh?" he asked. "Then why is it that you are here instead of at the front of the group?"

"It's not that," I said quickly. "It's only that—"

"I promise, if you join me at Roche's Point, I'll see to it that you're entertained."

"I don't know. My sister and I—"

"Bring her along," he insisted.

"I'll see." I stood to my feet. "It looks as though your tour is continuing without you."

He took several steps backward, heading back to the crowd. "Promise me you'll be there."

"We'll see."

He tipped his hat and nodded. "Fair enough."

·❧[7]❧·

"WWWhat should I wear tonight?" Astrid shouted into the bathroom as I stepped out of the tub. She sifted through the brown leather trimmed suitcase Momma had bought her last Christmas, looking for the perfect skirt. "I suppose this will do." She pulled a pea-green dress from her bag and held it up. "Since I wasn't invited to the Captain's table, I'll make sure I look better than everyone there. Then they'll allow me to sit at the Captain's table with the rest of the rich, snooty people or maybe even at the head, right next to the Captain himself. Can you imagine that, Corinne?"

"Why would you want to sit next to people you call 'snooty'?" I asked her, heading to my bed with a plush white towel wrapped around me. "Not to mention, first and second-class dine in separate halls. I don't even think there is a Captain's table in our hall."

"You don't get it. Rich is everything. I'm tired of being poor and being thought of as less. I want to wear tiaras and have people wait on me and rub my feet and fetch my slippers."

Astrid had an incredible imagination. On more than one occasion, she had been sent home by schoolteachers for making up lies about why she was late to class or why her housework wasn't completed. She once even told Mr. Boulanger, her boss at Jor'dan's, that she was late because I had fallen out of a tree and had broken my arm. She told him that she had taken me to the hospital where I was in bed with a 103-degree temperature. I only wished she had told me. Mr. Boulanger wasn't the only one surprised when the next evening, I sauntered into the bakery to give Astrid the stew Momma packed for her dinner that evening. That night Astrid lost her job at Jor'dan's. Forever after, she never hesitated to say it was my fault.

I threw down the towel, picked up the robe lying across my bed and fastened it tightly around me. As I brushed my wet hair, I caught Astrid studying me with a perplexed expression—like when a kitten sees a bird for the first time and can't quite figure out why it wants to pounce and devour the poor little thing.

"Why are you looking at me like that?" I asked.

"I bet Daddy has more money than he's letting on," she said. "He told us he sold the farmland. We must have money."

"Doesn't that seem odd that he sold the farm and didn't tell us right away?" I asked, scooching up to the foot of the single over-hanging bed. The stateroom was tiny and barely fit the both of us with our large suitcases. I didn't think it was possible, but those beds in the stateroom were even smaller than our twin beds back at home.

"Why is that odd?" Astrid asked. "We needed the money and Daddy sold the farm, so?"

"Where do you think Momma is?"

She turned back to the mirror and shrugged. "I don't know. Daddy took care of it. Momma is fine and we'll see her in a few months. I'm not worried and you shouldn't be either. I trust Daddy."

I shook my head. "It doesn't make sense, Astrid. Daddy told us she had to stay in Cherbourg because she had to work to make money. Now all of a sudden, he tells us that he made a big sale from the farm. Isn't that odd?"

"I don't know, Corinne. Personally, I think you're making much more out of this than needed."

"And what about her staying with *grandmère* and *grandpère*?" I asked. "We have never even met them. According to Momma, she had been cut from their lives years ago when she married Daddy."

"Would you stop it," Astrid complained. "Look at us." She hopped up on the bed and like a headless wild turkey, began flinging her arms in the air as she whirled around. "We're on the ship that the entire world wishes they could be on. We'll be famous and in a hundred years, our grandchildren's children will read about us in some thick, stuffy old history book. I can't believe you're sitting there worried about a stinky, old rundown farm. Enjoy yourself for once and stop whining."

I found that amusing coming from the likes of her.

She grabbed a pin and stuck it into the pouf of hair gathered at the crown of her head. As she looked into the mirror, I suddenly realized she was looking past her reflection. She was thinking, and for a second, I glimpsed a hint of worry in her eyes. "How does this look?" she asked as she turned around. "Does it look like I'm rich?"

Astrid reached down and picked off an imaginary piece of lint from her dress. Her hands trembled as she smoothed down the front of the already-straight-as-a-board skirt. She was as concerned as I was.

"Don't just sit there, staring," she said. "Help me with this corset. I can't seem to get it right."

I stood up and positioned myself behind her and pulled, coming nowhere near fastening the corset. "You're too big," I told her. "It's not going to close."

"It will," she insisted. "You have to pull tighter."

"I did and it won't close."

"Pull it tighter."

I planted my feet into the carpet and once again pulled with all my might. This time I got within an inch of closing. "It's not going to close."

"Try again!"

"It's all that food you've been stuffing in your face the past few weeks."

"It is not. Now pull!"

I pulled harder, burning the corset strings into the flesh of my fingers. "Take a deeper breath and arch your back."

She sucked in more air and dipped backward. I was almost there. "You have to breathe in deeper!" I commanded. A second later, the corset strings snapped. I stumbled backward, landing on the floor—backside down—with a hard thump.

"Look what you did." Astrid ripped off the corset and flung it onto her bed. "Now I'll have to find something else to wear."

She threw the pea-green dress onto the floor and flopped open her suitcase at the foot of her bed. Like a ravenous bear fishing for trout, she dipped her head into the suitcase, reached in and yanked out a lilac-colored dress with billowy white frills hanging loosely from the bottom. The dress was beautiful. The only problem was that she hadn't worn that thing in five years and in that time, she had gained a solid twenty pounds.

For the next fifteen minutes, I tugged, yanked and darn near pulled a shoulder muscle trying to get an extra twenty pounds into that dress without her popping out of it before the first course was served.

"How do I look?" she asked, admiring her reflection. She admired it so much I did not have the heart to tell her she looked like a stuffed sausage.

"It looks fine."

She exhaled carefully as she ran her hands down the front of the dress. "I think so, too."

"Are you serious about getting off the ship in New York?" I asked.

She didn't answer right away. Instead, she whirled around, inspecting every inch in the mirror, starting from the top of her pinned-up hair and finishing with her unlaced boot. Finally, she shrugged. "Maybe."

"What are you going to do in New York? You don't know anyone. You don't have any money. You'll be alone," I told her. "What can you possibly do in New York?"

She stuck another shiny barrette in her hair and then meticulously ran her fingers along the sides, taking care to make sure every strand was neatly in place. She turned to face me. The corners of her mouth slowly turned downward. "Things are changing, Corinne. Don't you feel it? Life is different. We're not kids anymore. The days of playing barefoot in the fields are long gone. It's time to grow up."

"Leaving the family doesn't mean you're growing up."

"That's exactly what it means," she said. "I'm going to start over in New York. I plan to do better, be better. I have big plans for myself." She grabbed her shawl and headed out the door. "If you see me at dinner, pretend you don't know me." With that, she sauntered out the door, slamming it behind her.

I flopped down onto the bed. At that moment, I had never missed our tiny farm so much in my life.

·∙≻‖ 8 ‖≺∙·

"Hi, sweetheart." Daddy leaned over and kissed my cheek, leaving behind a tiny trace of saliva. It made me feel like when I was a little girl and right before walking into church, Momma would lick her finger and wipe away the dirt from my face.

"You look beautiful tonight," he told me.

After Astrid left the stateroom, I had gotten dressed in the discarded pea-green gown she no longer fit and met Daddy in the dining room. She'd kill me for wearing it—more so because it fit me and not her. The only thing I brought even remotely resembling something formal was my sable-brown dress that Astrid referred to as a potato sack. Unlike Astrid, I despised shopping.

"Where's your sister?"

"She decided to eat early," I told him. "I don't think she's coming."

He looked over my shoulder and scanned the room for any sign of Astrid. Finally giving up, he said, "Well, it looks like it will just be me and my little girl tonight."

Like that little girl he constantly referred to me as, he grabbed my hand and led me out the door.

He stopped halfway down the hall. "What am I doing? You're not a baby anymore." He crooked his elbow. I took hold, feeling more like a lady with her gentleman caller as we headed toward the dining room.

When we reached the mile-high glass doors, Daddy reached ahead of me and held open the left side of the door. This was the first time I had actually seen the inside of the dining room. I found myself in awe of its spectacular decor. The space was elaborately set with its high ceilings and fancy chandeliers dangling over every table. The tables were sized according to, what I had assumed was, the importance of the family sitting there. At the very head of the room was an empty, large-sized table with a huge banner hanging over it that read, *Captain's Table*.

Astrid was right, I thought. The Captain's table existed. Whether or not the captain actually joined second- and third-class dining remained to be seen since, at that moment, the table was completely stripped of any silverware or fancy dressings.

Like Daddy and me, passengers were modestly dressed in simple gowns with minimal accessories or neat suits, some with ties; some without. I pictured third-class to be even more lax in their attire.

"Our table is over here." He led me farther toward the back of the spacious room until we settled at a tiny table in the corner. *Thank goodness Astrid wasn't here. Space was limited.*

As we sat down, I noticed all eyes on us. A sea of pale white faces washed throughout the room with the exception of a few sun-kissed ones. Daddy didn't seem to notice, though. He politely pulled out my chair for me.

One of those faces was staring at me particularly hard. It was a young girl around my age. Her face was so made up, she added ten years to her actual age. Huge, dazzling diamonds hung loosely from her earlobes. I hoped she had the good sense to either wear fake jewelry or have no less than ten beefy security guards in close proximity.

Her hair was dark brown and pulled back into a severe bun that looked like it hurt when she smiled. The scarlet lipstick was in complete contrast to her pale skin. It was the exact same color Claudette Beauchamp wore. In fact, the girl reminded me of Claudette, only this girl was even thinner and wasn't nearly as buxom. I wondered if Sébastien would have found her pretty.

"So what do you think of the ship?" Daddy asked. "It's beautiful, isn't it?"

I nodded as I took a sip from the glass of water in front of me. Immediately, I spat it back into the fancy crystal goblet. It tasted like toilet water. "So when is Momma coming?"

"Not sure. We'll decide that when we get there."

"If you sold the farm, where is she going to stay until she comes over?"

"She'll be with her family."

I raised the water glass to my lips once again, but quickly set it back down when I remembered its contents. "But she hasn't spoken to *grandmère* in years."

Daddy fidgeted in his seat. "This table sure is small, isn't it?"

"I didn't even know they were still alive."

"Corinne," he began. "I'm going to be honest, but I need for you to accept what I'm going to tell you." He hesitated a moment. "Your mother is not with your grandparents. In fact, she will not be coming back to Canada at all." He said it so matter-of-factly, as if we were talking about the weather.

"What do you mean, Daddy?" My heart began to race.

"Your mother and I have decided to continue our lives separately."

With his words, I felt a loss of breath. It was almost like he felt relief by revealing this bit of information. The more I tried to inhale, the more constricted my lungs became. "What do you mean, continue your lives 'separately'?"

"Oh, honey." He grabbed the napkin next to his plate, dipped the corner of it into the glass of water and lightly dabbed at his forehead. "I didn't want to have to tell you like this, but you're no longer a child and I think now is an appropriate time."

"And when *were* you going to tell me?" The flush rose up to my cheeks.

"I don't know, maybe when we got back to Canada."

"Why?" I asked. "I don't understand." My voice had risen.

"France is her home and Canada is mine."

"What does that mean? You are ending your marriage after twenty-two years because of geography? What about Astrid and me? We were born in Canada, but Cherbourg had been our home for the last four years. Don't we have a choice?"

"It's not that simple," Daddy said.

"It's not that difficult, either." I shot up out of my seat. "What did you do to make her leave us?"

He stood up. "Sit down, Corinne. We will discuss this later," he commanded. From the corner of his eye, he glanced around the room at the few passengers who had taken interest in our conversation.

"I will not," I said, through clenched teeth. It was because of him that there was no more of that irritating creaky floorboard in the middle of our room that I would kill to hear now. The farm that we had worked so hard to maintain was gone, sold right from under us as if it were nothing more than an empty barren lot. All of this because Daddy decided we were moving back to Canada and without his children's consent. How dare he make life plans without asking how we felt? Standing across from Daddy in that luxurious dining room, I had begun to feel nothing but an intense loathing toward him and the decision he so callously made regarding the rest of our lives.

"What did you do to Momma? No way would Momma agree to something like this. You must've done something."

"I will not repeat myself," he said. "*Now sit down!*"

"What did you do?"

"You are not a child. Stop acting like one."

When he realized I was not backing down, he softened his voice. "Corinne, that's not fair. Your mother and I made this decision together."

"Does Astrid know?"

"She understands up to a certain point. I wanted to explain everything to both of you this evening."

"It's not fair," I told him. "You never even asked what we wanted."

"This wasn't done to ruin your life. It was done to make it better."

"That's a lie! You did this without us and only after you lure us on this big, broken-down barnacle, you tell us that Momma isn't even coming at all?" A few patrons, as well as service waiters, glanced over, looking down at us from the tip of their noses.

"Sorry to interrupt your perfect supper!" I yelled to the diners.

"Corinne," Daddy whispered. "Sit. Down. Now."

Angry, I pushed back the chair to leave. Instead of making a hasty exit, I knocked into one of the service waiters. He went flying into another table with a tray full of food. The server landed on the lap of a woman whose husband immediately jerked up and shoved the server to the ground.

Angry and embarrassed, I turned and stomped toward the exit, nearly knocking into another couple and their young child.

"Sorry," I mumbled. I pushed open the double dining room doors and exited as quickly as possible.

Instead of taking the stairwell to my stateroom, I made a wrong turn somewhere between the galley and the third-class corridor. I ended up in an unrecognizable section of the ship. Momma used to tell me that if I ever got lost, make two rights and I'd be back on track again. So I did, but rather than find myself back in familiar territory, I wandered down another hall that looked like the one before it and the one before that.

I raced down one hall and then another, completely lost. Passengers stared with interest, but no one said anything—probably afraid to speak to the colored girl that was aimlessly roving the corridors. Finally, I came to a third hall. This one was a little different from the others with its posh lavender carpet and expensive-looking paintings hanging on the walls. Down the end of the hallway, a small sitting area was set up with intricately designed chairs. Two gentlemen in tuxedos and top hats sat in the formal area. One of the men drank tea. The other held an empty brandy glass in his hand.

Several doors down, on the right, a fancily dressed woman spotted me. She wore a purple laced dress and a wide-brimmed hat that had a large lavender flower pinned to the top. With a friendly smile, she asked, "May I help you?"

"Yes, ma'am," I told her, out of breath. "I'm looking for my stateroom. I believe I'm lost."

"I believe you are, too," the woman said. "This is first-class and you most certainly cannot be in first-class. You are probably looking for third-class and that's all the way down the hall and down the servants' steps. You can't miss it."

"No, ma'am," I said. "My family and I are in second-class."

She laughed. "You must be mistaken. Third-class is where you belong." She pointed a short, stubby finger down the hall. "Now, you'll need to follow that hall and go down the servants' steps. If you don't, I'll have to call the Captain."

I stared at this woman, debating on whether or not to yank that hideous purple flower off her ugly wide-brimmed hat and shove it down her throat. Instead, I forced a smile on my lips and curt-sied. I popped open my eyes. "Yes a ma'am. Thank goodness for kind ol' folk like y'all cuz I sho' don't know what I's do if I's got lost in this big ol' boat." I pinched the sides of my dress and took another bow. "Thank you for showin' a lil' ol' colored girl like me the way ta go." I rolled my eyes and stomped off in the opposite direction.

Behind me, hat lady nervously called for one of the fancy men sitting at the end of the hall. I stepped up my pace. When I turned the corner, I slowed down to catch my breath. All I wanted to do was find my stateroom so I could pout in peace. Tears began to run down my face as snot dripped from my nose. With the back of my hand, I wiped at my cheeks and nose. The only thing that achieved was leaving an unsightly trail from my nose to the back of my hand.

"Excuse me, are you all right?"

Startled, I whipped around. There stood the boy from the gangway and the tour, looking like an adult with such a look of concern. The way he was staring, I figured I must've had another head growing from the side of my neck. It was only when he glanced down at my hand and at the trail of snot resting on it did I realize it wasn't a look of concern on his face; it was probably disgust.

I lifted the tattered ball of tissue and fruitlessly dabbed at the back of my hand.

"Take this." He reached into his tuxedo jacket pocket and handed me an embroidered handkerchief. I took it from his hand, but before wildly blowing into it, I glanced at the meticulously embroidered initials, *CAS*. On the right side of the initials was a colorfully embroidered crest with a sword piercing through it.

"Thank you," I said, handing the handkerchief back to him.

"Keep it," he told me. His smile was so bright and wide.

Standing in the middle of the hall and under the bright lighting, I finally got a good look at CAS. He was even more handsome than I had remembered. His brown hair was slicked back and he was very tall. He towered over me like a large, lean, sturdy oak tree would a tiny, round shrub.

Depending on taste, he was a little on the thin side, but what he lacked in weight, he more than made up for facial feature-wise. His eyes were brown and his skin, tanned. He could have been mistaken for being of mixed race, like I was. If I hadn't seen him in full uniform earlier, I would have assumed just that. Seconds later, two adults peeked out of the stateroom behind him.

"Christopher, I thought I told you to hurry and get ready," the lady said. "We don't want to be late." She stepped into the hallway wearing a fancy embroidered, bright-pink, floral cotton housedress and her hair was wrapped neatly under a silk scarf of the same color.

The slightly older man peered out of the room behind the lady, fastening gold cufflinks to his crisp white shirt that hung freely over the top of his trousers. The lady was olive-complexioned, but her hair was practically white, which was strange seeing as she appeared to be only in her mid-forties. The man had white hair that matched his beard perfectly, but his skin was pale. He was tall and thin like the boy and quite handsome and well-kept. He was very much unlike those pictures of Gran Daddy LaRoche that hung in our living room back in Cherbourg. In at least half of those pictures, Gran Daddy wore a scruffy beard that always appeared unkempt and his eyes were weary and sad.

When the lady saw me, she stepped out of her stateroom and into the hall. She had a wide but inquisitive smile on her neatly painted face.

"And who is this?"

"Mother, this is uh, I'm afraid I don't even know your name." He smiled warmly.

"Corinne."

"Mother, this is Corinne."

"Well, dear, it's wonderful to meet you. Excuse my dress, but we were preparing to dine." She extended a well-manicured hand. I gently shook it. "I really don't mean to be rude, but I'm afraid we're running a little late." She placed her porcelain hand onto her son's shoulder, steering him back into the room. "Maybe we'll see you later, young lady, perhaps dining this evening."

Before she steered her son back into the room, he turned back to me and stuck his hand high in the air. With his brow raised, he said, "Good night, Miss Corinne. Even though you disappointed me at Roche's Point, I still look forward to seeing you again."

·❧[9]❧·

*W*hen I finally found my way back to my stateroom, I was tired and ready to flop into my bed and pull the covers up over my head. I was thankful that when I opened the door, it was completely dark. Astrid was still out.

Quickly, I stepped out of Astrid's too-tight-for-her formal pea-green dress and the twill bustle skirt underneath and carefully folded them up. I placed the dress back into her suitcase and the bustle back into mine. After putting on my nightdress, I proceeded to the bathroom to wash my face.

With soap and water dripping from my face, I thought about Astrid. I wondered how she would take the news of Momma not coming to Canada. Knowing her, she would somehow manage to make it all about her, complaining that now she was going to have to travel back and forth from Cherbourg to Canada and how tiresome that would be for her. Then I thought about what Daddy had said tonight. *Astrid understood up to a certain point.* What exactly did that mean?

I flicked off the light, fell into bed and lay there for a few minutes, listening for faint sounds of larger waves crashing against the side of the ship. It was completely quiet. It took less than five minutes before I fell into a deep sleep.

Creeeeeeeeaaak!

Baaam!

The door barged open.

I opened my eyes and was greeted with insanely bright hall lights shining in my face.

A bulky shadow stood in the doorway. The smell coming from that shadow was of liquor and some unidentifiable pungent odor.

"Hey, little sis." With her shoeless foot, Astrid slammed the door closed. She reached over and flicked on the light.

I rubbed my eyes and focused. *Vomit!* That's what the other smell was.

Strands of Astrid's curly hair hung limply around her shoulders and her dress had a big wet stain running down the front. She carried one of her shoes in her left hand, and the whereabouts of the other shoe was anybody's guess. Her shifty, bloodshot eyes scanned the room, as if expecting someone to pop out from the closet, yelling, *Surprise!* Without warning, she burst out laughing and fell to the floor.

She rolled around on the floor for a few minutes until rolling herself up into a kneeling position. She looked up at me with a vacant expression. Her face had turned a greenish-white as she struggled, on all fours, to make it to the bathroom. She slammed the door shut.

I scrambled out of bed and put my ear to the door. "Are you all right?"

She flung open the door. She flounced past me, knocking me in the shoulder, and collapsed down onto her bed. "Look at me. Does it look like I'm all right?" she slurred.

She flopped back onto her pillow. "Oh, God. Somebody kill me, please. Take a pistol and put me out of this misery."

"What is wrong with you?" I asked.

She took her hands and rummaged through her untidy mane. "Why is the world not fair? Can you tell me that, Corinne?" Before I could offer an answer, she crooked her head to the side and asked, "Well?"

"I don't know what to say."

"Of course you don't. Because you, little darling, are safe and secure in your little world. You have no idea what really goes on out there, do you? You would just love to be Daddy's little girl forever." Lazily, she pointed to the door. "A little girl like you will be devoured out there."

"In the hallway?"

Astrid stared at me and then slowly, a smile formed across her lipstick-smeared lips. "You're being funny, aren't you? The funny yet timid girl is attempting her hand at a jest." She brought her index finger to her lips. "Shhhhh. Don't tell anyone, but I'm going to let you in on a little secret. Life is not funny. You're going to have to grow up someday. You're born, you live and then you die. Hopefully, you will have done something meaningful with your life before taking the big dirt nap. You probably will, but me? I'm hopeless. The good news is, I'll never give up trying."

"Astrid, are you feeling ill?"

"If I wasn't feeling ill, would I be throwing up all evening?"

"Did you eat or drink something spoiled?" I asked, immediately thinking of the water served at dinner.

"If you call three glasses of wine something bad, then yes, maybe. Or was it four?" She burst out laughing.

"How did you get wine?"

Again, she raised a single finger to her lips and with a sneaky grin, she said, "Shhhh, that's a secret."

"Maybe you should see the ship's doctor." I took a seat next to her on the bed. Immediately, I regretted it. The putrid smell was so overwhelming. If I didn't think she would go into a drunken rant about it, I would have gotten up and moved to the other side of the stateroom. Instead, I held her limp body up with my shoulder, making sure to only take breaths when absolutely needed. "I talked to Daddy tonight at dinner."

"Awww, and how is Daddy dear?" She reached over and flung her arms across me. Her breath smelled sour. "You're a good sister." With every word, the strong toxic odor escaped. It was so strong, it almost made *me* pass out—something I gathered she would be doing very soon.

"You're such the good little girl and I'm the mean, ferocious one." She started growling like a tiger and then broke out in laughter once again. She laughed so hard, she would have rolled off the bed if I hadn't grabbed her arm.

"I talked to Daddy tonight," I said again. "I need to tell you something."

Astrid shot up and darted for the bathroom. This time she didn't make it to the sink. She threw up all over the floor.

"I hope you don't expect me to clean that up," I said angrily.

Astrid turned green and released once again. The really infuriating part was when she looked me in the eye and then began laughing hysterically. In a mocking tone, she repeated, "I hope you don't expect me to clean that up."

"I told you I won't clean that up. I'm sick and tired of cleaning up all your messes."

Astrid, who by this time was leaning on all fours again, rolled over onto her back and wrapped her arms around her stomach. I thought she was going to vomit again. Instead, she started laughing and hiccupping at the same time.

"You can be such a witch."

That made her laugh even more.

There was a knock at the door. By its force, I knew it was Daddy. In a panic, I shot Astrid a warning look. "Yes?"

"Corinne," Daddy said from the other side. "We need to talk."

"Would you be quiet?" I whispered to Astrid. I turned back toward the door. "I'm really tired now, Daddy. Could we please talk about this tomorrow?"

Astrid raised her voice an octave and imitated, "Can we please talk about this tomorrow, Daddy, because I'm perfect and delicate and I need my perfect and delicate sleep?" To finish off her impersonation, she smiled sweetly and batted her eyelashes.

"Be quiet!" I demanded. "I hate you!"

"Is everything all right? Is Astrid in there with you?" Daddy asked.

"Everything is fine," I called back.

There was a pause.

"Okay. I'll return later and we'll talk."

"Okay."

His shadow disappeared from under the door, so I turned back to my sister, who was sprawled out on the carpet. Thankfully, she had stopped cackling like a sickly chicken. "If Daddy sees you were drinking, he's going to kill the both of us." I helped her up from the pool of vomit she was lying in.

With a serious expression, she said, "Oh, no, no, no, little girl." She lowered her voice to a whisper. "When Daddy finds out his eldest daughter is with child, *that's* when he'll kill me." She burst out laughing, hiccupped and threw up once again.

2 days until...

·❧ 10 ❧·

The next morning I awoke early. Astrid had still been asleep-slash-passed out, so I headed to breakfast alone.

"Corinne?" Daddy's voice whispered from behind the door. "I know it's early, but I really would like to talk to you and your sister as soon as possible."

Sitting on the edge of my bed fully dressed, I glanced down at Astrid sleeping in the bed under me. I decided it would be better if I didn't open the door. The room still contained a foul stench even after scrubbing for hours, plus, I wasn't exactly sure what condition my dear, inebriated sister was in.

"Corinne?" Daddy whispered.

I sat still for another second before hopping off the bed and placing my ear to the door, listening for his breathing.

He was gone.

I hadn't talked to Daddy since dinner last night and was feeling guilty about that. Even so, my head throbbed at the thought of another uncomfortable conversation, which I was sure would result in more questions rather than answers.

Even after shooing him away yesterday evening in an attempt

to keep Astrid's condition a secret, he had come back an hour later. I had heard his faint knock through the door, but I pretended to be asleep. I was still angry and I was mentally exhausted.

This morning, nothing had changed.

Was Astrid really pregnant? She constantly exaggerated, but from what I could tell, she always told some form of the truth. If Astrid didn't want you to know something, rather than lie, she would keep it secret. Without her being sober, I couldn't know for sure.

Dressed in a simple Irish linen crochet tea dress with a matching ivory lace shawl, I made my way down the hall and toward the outside deck for breakfast. For full service, the dining room was set for each seating, but I had opted for the mini-breakfast served on the deck. The buffet was meticulously laid out with a vast array of delicacies with coffee and juices situated at the very end of the culinary display. The morning time air was slightly chilled but by the afternoon, the sun had begun to burst beyond the clouds and heat up the deck.

I grabbed a piece of fruit and some toast and headed up the stairs toward the upper deck. Once sitting directly in the sun, I began to warm up, so much so, that I pulled the neighboring chair closer and rested the shawl in the seat next to me.

Before I could take a bite of my fruit, two people walked up and stood over me. With the sun's glare, I couldn't see their faces, so with my hand, I shielded my eyes and glanced up. It was hat lady from yesterday evening. She wore an angry expression. The man next to her was in full uniform and frowned at me with an equally somber expression. The glare from the silver metals pinned to his uniform jacket shone directly into my eyes.

"Is this the girl, ma'am?" the man in uniform asked.

"Yes it is."

The uniformed man reached out and grabbed me, pinching at the fleshy part of my upper arm. "You'll need to come with me."

"Why?" I asked. "I didn't do anything."

"Mrs. Ashcroft says different."

I snatched back my arm. "I will not."

"Good morning, sir and madam." The boy from yesterday evening had come up to the table and nodded a polite greeting to Mrs. Ashcroft and the man in uniform. "Is there a problem?" He wore a clean, starched white uniform outlined in black. His hat was white with black trim. I tried to read the nametag fastened to his left breast pocket, but the sun's rays bounced off it. All I saw was the glare.

The other uniformed man cleared his throat and spoke first. "Mrs. Ashcroft says this girl created a disturbance while aimlessly wandering the halls yesterday evening."

"Is that so?" the boy asked, turning to hat lady.

"Yes she was."

"Well, she's with me. I can assure you there will no longer be a problem."

"Just keep her where she belongs," Mrs. Ashcroft said and stomped off. The uniformed seaman followed.

"Why did you tell her that?" I asked.

"Who?"

"Mrs. Ashley, Ashcomb—"

He laughed. "You mean Mrs. Ashcroft."

"Ash, whatever," I said angrily. "I did no such thing. I was lost and...and...I...I couldn't—" I was so angry, the words wouldn't come out.

The boy smiled. "Of course you didn't, I know that. Mrs. Ashcroft is the type to rant on about the food not being to her liking, or the ship being too cold. She's the type you have to appease just to get her out of your hair. One time, I even heard her complaining about the sea being too watery."

I grinned.

"May I sit down?" he asked.

I nodded.

He pulled out the chair across from me and flopped down into it with tiresome ease. "It certainly looks like you're feeling much better than you were last night."

Without lifting my eyes from my plate, I gave a slight nod.

"Except for those dark circles under your eyes."

This time I looked up.

Quickly, he recanted. "Wait. I didn't mean that. It's only that you look a little fatigued. Many passengers have sleepless evenings on a ship. Most times they look worse than you."

I cut my eyes at him. "Excuse me?"

"I didn't mean that either." He took a deep breath. "Allow me to start again."

"It's fine," I told him, taking a bite of my peach.

"Is that all you're eating?"

I looked down at the fruit and bread on my plate. Did he think I got this size by just eating this bird food? My plan was to start out with the fruit and finish with the flapjacks dripping in butter and maple syrup.

"You didn't have to come to my rescue," I told him. "I could've handled it myself."

"Surely, you jest. Before I came, it looked like Officer MacDougal was about to take you to the brig and shout, *'Off with her head!'*" he said, chuckling.

"Really?" Anger flushed my cheeks. "I guess it's my skin color that scares all of you big-deal first-classers on this stupid ship."

He stopped laughing. His amused expression abruptly turned

into an astonished one. "I didn't know—" he stammered. "I mean, I assumed you were white." Then he quickly added, "Not that it's a problem. I apologize if I offended you in any way. All I meant was—"

"I know what you meant. You meant to do your good deed for the day by coming to the poor colored girl's rescue. Well, I don't need your, or anyone else's condescension."

"Don't be ridiculous," he began, "I assure you that was not the case at all."

I gathered up my plate and huffed off, nearly stumbling over a nearby table. With this sudden race revelation, I assumed an exchange of names was no longer necessary. I dumped the full platter into the garbage and headed for the doors leading back inside.

"Wait!" He ran up to me and extended his arm. "Did I do something wrong? I apologize if I've offended you."

I sighed. It wasn't him that was bothering me. He was only the target on the receiving end of my frustration. "I'm sorry. It's like you said, I had a restless evening and right now I'm out of sorts."

"Whew. I was beginning to think it was me."

I started to walk away before he called, "Wait! You forgot this." I looked down at my shawl slung neatly over his outstretched arm. I reached for it, but he yanked it away before I could grab it.

"First, let me say that I am truly sorry." His brown eyes softened. "I most certainly did not mean to offend you in any way. And if you must know, I only came up to you because I thought you needed assistance. I see I was wrong, and so again, I apologize."

"No harm done," I said, relenting a bit.

"If you don't remember, my name is Christopher," he offered. "And I believe you are Corinne."

"How do you know that?"

He laughed. "You told me yesterday and I never forget the name of a girl that holds such beauty."

The heat rushed to my ears. "Thank you," I muttered. I extended my hand. "Now, if I could have my shawl, please?"

"You may." Instead of placing it in my hand, he reached over and gently draped it over my shoulders. "I hope I can see you again," he whispered. His breath was sweet and warm as it caressed my ear.

"You don't have to pretend to be interested," I said. "Although I may have been a little harsh earlier, I do appreciate your help."

"A *little* harsh?"

His arm stretched around me and pulled open the door. I felt the light touch of his chest brush up against my shoulder. "Meet me for dinner tonight."

"Why?"

"Uh—"

After all his confidence displayed earlier, I had actually left him speechless.

"I thought it would be nice to have dinner with you," he finally said.

"Really?" There was a little more sarcasm in my voice than intended.

"Yes, really," he answered with more confidence. "What stateroom are you in?"

I hesitated a moment and then said, "Forty-two C."

"Well, Corinne in forty-two C, consider me there."

"I would prefer if we met someplace," I said, not eager for Astrid to meet him. She and Daddy shared the same views when it came to white people.

He grinned. "That's fine by me."

As I walked through the opened door, secretly I prayed that he was not watching me. When I turned back around, I saw him staring, but he wasn't wearing a frown of realization. Instead, he displayed a wide grin of satisfaction.

As tired as I felt, I could not help but smile as I headed back to my stateroom. Christopher seemed like a nice boy. A small part of me wanted to kick myself for even thinking such things about any boy after what Sébastien had done to me.

"With that smile on your face, I'd assume you were having a grand time." Christopher's mom smiled at me. Her white hair was pulled back into a tight bun. Standing alongside her was a young girl wearing a white flirty dress and carrying a matching lace umbrella. Immediately, I recognized her as the one who had been in second-class dining last evening.

"If I remember correctly, your name is Corinne?" the white-haired woman said.

"Yes, ma'am."

"I'm Mrs. Smith and this is Sophia Calloway."

"Nice to meet you again." I held out my hand.

"No need to be so formal." Mrs. Smith grabbed my shoulders and tightly embraced me. When we parted, I stuck out my hand to Sophia. In contrast, she hesitated before cautiously taking my fingertips.

"Sophia and I were headed on the deck to get a few rays," Mrs. Smith said. "Would you like to join us?" She then leaned in and whispered, "Not really, though. Us girls have to keep our skin powder-like, don't we? But even so, it's nice to get some fresh air every so often."

Sophia stared off in the distance. She mumbled something as

she tipped the umbrella slightly to the side, shielding her delicate features from the sun.

"I would love to, but—," I began.

"But what, dear? Where could you possibly be rushing off to on a ship?" She grabbed my elbow, pulling me toward the direction from which I had just come. "I won't accept a decline. You must sit and chat with us. Please do tell us more about you." Still gripping my elbow, she hastened her steps. Sophia followed closely behind.

As soon as we took a seat on the deck, Sophia asked, "Where exactly did you say you were from? And what stateroom are you in?"

"Well," I began, "I've lived in several places."

Mrs. Smith's eyes widened. "How exciting for you," she interrupted. "The same for my Christopher, he was born and raised in England, of course, but was schooled in Sweden as well as other countries for quite a few years."

Sophia pouted. She folded her arms across her chest and asked again, "What stateroom would you be in?"

"Sophia, dear, let her finish telling us about her well-traveled life." She turned back to me. "The minute I saw you I understood that you must be a well-traveled young lady. There are certain things I can tell upon a first meeting."

"Ladies." A server with a round silver tray filled with water and juice glasses approached us. "Would you like something to drink?"

Sophia reached for a tall glass of water. Mrs. Smith, with her eyes still fastened on me, shook her head and with a flick of her wrist, shooed the server away.

"So where were you coming from with that beautiful smile upon your face?" Mrs. Smith asked.

"Actually," I told her, "I was just speaking to your son."

"You were up here with Christopher?" Sophia asked.

I turned to Sophia. "Unless Mrs. Smith has another son, I'd have to say yes."

"That's delightful, dear. My son is great company. He is smart and has a wonderful personality, but I'm sure you found that out when you spoke with him."

"Yes, ma'am."

"Oh my, Sophia," Mrs. Smith said. "I do believe you have competition for my son's affections." She chuckled.

Sophia's expression remained concrete. "Hardly," she said as she rolled her eyes and stuck her nose in the air.

"Oh, no," I began. "It's not like that."

"Not yet," Mrs. Smith said, playfully nudging my shoulder. "My son is quite the charmer." She looked over toward a miffed Sophia. "You know that, dear."

Sophia took another sip of water.

"Oh, Sophia," Mrs. Smith began, "before I forget, please tell your mother that I would be willing to take one of her servants off her hands temporarily. I believe she mentioned Millie?"

"I will definitely tell her," Sophia said. "But I must inform you that Millie is one colored gal that does nothing but cause a ruckus, constantly wanting time off. Her daughter must be the sickest child in England with her constant coughing and wheezing."

"If the girl is sick," I said, "I see nothing wrong with needing her mother."

Sophia looked directly at me. "And I don't think that's really any of your business."

"I think I should go." I stood up.

"Are you sure?" Mrs. Smith said. "We're having such a lovely chat."

I stood. "Yes, I have a few things to do this afternoon." As I headed toward the exit, I felt Sophia's eyes searing a hole right in the back of my head.

·∘⟮ 11 ⟯∘·

I looked at Daddy and then to Astrid, who was turning a pale shade of green. It was questionable as to whether she would be able to hold out much longer before having to run to the bathroom. She had been vomiting all morning long. That last hiccup, I thought it was surely coming, but it was another false alarm.

After my brief encounter with Christopher, his mother and Sophia, I had gone back to the stateroom to find Astrid leaning over the toilet. An hour after that, Daddy had knocked on our stateroom door again. His tone was pleading, but firm, when he asked to speak with us. Here we were, side by side, on Astrid's bed. Daddy hovered over us, pacing back and forth.

"I don't know how much your sister has told you," he said, looking at a pale Astrid. "But I think it's time we discuss a few things."

Astrid glanced at me from the corner of her eye. She took a deep breath and then wrapped her arms around her stomach. If it wasn't for her waking up with a terrible hangover in her own bed this morning, she probably wouldn't have even remembered returning at all yesterday evening.

"I feel terrible discussing this with you, but it is something you will find out about sooner rather than later," Daddy continued.

My gaze fell to the large circle stain on the carpeted floor. I had spent two hours on all fours trying to scrub out that awful smell. I must've sprayed at least half a bottle of cologne on that stain and still the faint stench of vomit seeped through.

My thoughts drifted, first remembering Cherbourg and then thinking about how, in just two days, my life had changed. I closed my eyes and could almost smell the turkey basting and a special dish Momma called Chef Supreme, which we all knew was onions simmered in a cream sauce seasoned with dried currants and parsnips. Only one week ago, I had made a special trip to the downtown fruit sellers for Momma. She was baking a pie and needed fresh cherries from Mr. Horsence's fruit stand.

Hearing Daddy speak about Momma angered me. This was an emotional path that I did not care to tread. Last night was enough.

"What do you mean?" Astrid asked when Daddy gave the dreaded news. "Momma is not coming to Canada with us?"

"I'm afraid not." He looked at me. Quickly, I looked away, hopped up to my top bunk and flopped down onto my pillow. I swung my legs over the edge and lay down with my hands comfortably resting behind my head. I no longer wished to continue a conversation that only frustrated me.

"What happened?" Astrid asked. Daddy never noticed each time she spoke, she would put her hand to her mouth to keep from spitting up. "Does that mean we're never going to see her again?"

"Of course it doesn't mean that," I said. "I'm going back to see her anytime I want." I looked at Daddy. "Isn't that right?"

He scratched his head, shifting from his right foot to his left. When he didn't answer right away, my heart dropped inside my chest so far, it was likely to hit the bottom of the ocean.

I sat up in my bed. "It doesn't mean that, does it, Daddy?"

He forced a smile and perked up his brow. "Of course we can see her again. We'll discuss all that when we get to Canada." He turned to reach for the doorknob.

He was lying. I knew it.

Daddy pulled open the door. "I'll see you for dinner this evening? In the meantime, you girls should relax and enjoy the ship."

"I can't," I told him.

"Can't what?"

"Meet you for dinner."

Daddy looked to Astrid, waiting for an explanation. She shrugged and looked to me. I expected Daddy to turn on his stern voice, telling me that I was expected to be there. Instead, he said, "Fine then. I'll see you for breakfast."

Daddy left the room with me feeling worse with this discussion than the one last evening. There were still so many unanswered questions. Why wasn't he telling us the truth?

"Do you believe what he told us?" I asked, peering down at Astrid from my bed.

She stood. "Of course I do."

"There are so many unexplained things," I said. "I feel like he's not telling us the entire truth. What about—"

"What about nothing, Corinne. You're going to do what you always do and make this something more than it is." She hiccupped and her face turned a sickly shade of purple. She wrapped her arms around her stomach and threw her head back. Suddenly, she shot like a bullet toward the bathroom, slamming the door shut behind her. Minutes later, she emerged paler than when she'd gone in.

"What about you?" I asked.

"What about me?" She hobbled over to her bed, collapsing onto her rumpled, unmade sheets.

"Were you drinking alcohol last night?" I asked.

She cut her eyes. "I'm fine."

"Are you really pregnant or is this you trying to get attention again?" I asked.

She shot me another look. "What is that supposed to mean?"

"Never mind."

She squirmed and moaned a bit before swinging her legs over her bed and settling into a fetal position. "Seriously, what is that supposed to mean? Does it threaten you that I may take away some of Daddy's attention? Don't worry, little sister, I'll always be the bad sister who stays in trouble, and you'll be the perfect little one who doesn't want to grow up." She stood up and took a deep breath. "And yes, I am pregnant. You can't be surprised by this news."

"Are you absolutely sure, Astrid?"

She nodded.

"Want to talk about it?"

"No."

I jumped off my bed and stood over her. I felt badly for her. As strange as it may have sounded, I even felt somewhat responsible.

"So what are you going to do?"

"I said I don't want to talk about it, Corinne!" she snapped. "Would you go away and leave me alone?"

"Fine!" I said, heading for the door. "If you don't want me here, I don't have to be here."

Before my fingers touched the knob, Astrid said, "I'm scared, Corinne." A single teardrop fell from her left eye. That was the first time I had seen her cry. I walked over and sat down next to her. To my surprise, she laid her head on my shoulder. "I don't know what I'm going to do, Corinne. That's why I'm getting off in New York. I'm going to have this whole thing go away."

"You can't do that. Is that even possible?"

"Of course it's possible. I know someone who knows someone who had hers taken care of. But you can't tell anyone."

"You don't have to do that." I had heard the story about a girl back in Cherbourg who had died on the table when trying to get rid of a baby. I didn't want that same fate for Astrid or even a tiny, innocent baby.

"What about God?" I asked.

Astrid lifted her head. "What kind of question is that?"

"I don't know," I responded, not even sure of where that question came from myself.

Astrid laughed. "You can't be serious. If God cared about me, he wouldn't have put me in this position in the first place, now would He?"

"It's not that simple," I told her. "God gives us free will. Don't blame Him for your actions. God's there to fix the messes in your life that you have created. Don't do this, please," I begged. "With His help, we can fix this."

"What is this, Sunday school?" Astrid asked. "I tried so hard to be perfect…like you. No one is ever going to let me live down my past actions. Not you, not Momma and definitely not Daddy."

"I'm not perfect," I argued.

"Put it this way, if there's only one place left in heaven and it's between you and me, you can be damn sure I'll be taking the elevator downstairs."

"What about the baby's father?" I asked, steering the conversation back on topic. By her actions and behavior, I most certainly believed that she had quite a few boys on a string. "Where is he?"

"I can tell you where he isn't, and that's on this ship," she responded flippantly. "It doesn't matter. I'm doing what I have to do. I'll make a better life for myself there."

"Do you even know who the father is?"

"See what I mean?" she asked. "Never let me live it down. For your information, I've only been with one boy and we were supposed to get married before he cheated on me. That's why I had to tell you about Sébastien before you ruined your life like I did."

"What will you do? Where will you live? How will you get money?"

"Remember Luc from Jor'dan's bakery?"

How could I forget, was the more appropriate question. Luc had worked at Jor'dan's and was at least thirty-five years old. He was rumored to have been married to a woman from the Cherbourg Mill, which he emphatically denied. Consequently, the woman had left town two weeks before Luc decided to take off. He always looked at me funny whenever I went into the bakery for Astrid. To me, Luc was eerie.

"Luc moved to New York last year. I'll get in touch with him."

"Is he the father?" I asked.

"God, no!"

"Then, who?"

"That's none of your business."

This was one truth she would undoubtedly take to her grave. "But you don't even know what town Luc is living in, or even if he's still in New York."

"I'll find him."

That was her plan? To get off the ship in New York, rid herself of a child and then find some man who supposedly moved there a year ago?

"Don't do this, Astrid," I begged. "We'll tell Daddy together and we'll work it out. Just please come to Winnipeg with us." How was I supposed to go back to Canada without Momma *and* Astrid?

I looked into my sister's eyes. She was really scared. Now wasn't the time to tell her how ridiculous she was for even contemplating such a thing. She didn't want to do this any more than I wanted her to. For her, it was the only option. Then I did something I hadn't done since we were kids. I placed my arm around her and held on tight. "Everything will be fine." The problem was, even with a safe, generic statement like that, I didn't necessarily believe it.

·❧[12]❧·

Astrid was in bed so sick, she had to beg me not to go for the doctor. In her favorite chiffon morning gown, she had rested all morning long, telling me that it was the pregnancy sickness that made her feel this way. I had no choice but to believe her.

About a half-hour later and another two trips to the bathroom, she began to feel a little better. She even sat up while nibbling on some salt crackers I had brought from the dining hall.

"I think it's the motion of the ship that's making me so ill." She took a small bite from the corner of one of the crackers. "I should be fine for the rest of the evening."

I started to tell her that there was no way you could feel relevant motion from a ship this size, but as soon as I sat on the edge of the bed, there was a knock at the door. In a panic, both of us looked at each other as if staring into one another's face would magically tell us who was behind the door.

"Daddy did say he'd meet us for dinner, didn't he?" Astrid asked in a panic.

I mentally replayed the earlier conversation. Daddy wanted to meet us for dinner. I told him I couldn't. He said he'd see us for breakfast then. It couldn't have been Daddy. Then, I realized who it was. Quickly, I hopped up from the bed and pulled open the door.

"Good evening, ma' lady." Christopher took a playful bow and tipped his top hat. When he saw me in my casual twill bustle skirt, he straightened up. "I'm not too early, am I?"

"Who is that?" Astrid called from her bed.

I took a step out into the hall, pulling up the door behind me. "I'm really sorry, but I won't be able to go to dinner with you tonight."

"Really?" he asked, concerned. "Well then, I'm quite disappointed. Is there anything wrong?"

I shook my head. "Oh no. It's just that—" I stopped mid-sentence, deciding whether or not to tell the truth. I settled for half-truth. "My sister has fallen ill and she's very weak."

"I'm sorry to hear that."

"She can barely speak. It's that bad."

From the other side of the door, Astrid boomed, "Corinne, who is that at the door?" If she were any louder, the engine room attendants would have been able to hear her.

Christopher raised his brow. "Is *that* your sister?"

I nodded weakly. "Y-y-y yes, but she's not really eating well. I think I should stay with her tonight and keep a watchful eye on her."

"Corinne?" Astrid yelled once again. "Whoever it is, tell them to go fetch me something from the dining room. I am starving."

The rush of embarrassment flushed my cheeks. I couldn't even look at him.

"If you don't want to go to dinner with me, then please say so. You don't have to make up stories about having a sister that is ill."

"No," I said quickly, "it's not that. She really is sick, but I guess she's feeling better, so yes, I'd love to go with you."

His expression lifted. "You sure? I wouldn't want to force you."

"Of course I'm sure. Give me a few minutes to get dressed. I'll meet you upstairs in the dining hall."

"Very well then," he said and sauntered off. I waited until he turned the corner before I opened the door and headed back into the stateroom. Astrid wasn't in her bed and the bathroom door was closed.

Oh, now she wants to play sick, I thought. I pulled up my sleeves and headed toward the bathroom, preparing to hold her hair back for the millionth time today.

"Who was that?" Astrid asked, shuffling back to her bed. "Is he going to get me something to eat? I am so hungry." She flopped down onto the bed, pulling the covers up to her chin.

"I know," I told her. "The entire ship knows you're hungry."

She shot off one of her looks. "What's wrong with you?"

"I'm going to the dining room tonight."

"You can't leave me here alone," she said, sitting up. "What if I get sick again?"

"You're fine, Astrid. You said so yourself. You can do without me for an hour. That will be the perfect time for you to get some rest."

"I don't want rest. I've been resting the whole cock-a-doodle day."

"I'm going to dinner," I told her. "You are not going to ruin this."

"No, you're not!"

"I am."

"You're not!"

"Astrid, I'm not going to argue with you. I'll be back before you know it."

"You are so selfish, Corinne. You've always been selfish. Think of someone else besides yourself for a change."

"Are you serious!" I yelled. "You're the one that always makes me cover for you, knowing I could get into trouble for it. But you don't care about that, do you? How many times have I been punished because I covered for you? You'd never do anything like that for me—not that I would ask because I'm not the one who's selfish."

I had one of those moments where I purposely paused to refrain from speaking something hurtful. It usually worked, however, this time it did not. "Apparently, I may have covered for you one too many times seeing the condition you find yourself in."

Stunned, Astrid reached over to the nightstand table for the first thing she could find—a half-filled cup of water. "You wretched little rat!" She picked up the cup and tossed it at me. I ducked and the cup banged against the door. A few speckles of water splashed across the front of my dress.

This time, I reached for the first thing *I* saw—a hairbrush—and hurled it at her. She pulled the bed sheet over her head, but the brush bounced off her covered head and fell to the ground. "Owwwww!"

I rushed toward the door and quickly exited before she had the chance to retaliate. When I slammed the door behind me, I heard the brush crash against it.

From the other side of the door, she screamed, "You are so selfish, Corinne. I hate you!"

I stood outside in the hallway, trying to regain my composure. What I really felt like doing was screaming and pulling out all my hair at the roots. Was one night of peace too much to ask? I didn't want to think about my parents' separation. I did not want to think about Astrid or the baby she was carrying. *Was that too much to ask—one night?* One dinner and then I would go back to carrying the weight of the world on my shoulders.

··❧[13]❧··

"You look nice," Christopher said when I met him in front of the dining hall. His eyes scanned from the crown of my head to the tips of my toes that were trapped in Astrid's too-tight, pointed-toe kidskin boots. I was lucky she was too busy hurling water glasses at me to even notice I had on her pale-blue batiste dress with the blue false bolero bodice.

Wanting to look special for tonight, I had even attempted to wear the never-worn-before Curved Busk Waspie I had bought a few years ago. But with its twenty-one-inch waist, there was no way I was ever going to fit into that thing. I settled for the Matron's Summer Corset.

"Let me do this properly," he said, taking a bow before me. "My, the lady certainly does look beautiful this fine evening." He swiped at the slicked back strands of hair that had fallen into his face.

Enjoying the amusing sight, I giggled at his silliness.

He straightened up and took a step closer. My legs felt like they would give out as I closed my eyes and took in a deep breath. I prepared myself for that kiss that had crossed my mind since first laying eyes on him when he greeted us on the ship. Instead, he reached up and pulled something from my hair. Disappointed, I slowly exhaled.

"Don't want this poking your eye out later in the evening." He held up a rust-colored hair pin.

It had taken over an hour to stick thirty hairpins into my bushy mane in order to create my upswept look. When I had inspected myself in the mirror, the combination of the pins plus the Matron's Corset tagged twenty years onto my otherwise youthful appearance. I had yanked out every one of those pins—or at least I thought I had.

"Thank you," I mumbled, wishing I could crawl under a table.

"Shall we go?" he asked.

"We shall," I said, relaxing a little more.

He held open the dining hall door. That was the first time it dawned on me that this was first-class dining. The immaculate hall looked completely different from second-class seating. The cheaper individual gold-plated chandeliers that hung over every table in second seating were replaced with shiny, crystal ones. The tablecloths were made from a silky material and had multi-colored flowers stitched into each corner. In the center of each table, a tiny candle encased in a glass covering flickered. The previously vacant Captain's table in second-class seating was filled with smiling, chatty people that looked important with their overly decorated gowns and expensive-looking, crisp tuxedos. I glanced down at my dress, afraid that my less-than-extraordinary attire would stand out.

With his arm interlocked in mine, we sauntered through the dining room with surprising ease. As we moved to the head of the hall, I figured we would be seated somewhere up front. We passed one table, then another, and then another. I soon realized we were headed to the front, toward the Captain's table. Christopher's mother was seated next to the well-groomed older gentleman I had seen with them in the first-class corridor. Realization walloped me right in the face.

"Christopher, are you related to the Captain?"

He laughed. "Why did you think I was in uniform every time we ran across each other? He's my uncle."

"I only assumed you worked on the ship, not related to the Captain," I told him. "So, your mother is the Captain's sister?" I began mentally putting the pieces together.

"Yes."

My mouth hung open as he continued directing me toward the table full of those fancy dresses and tuxedo tails.

"Relax," he said. "You'll enjoy these people. They'll provide the entertainment, trust me. Keep an eye out for old man Percy Harland, though."

"Who's he, another uncle?"

He laughed. "No, Mr. Harland is the guy with the double chin that waddles when he talks. He wears his collar so starched, it looks like he's going to strangle himself with it. He's a smart man, though. He and my uncle have been business partners for years. I'll only say he loves to joke. Years ago, he was a magician's apprentice and had even worked under the great Harry Houdini."

"Wow! That sounds fascinating."

"Then there's Angelica Pennyworth," he continued. "You'll recognize her by her nose."

"What's wrong with her nose?"

"It's stuck up in the air so high, it'll take an anchor to pull it down. Then there's Margaret Brown. You'll enjoy Molly. She'll talk for days if you let her. I believe you met her on the tour."

I spotted Ms. Brown sitting toward the end of the table, chatting away with another lady.

When we reached the large table, one-by-one, heads turned in our direction. Conversations ceased mid-sentence in order to get a glimpse of me—the interloper.

I quickly glanced at all the white faces staring back at me, starting from the end of the table and working my way down. Angelica Pennyworth stared at me with her nose hoisted in the air. Her glasses had slipped to the tip, giving her that schoolmarm look. Two seats up was an older, stodgy woman bejeweled with way too many diamonds. When Christopher saw me staring, he whispered, "That's Penelope Harland, Percy's wife. You wouldn't believe it, but they have four adult children named Penny, Parker, Peter and Pablo."

"Pablo?" I questioned.

"Mrs. Harland wasn't always the doting, faithful wife she pretends to be. Big scandal. Never mention it," he warned.

I looked at the entire table. The common denominator was their wealth. I could practically smell the rich dripping off them.

"The contest is over," Mr. Harland yelled, throwing his hands in the air.

A few of the curious people at the table glanced over, but on the whole, most ignored him and continued on with their conversations.

I leaned over. "What contest?"

"For the prettiest girl, of course," he said.

I turned around, expecting to find some strikingly beautiful woman walking up behind me. I only saw a server meticulously placing water glasses onto the table.

"He means you," Christopher whispered.

Mr. Harland nodded. His smile was welcoming and I was thankful for that. Right away, I liked him.

"Thank you."

"And modest as well. They don't make them like you anymore."

Mr. Harland suddenly reached behind me, pulling a single rose from behind my back. "And she has even brought flowers," he said, handing me the rose.

"Percy, would you stop that nonsense?" Mrs. Harland scolded. "No one wants to see your inane tricks."

"Thank you," I said, taking the rose. His wife may not have enjoyed the trick, but I most certainly did.

"Please excuse him, dear," Mrs. Harland said. "The only thing Percy loves more than magic is making ships. If I'm lucky, I may fit somewhere on that list."

"You make ships?" I asked, impressed.

Mr. Harland's eyes lit up like a child in a toy factory. "Why, yes, and I'll let you in on a little secret. This one isn't my favorite. You should see the Olympic. Now *that's* a ship. My partner, Wolff, and I plan to build a third ship and call it the Gigantic." He lowered his voice and whispered, "After my wife, of course."

"I told you I despise that name," Mrs. Harland said. "I would much more prefer—" She thought a moment and then said, "I prefer the Britannic. That's a perfect name for a ship."

We finally reached his mother and uncle. With my arm still locked in Christopher's, he cleared his throat and announced, "Mother, Uncle Edward, this is Corinne."

"How nice to see you again," his mother said. His uncle, whom I had barely seen, stood up. He cleared his throat and extended his large hand. "Good evening, Corinne. I'm Captain Edward J. Smith and I believe you already met my sister, Eloise," he said, nodding toward Mrs. Smith.

I was so nervous my stomach turned. If Christopher hadn't been still hanging onto my arm, I would have turned and dashed out of there so quickly, it would have probably blown the wigs and hair pieces off of those people.

"Do you mind if Corinne dines with us this evening?" Christopher asked.

His mother smiled graciously as she reached for her glass and took a long sip. "Of course not, son. It'll be our pleasure. But you do know that Sophia will be dining with us tonight as well?" Her deep voice cracked.

Christopher finally released my arm. "As expected." His smile faded and his tone was cold. "But remember, she's dining with you, not me."

His uncle, the Captain, dipped his head and looked at his nephew disapprovingly.

"I apologize," Christopher corrected, looking at his mother. "I understand her coming, but sometimes it feels as though you spend unnecessary time attempting to put us together."

"I simply assumed you would enjoy spending time with someone your age." His mother looked at me and then said, "But I'm sure Corinne wouldn't mind keeping you company."

I politely smiled, disregarding the prickly conversation, which had somehow managed to include me.

"You have to understand, son, that Sophia is the daughter of our dearest and closest friends who entrust us to see she is well taken care of when she joins the family for holidays." Mrs. Smith took another dainty sip of water. She laid down her glass and exclaimed, "Oh! Did I happen to mention that Langston Calloway secured another deal? Blythe is over the moon."

"Who are Langston and Blythe Calloway?" I asked Christopher.

"They are only the most prominent couple in England," Mrs. Smith offered.

"They're also Sophia's parents," Christopher added. "And apparently admired by my mother."

"I do believe Blythe's great-great aunt is the queen's cousin twice removed," Mrs. Smith said. "Or is it her mother's father is the—"

Ms. Brown called up from her end of the table, "Or perhaps she's married to Rover, the official mutt to the King of England."

"Mother," Christopher complained. "What does that have to do with me? Not to mention I don't think Corinne cares about that."

His mother shrugged. "I may not remember the family lineage exactly, however, I do know that they are quite important. My point is, I am only attempting to keep Sophia well occupied. I wouldn't want to cause any dissension with her family." She turned to me. "Christopher and little Sophie have known each other since they were small children. We used to say they were going to marry one day." She turned back to Christopher. "Remember that, son?"

Christopher sighed. "I've known Nicholas and Robbie for years as well. Does that mean I'm going to have to marry them?"

From the other end, Molly Brown gave a hearty laugh. "The kid's got a good point there, Ellie."

"Christopher!" his uncle exclaimed. "Please tone down the sarcasm and do not speak to your mother in such a manner."

"Maybe I should join you for dinner some other time," I chimed in, feeling a bit uncomfortable.

"Oh no, dear," his mother said. "Please have a seat and join us as planned. My son has always been the little court jester of the family. What he failed to understand was that I was simply trying to explain why it is important to keep little Sophie happy. That's all."

I didn't have to look at Christopher to sense his frustration.

"Please do have a seat." With a nod, his mother motioned toward the empty chair across the table.

When I sat down, his mother's eyes probed my every move.

She watched as I picked up the cotton napkin and gently placed it in my lap. When I reached for the glass of water, she quietly observed. Feeling nervous, I quickly set down the glass.

"Oh dear," she said, reaching across the table and picking up the fork next to my plate. "This is filthy. This will not do at all."

I glanced down at the spotless fork. "Oh, no, it's fine, really."

"No, this is unacceptable. I'll get you a new one." With one wave of her arm, in less than two seconds, a service waiter hovered over the table. Without saying a word, she thrust the fork in his face. He took it, inspected every inch and then with a furrowed brow, looked at me. I shrugged.

The service waiter reached into the pressed white apron fastened around his waist and pulled out another shiny fork. He held it up to the brilliant light of the crystal chandelier, twisting it back and forth before finally resting it on the table next to my plate.

"Thank you," I said as the waiter turned to leave.

Christopher leaned over and whispered, "She does that sometimes. I think it's some sort of complex she has because she grew up in an orphanage most of her childhood."

"Orphanage?"

Christopher nodded. "When she was twelve, my mother was adopted by my grandfather and his wife, Catherine Hancock. When she goes on like this, I ignore her rants. She's a good person, but sometimes feels as though she needs to prove her worth."

"Understood," I said, with a smile.

Christopher and I locked gazes. From under the table he reached for my hand and gently squeezed it.

"Hello? Young lady?" Mrs. Pennyworth called from the middle of the table and waved her hand in the air in an attempt to capture my attention.

"Yes, ma'am."

"I'm curious," she began, "about that dress you are wearing. It's quite different, but in an eclectic sort of way. Seeing as stitching is a hobby of mine, I do find the details quite fascinating. Would you mind telling me who designed such a beautiful dress?"

"I'm not sure," I told her, glancing down at Astrid's borrowed gown. "I believe it was bought at a shop in Cherbourg back in France."

"Ah yes," Mrs. Smith said. "I've been to Paris several times and enjoy the cuisine very much. However, the sauces are a bit rich for my taste. I haven't been to Cherbourg, though. Is that outside of Paris? Do they have high-end boutiques there? Please don't tell me I've missed a town to shop for gowns."

"The dress," Mrs. Pennyworth reminded. "Do tell us where you purchased such an interesting piece?"

"Honestly," I said, "I really can't remember where it was bought."

Mrs. Harland wagged her finger in the air. "My, you are a crafty little one."

"Excuse me?" I asked.

Mrs. Harland gave a sly wink. "Keeping the secrets of your designer, eh?"

"Or," Molly Brown called out, "maybe she knows that telling Angie here is like reporting it in the *Daily News*. She'll have on your dress faster than you can say 'thief.'"

Mrs. Pennyworth's expression soured. She leaned over to Christopher's mother and whispered, "I thought we seated her down there for a reason. How is it that she still manages to include herself in our private conversations?"

His mother scooted to the edge of her seat, eager to catch every single word. "Tell me dear, what is it your father does exactly? What is his field of study? I don't believe I remember you mentioning it before."

"Well," I began, "he has an engineering degree."

Her brown eyes sparkled. With an approving nod of her head,

she responded to the ladies at the table, "Very impressive." She turned to Christopher. "Did you know that Corinne has traveled the world and has been schooled in some of the best boarding institutions in Europe?"

"Actually," I corrected, "I never said I was in the best boarding schools in Europe."

"Oh."

"And my father has an engineering degree," I continued, "but currently he is a farmer." I thought a moment. "Actually, he's out of work right now, which is why we are returning to Canada."

The glimmer in her eyes slowly dimmed. "Out of work?"

"Yes, ma'am."

"I see. If you don't mind me asking, how is it that you are able to afford first-class?"

"Mother!" Christopher warned.

"Oh, I'm not in first-class."

"But…but…I saw you in the halls."

"I was lost."

While a few of the women cleared their throats and dipped their heads, Molly called out, "Don't feel bad, honey. I get lost down these halls all the time. If it weren't for the smell of money emanating from the first-class corridor, I'd probably end up walking in circles until I walked clear off this ship and into the ocean."

"If only we could be so lucky," Mrs. Pennyworth muttered.

With her head dipped, Christopher's mother reached for the glass in front of her. With both hands cupped around it, she gulped down the water in one gigantic swallow. "A farmer. I see," she said again. She turned to Christopher. "I suppose Sophia should be along any moment now. I wonder what's keeping her."

No sooner than she said it, behind us a tiny high-pitched voice with a hard British accent asked, "I'm not late, am I?"

14

"No, dear," Christopher's mother said. "On the contrary, you're right on time."

"Good," Sophia's said, cutting her eyes to me. Her British accent was seasoned with a pinch of arrogance.

The men at the table, including Christopher, stood in her presence. The women smiled graciously and gave subtle, approving nods at Sophia's chosen attire. Sophia went around the table, giving polite hugs and double-cheek kisses to everyone—except me.

Like the others, Sophia's choice of apparel was rather expensive-looking. She wore a tailor-made black silk brocade and chiffon dress. The material was so thin, the bones of her shoulders peeked through. Wrapped around her shoulders she wore an ostrich feather cape that was in complete contrast to the simple but elegant dress.

With her gloved hand, she reached up and grabbed a handful of feathers and carelessly flung the cape over an empty seat. The dark color of her gown accentuated her porcelain skin. Unlike mine, her dark-brown hair was pinned up with curly tendrils cascading down her face. I would have bet anything that under her pricey dress was one of those Curved Busk Waspie corsets I couldn't have begged my portly waist to squeeze into.

On several occasions, she glanced over at me with the same expression as Angelica "Schoolmarm" Pennyworth.

Christopher's mother motioned toward the other empty seat next to her son. "Sophia, please sit down."

Sophia stood behind the chair and waited. Appalled, Christopher's mother exclaimed, "Christopher! Years of etiquette training at the most expensive schools and this is how you behave?"

The corners of Sophia's crimson-painted lips curved upward as she nodded her approval to Mrs. Smith.

For at least thirty minutes, Christopher's mother chatted directly to Sophia about old times, retelling the story of how "little Sophie" and her son were to be married some day. When Sophia attempted her hand at a humorous tale, Christopher's mother placed her hand on her chest and laughed as if it was the funniest thing she had ever heard. Maybe I did not understand the wittiness of the rich, but I hardly found Sophia's tasteless tale of a servant fired for stealing a silver candelabra amusing.

Every so often, his mother would graciously give me a courteous smile from across the table and then ask if I was all right. Once, she even asked if I would like my water glass refilled. That was the extent of our conversation.

Captain Smith, however, spent most of the time rallying back and forth with business colleagues about the upcoming election. During the heated discussion, he and Mr. Harland let it be known that they planned to vote for Wilson. Most of the other gents preferred Taft. From there, the conversation turned into a heated debate.

"Are you enjoying yourself?" Christopher asked.

I nodded. "I'm having a wonderful time. What about you? Am I doing a good job of keeping you company this evening?"

"Of course," he said. "I'm having the best time."

"I do hate to complain," Sophia interrupted.

"Since when?" Molly interjected from the other end of the table.

"But I must say," Sophia continued on, ignoring Ms. Brown, "second-class seating is quite horrific. Do you know they had the audacity to tell me I had to stay in that seating because of my misfortune of being tardy?"

She glanced around the table with her mouth hung open, looking for sympathy for her abominable calamity. Sophia was amusing to watch. Even more amusing was watching the same expression on the women's faces when she explained how the roasted mutton tasted like rotting day-old bangers.

"Was it that bad?" Christopher's mother asked with genuine concern.

"Of course it was. The diners were stuck so close together, I practically bumped elbows with the gents at the next table. And the food…" She placed a hand over her chest and drew in a deep breath before continuing, "As I have explained, the food was horrific. I wouldn't even feed my servants the peasant food they tried to give us."

"Actually the food wasn't that bad," I chimed in.

Sophia slowly turned her head in my direction. In fact, up until that time, I honestly believed she forgot I was sitting at the table.

"The only thing that was disgusting," I continued, "was the water." I picked up the glass in front of me and took a sip. "From what I can tell, first-class and second-class water come from the same toilet."

Christopher chuckled. Sophia squinted and stared hard at me. Suddenly, her eyes popped open and lit up like a Christmas tree. "I knew you looked familiar when I saw you on the deck this morning! You're the girl I saw in second-class dining that night."

Mrs. Smith gulped down more water. The entire table hushed

while Sophia continued, "You were with that tall, Negro man, yes?"

Every pair of eyes at the table were set on me. "Yes, I was. And that Negro man is my father."

Shocked into an even paler complexion, Sophia choked back her surprise. She reached for her glass of water and took a huge gulp. Subtle, she was not. I wasn't taken aback by her reaction. It was quite common lately.

Mrs. Smith's head whipped around to Christopher. "Did you know that she was a…that she was…" She lowered her voice and whispered across the table. "…a Negro?"

"Yes, Mother, I did. I assumed you knew."

His mother's jaw practically dropped to the embroidered table-cloth. I felt compelled to speak up in her defense. "Truth be told, Christopher, you didn't know until I told you." I turned back to Mrs. Smith. "This reaction is quite common. Some know and some don't."

"But I don't understand," Mrs. Smith said. "You are so well-spoken, so attractive."

"Mother!"

"Do not take that as an offense," she explained. "I'm just quite shocked. I had no idea."

"How are you in first-class if you're a Negro," Angelica Pennyworth called from the middle of the table.

"As I explained to Mrs. Smith earlier, we aren't."

"You aren't Negro?" Miss Pennyworth asked.

"No, I mean we aren't in first-class."

There was a gasp. All eyes were fixed on Mrs. Smith, perhaps attempting to figure out how she could allow such a travesty to occur.

"That can't be," Mrs. Harland said. "This must be some sort of joke, no?"

"Well, personally, I don't care if you're purple," Molly said.

"The more the merrier." She held up her wine glass and toasted. "Here's to just being alive." She chugged down the contents and proudly let out a burp.

"Oh, hush," Mrs. Pennyworth said.

I looked to Christopher for reassurance. Once again, he squeezed my hand from under the table. "Here, ye, here ye, allow me to announce that Corinne LaRoche is Black. There, everyone knows, so let's please continue to enjoy our supper."

"That's hardly funny, Christopher," Mrs. Smith said.

Eventually, the women resumed conversing with one another. They whispered back and forth and occasionally gave me side-glances. I swore at some point in the evening, some had even removed pieces of their jewels.

Sophia leaned back in her chair, positioning herself so that her back was to me and she was facing Christopher's mother. "*Que cette fille fait-elle ici?*"

So, she wants to know why I'm here?

I straightened up in my chair. I patted down the front of my gown with the back of my hand and calmly said, "*Je suis ici parce que j'ai un droit d'être.*"

I'm here because like you, I have a right to be.

Sophia's mouth gaped open. I took pleasure in watching her face turn bright red.

"What did you say?" Christopher asked, impressed.

I looked at Mrs. Smith. With her eyes, she pleaded with me not to let her son know what a rude person Sophia was, seeing as she thought so highly of her and her family.

"Nothing really," I told him. "I gather Sophia wanted to know more about me but apparently was too shy to ask."

Embarrassed, Sophia resumed a less disdainful conversation with Mrs. Smith—in English.

"I'm glad you came," Christopher told me.

It was my turn to blush. "I'm glad I did, too."

A uniformed man walked up to the table. "Excuse me, ladies," he said, giving a head nod to all women in the near vicinity—myself included. He leaned over and whispered into the Captain's ear. When the man looked in my direction, I realized he was the steward who had, only a day ago, accosted me at breakfast with Hat Lady. I bowed my head, fearing that I would be confronted again, only this time, more was at stake.

With a troubled expression that no one else seemed to notice, Christopher's uncle rose. With a quick nod, he excused himself.

"Christopher, honey," his mother called from the other side of the table, "why don't you tell us how you are going to be the captain of this beautiful ship one day?"

"Mother," Christopher sighed, "I'm really not in the mood tonight."

His mother's eyes shifted down to her plate. I felt sorry for her. She was annoying, but like any mother, she only had the best intentions for her son, just as Momma did Corinne and me.

Sophia's eyes inspected me from head to toe until finally, she asked. "Will you be joining us *every* evening?"

I looked toward Christopher. He turned to her and said, "I'd be honored if she did."

Sophia glanced at Christopher's mother and then reached for her glass again. This time it was empty. That didn't stop her from pretending to take another sip. Trembling, she set the empty glass back onto the table. She shifted uncomfortably in her seat and tried her hardest to avoid eye contact.

The servers arrived and set down fancy dining plates containing hors d'oeuvre of various oysters. Not particularly fond of oysters, I allowed Christopher to nibble off my plate.

"Christopher," his mother said disdainfully, "it is not proper to eat from another's plate."

The servers returned with lamb with mint sauce and *parmentier* and boiled new potatoes served on a bed of white rice.

For the rest of the meal, Sophia quietly nibbled on a few morsels of her lamb while Mrs. Smith attempted to make forced, but polite, conversation at the table.

"So is there anything else I should know about you, Miss Corinne?" Christopher joked. "Within the last several hours, I found out you're Black, you speak French fluently, and you don't particularly enjoy the taste of an oyster."

"Are any of those a problem for you?" I asked.

He shook his head. "Your skin is beautiful and I think it's most attractive that you speak another language. However, I will have to say a line might need to be drawn with your distaste of oysters. They are quite the aphrodisiac, you know?"

"Christopher!" His mother choked from across the table. "Please be a gentleman before Sophia. I mean, before the...ladies."

I grinned. His silliness was a redeeming quality that I had not witnessed in many boys. Sébastien had always been so serious and self-righteous—right up to the day I caught him cheating.

"Relax, Mother," he said. "It's an old wives' tale."

Our faces were so close, his breath warmed my cheek. Sophia must have noticed. She started coughing. No one took notice until she wrapped her thin, white fingers around her throat.

"Sophia!" Christopher exclaimed, jumping out of his chair. "Take a deep breath." He poured water into her empty glass and handed it to her. "Drink some of this."

She placed her hand on her forehead as she took a tiny sip. "Christopher, could you please take me back to the stateroom? For some reason, I have fallen quite ill."

Just then, Captain Smith returned to the table. The smile he so cheerfully wore at the beginning of the evening was conspicuously missing. In its place was a furrowed brow and elongated creases around the corners of his mouth, giving the telltale sign that something was terribly wrong.

Captain Smith leaned over to Percy Harland, who had just made a coin disappear for the gent next to him. I watched for several minutes. As Captain Smith relayed his message, Mr. Harland's expression went from disappointment to shock. Moments later, Mr. Harland hopped up from his chair. Both were gone without so much as a word to anyone.

"What do you suppose that was all about?" I asked Christopher.

"What?"

"Your uncle and Mr. Harland?"

"Oh that," he said casually. "Probably some business venture gone bad. Would you like to take a walk on the deck?"

"Christopher?" his mother called. "Maybe you should escort Sophia back to her stateroom. You can see she's not feeling well."

Sophia began coughing furiously.

Christopher turned back to me. "Sorry, Corinne, I really should—"

"Oh, don't worry, Christopher," Molly shouted from across the table. "You two please go on and resume what you were doing. Your mother and I can take Sophia back to her stateroom. Besides, I do believe your mother owes me some gossip, don't you, Ellie?"

"But I really—" Mrs. Smith began.

"Oh, no, no, no," Molly said, lifting up Sophia from the chair by her elbow. "I won't wait any longer."

"Christopher," his mother said, "Ms. Brown and I will be able to catch up anytime. I *need* for you to escort Sophia back right away." She stared down at her son, daring him to defy her wishes.

"I'm sure you and Ms. Brown are quite capable," he said. "However, I will check in on her later if you like."

His mother's lips pursed as she shot up from her chair. She threw her napkin onto the table and took Sophia's elbow. Ms. Brown held the other.

I glanced up at the round, silver-plated clock hanging over the Captain's table. It was getting late. I told Astrid I would be back soon, but I was having such a good time. It pained me to think about spending the rest of the evening holding back her hair while she leaned over the toilet. "I really should go," I told Christopher.

"Don't worry about Sophia," he said. "She'll be fine."

Sophia? I was hardly concerned with her!

"Let's enjoy the evening," he begged. "The night is so beautiful."

His brown eyes sparkled under the crystal lights. He pushed his chair back and stood up and then placed his hand on my arm and helped me from my chair.

"Thank you."

"You're very welcome."

As we headed out of the dining room, I looked back. With a helpless expression, Sophia watched us exit.

·∘⟨ 15 ⟩∘·

*T*his side of the ship's lower promenade deck was slightly different from the other side. There were no tiny circular eating tables or the frilly umbrellas used to shade them. The eastern side of the ship had long wooden lounge chairs situated in line formation alongside the metal rail, starting from the bow to as far as my eyes could see. Aside from a few passengers, this side was desolate. On the above level, a young boy and girl ran through irritated couples, tagging each other and yelling, "*Your turn!*"

"It must be great having your uncle as a captain of such a magnificent ship," I said. "You're able to sail all over the world, meeting different people while learning about their cultures. It must be wonderful."

Christopher shrugged. "That depends on the perception. While I do like sailing, I don't visit as many places as you would think. For instance, my mother and I will get off in New York and then my uncle—the Captain—will continue back to Europe." He exaggerated the words, *the Captain*, implying something other than pride. "During the Olympic's maiden voyage, I rarely saw my uncle. My mother was so seasick, she remained in the cabin most of the time. Most often than not, the passengers are adults, so it's rare that I actually have any company at all."

"But still," I said, "I can't see how you don't see this as a great opportunity."

"That's your opinion. I'll respect that. I'll only say that no one really knows what goes on in another person's head."

He looked over the ship's rail, down at the ocean, with a thoughtful yet troubled expression.

"Do you think you'll ever take over as Captain one day?"

He laughed. "Ships aren't willed to family members by the Captain. Like my uncle, I'd have to be appointed. He has a long and extensive history with ships that began with him joining the White Star Line years ago as a fourth officer. My mother would love it if it were that easy. However, it is a possibility seeing as my uncle has only a daughter, cousin Helen, not to mention my mother is pressuring certain officers for my appointment."

"And you don't want that?"

He shrugged. "I suppose. Although I don't have my uncle's extensive background, on several occasions he has referred to me as second in command. I do take that appointment seriously. Between you and me, Mother is even pushing my uncle to have his contacts allow me to bypass some of the stringent rules. I'm not supposed to know that, though."

"I guess it's convenient to have friends in high places," I said.

"It is and it isn't."

"If not Captain, what would you rather do?"

"I'd rather build the ships than sail them. I've always wanted to be an engineer."

"Really? My father is an engineer."

Christopher's eyes sparkled with excitement. "You mentioned that. I'd love to meet him."

My enthusiasm quickly diminished. Daddy and Astrid were

similar in that they both distrusted white people. Like my sister, Daddy tolerated them, but if he had a choice, he would prefer to have no dealings with them at all—especially after the Cherbourg incident.

"Maybe," I lied.

Christopher playfully grabbed my hand and pulled me further down the ship's bow. "So tell me, Corinne, what about all your gentlemen suitors? I know you left a pack of them back in France."

I sighed while glancing up at the stars that shone in the dark sky. The evening could not have been more perfect than if I had asked for it. The night was chilly and visibility, clear. I looked off into the distance, admiring the pointy tips of tall icebergs. They stood strong in the darkness.

"What suitors might you be referring to?" I asked.

"You know what callers I'm referring to. Those boys that follow you around like lovesick puppies and come to your residence at all hours of the evening in hopes of catching a tiny glimpse of the object of their affection—those suitors." He slipped out of his coat and wrapped it around my shoulders. In turn, I stepped closer so we could share the warmth. "Those hearts you broke when you left France. And speaking of France, how long have you lived there? You speak the language so fluently. If I didn't know better, I would have assumed you were born and raised there."

"Four years," I told him. "My mother is French and encouraged us to speak the language as often as possible. I think she knew someday we'd live in Cherbourg since her family is there."

"I imagine you with a big family—aunts, uncles, a ton of cousins. Do you visit them often?"

I paused, attempting to figure out how to respond. Finally, I said, "I've never met them since my mother was disowned for marrying a Black man."

"I'm sorry. I didn't mean to pry."

"It doesn't really bother me anymore," I admitted. "It's been so long that I've always thought of her family as never existing—the same way they did us. My mother is a strong woman for doing that. I would love to be like her one day."

"I bet you look like her."

I started becoming uneasy with the direction the conversation was turning. Sensing the discomfort, Christopher took hold of my hands. "You never did tell me about all the hearts you broke back home."

"There was one boy," I admitted.

"See, I knew it!"

"But," I quickly interrupted, "he wasn't the one for me and fortunately I see that now."

"What made you come to that conclusion?"

"I don't know," I told him.

"I think you do."

Christopher reached inside the coat and wrapped his arms around my waist, holding on tight. Granted, it was cold and I was shivering, so maybe he was warming me up, but this embrace felt like there was more behind it.

I quickly pulled away.

"Did I do something wrong?" he asked.

I struggled with the words, eventually deciding on, "My life is rather complicated, Christopher."

He laughed. "I know that you charmed Old Man Harland and he is a hard one to please. What could be more complicated than that?"

"Stop it," I commanded. "I'm serious. You don't understand. I wish I had someone to talk to about these things, but I just can't right now."

"Are you in trouble?"

I didn't want to reveal too much. "I'm not the person you think I am," I finally settled on. "My family is falling apart right before my eyes and it only seems to be getting worse."

"We all have problems."

"Don't you dare try to discredit what I'm dealing with," I said angrily. "You have absolutely no idea."

His expression softened. "I'm sorry. I wasn't trying to do that. I was simply trying to comfort you. It's just that you're smart, pretty and funny, so I guess I focused on that rather than the fact that you're human like everyone else. For that, I apologize."

"You said yourself that appearances are never what they seem, or does that only apply to you? Maybe it would be better if I kept up a façade, forgetting that my life was crumbling down around me."

"You're right. I'm sorry." He wrapped his arms around me tighter. My head nestled against a chest that was much broader than I expected. His embrace was so strong and comforting, I could've stayed in his arms for the rest of the evening…or forever.

I inhaled, taking in the salty aroma of the sea surrounding us. Every so often, a wave crashed against the ship and a few trickles of water splashed onto my face. A few times the ship hit rough waters and rocked. The gentle rocking reminded me of when Momma used to sing a simple song to Astrid and me as children in order to get us to fall asleep:

The sea is a piece of heaven
For all the world to see
The sea holds our deepest dreams
For us, for eternity

"Are you all right?" Christopher asked.

"Yes, I'm fine," I said, closing my eyes tightly. I absorbed every single moment, realizing life was rarely this peaceful. I had to appreciate it as often as possible. "Honestly, Christopher, I don't usually get upset like this, but—"

"You don't have to apologize."

"Yes, I do. I don't want you to think I whine like a baby, whose rattle was snatched away. Really, I'm not like this. In fact, I can't remember the last time I was so flustered."

"Yesterday in the hall, remember?"

That made me laugh.

"It's quite all right, Corinne. Half the time I feel frustrated, too, but then I say or do something to laugh instead."

"I know," I told him. "I haven't stopped laughing since being with you."

"And I don't want you to."

A huge wave struck the side of the ship, causing us to lose our footing. With his arms securely around me, he leaned our bodies against the railing and held on.

"Are you sure everything is all right?" he asked.

I nodded.

He leaned in closer. Not wanting to be fooled like last time, I kept my eyes open as I stood in place against the ship's rail. His face was inches from mine, but still our lips remained unconnected.

"We haven't even had a first dance yet," he said.

He pulled me to him and playfully spun me around and around until I thought I would fall to the ground with dizziness. I laughed and enjoyed every moment out there on the Titanic's cold and windy deck. I enjoyed myself so much I didn't notice Sophia standing on the deck stairwell, watching us.

APRIL 12

11:12 P.M.

"Where the hell were you?" Astrid inquired as soon as I opened the door. The stateroom light was off and I had tried sneaking in without being noticed, but unfortunately, Astrid could hear a chicken feather drop at a cotillion. She had been waiting up so she could call me a liar for first, not coming back early as I had told her, but for also not bringing back dinner as promised.

"You said you'd only be gone an hour. Do you know how many times I felt like passing out in that hour? I'm sure you don't, because as I've stated before, you are so selfish. What do you think I was supposed to do all alone by myself? Did you expect that I would be able to feed myself and clean up after myself? You really don't care about me, do you? And is that *my* dress?"

"Astrid, please," I sighed. "I'm tired."

"I guess you would be, seeing as you stayed out for hours doing who knows what. I could have been starving for all you cared."

Before she had the chance to complain more, someone knocked at the door.

"Who is that?" Astrid asked.

"I won't know until I open the door, now will I?"

"It can't be Daddy," Astrid said. "He just left."

I opened the door. It was Christopher. "I'm sorry to be here so late, especially after we just left each other, but I wanted to make sure you were all right. On the deck I got the feeling that I may have overstepped my bounds a bit."

"Who is that?" Astrid yelled.

"Go back to bed," I yelled back.

"I would if you'd be quiet."

I took a step out into the hallway and shut the door behind me.

"Did I wake your sister?" he asked.

"Never mind her. Go on."

"The more I thought about it, the worse I felt." He gently touched my cheek with his fingertips. "I should have known when to stop with the questions. Instead I made you uncomfortable and for that, Corinne, I apologize."

"Christopher," I began, "you did not make me feel uncomfortable."

"Are you sure?"

"Yes, so please stop apologizing," I said lightheartedly. "I had a wonderful time this evening." Better than he could ever imagine.

"I'm glad to hear that," he said. "And since you're still dressed, perhaps you would like to watch the moon while relaxing on the deck with me."

"Now? At this hour?"

"This is the most beautiful time. The passengers are asleep and we can be alone."

The thought was tempting. I almost said yes, but then glanced back at my cabin door and thought about Astrid. As much as I wanted to, I'd never hear the end of it if I disappeared again.

"I can't," I told him.

He nodded. "I figured it was a little too late but thought I'd try anyway. Besides, I have another tour in the morning. Can I see you again?"

"I'd like that."

He kissed my forehead and gave me a hug. Then he reached around me and pushed open the door. "Apologize to your sister for me," he whispered.

"I will."

"Good night."

"Good night."

He waited as I pushed the door open and went in.

"I take it that wasn't Daddy," Astrid said when I shut the door.

"No, it wasn't." I undressed and placed her dress back into the closet.

"I feel like I'm going out of my mind," Astrid said. "It's like everything is closing in on me. What should I do?"

I looked at my sister. It really wasn't her fault—at least not everything. She was in the same predicament I was, but even more so. This was the first time I felt we were finally on the same page.

"What are we going to do?" I asked.

"I don't know, Corinne," she said. "But it doesn't help matters when you desert me and leave me here with tons of horrid thoughts running through my convoluted brain."

"I didn't leave you," I said. "I only went to dinner. I wasn't gone that long."

"How would you like it if I left you?" she asked.

"You *are* leaving me," I reminded. "Remember?"

"That's different. Besides, I thought I'd be doing you a favor by disappearing." She stared at me, waiting for my response. I wanted to tell her that wasn't the case—I really did—but for the past few days, I couldn't help thinking about life without her constant pestering and whining. Maybe being apart was best.

"I told you so." She frowned. "You don't want me around any

more than I want to be around your bratty, better-than-thou attitude."

"It's not that, Astrid. It's just that—"

"Oh save it!" she interrupted.

I headed into the bathroom to draw a bath, leaving her ranting about how selfish I was and how much better I thought I was.

I slipped into the bathwater, allowing the warmth to envelop my body. "If you're hungry, I can get you something as soon as I finish," I told her, interrupting her rant. "Are you hungry?"

"No, I'm not! But you didn't know that."

I sighed, slipping neck-high into the tub.

"Momma would be so disappointed in you for treating your sister like this. She always thought you were the smart, considerate one. I guess you've exposed one of *her* faults—the trust she held in you."

"Don't you dare talk about her like that!" I screamed from the tub. "You were never around long enough for her to put *any* trust in you. You were too busy sneaking around."

"Oh really?" she yelled back. "And how could Momma trust you? You were the one covering for me, weren't you? So, in essence, my situation is as much my fault as it is yours."

"That doesn't even make sense."

"It's the truth. You—"

I dunked my head completely under the water. I did not want to hear any more of her lies. I held my breath for as long as I could, struggling for one more second of silence. When I ran out of air, I lifted my head and with my bath towel, wiped the water from my face.

"You're probably the reason Momma left us—" Astrid said, continuing her rant.

I took in a deep breath and then dipped my head back under the water. As I lay there at the bottom of the tub, I opened my eyes and wished I were back on the promenade deck with Christopher. I blew tiny air bubbles and watched as they rose to the surface and burst. If I surfaced, I'd probably do the same.

I contemplated what would happen if I let myself run out of air. Not necessarily in a serious way, more like a would-I-even-be-missed type of way. I didn't feel I was a deeply religious person, but Momma always told us that those who took their own lives condemned themselves to hell. I wasn't itching to find out whether or not that was true.

Out of breath, I lifted my head.

It was quiet.

I listened for a second. When I didn't hear anything, I relaxed and continued my bath. When I finished soaking my tired body, I grabbed my towel, sat on the tub's edge and dried off every inch, beginning with my toes and finishing with my face. I reached for another towel and wrapped it tightly around my head. I then creaked open the door halfway, hoping Astrid had nagged herself into a deep sleep.

"Astrid?" I called. "Are you asleep?"

No answer.

Good, I thought, *finally some quiet.*

The room was dark except for the moonlight peeking through the tiny cabin window. I caught a glimpse of Astrid's shadow as she lay peacefully on her bed. She was on her side with her back to me and the sheets crumpled down by her ankles.

I went over to her and reached down to pull up her sheet. When I did, I felt something damp. At first, I thought it was sweat, but the cabin was hardly hot enough for that. I flicked on the light, and to my horror, Astrid's limp body lay there in a pool of her own blood.

1 day until…

❧ 17 ❧

I dashed down the corridor in nothing but my nightdress. My hair was sopping wet and mixed with the sweat from my forehead. I turned down one hall, realized it was the wrong one and immediately switched directions. *Which one was it? They all looked the same.*

When I came to the hall with the fancy paintings and the sitting area at the end, I knew I was headed in the right direction. *But which door?* It was at least halfway down the hall.

"Excuse me, miss." A warm hand lightly touched my cold shoulder. I turned and saw a man in full uniform. With a stern look, he asked, "Do you belong in first-class?" He glanced down at my nightdress. I gathered he already knew the answer. "Are you in need of assistance?"

I thought about asking him for help but decided against it. His inclusion may have been more of a hindrance than help. "I can escort you back to your room," he said.

"Thank you, no," I told him. "I suppose I got lost. I can find my own way back, thank you."

He dipped his head and said slowly, "I really think I should escort you back to your room, miss. We can't have just anyone roaming the first-class halls." He grabbed my elbow and began forcing me back down the hall.

"Oh, there you are, Mr. LaPierre." A tiny woman wrapped in fur waved toward the uniformed man. "I need your assistance, please. I'm afraid I've forgotten the number to my safe again."

Mr. LaPierre looked down at me. "Head back to your room, miss. I don't want to see you down this corridor again." He let go of my elbow. As soon as he did, his demeanor changed. "Why yes, Mrs. Godfrey. I'd be happy to help."

When it was safe to do so, I headed back down the hall. I knocked on a door, but there was no answer. The second door, a young woman answered. "I apologize," I said, out of breath. "I must have the wrong room. I'm looking for Captain Smith's stateroom."

The woman eyed me up and down and then finally pointed two doors down.

"Thank you."

Softly, I rapped on the door. There was no answer. I knocked again, only this time with more urgency. A few seconds later, Mrs. Smith emerged.

"Yes?" she asked. She glanced down at my disheveled appearance. "Is there something wrong?"

"Please, Mrs. Smith," I begged. "I need to speak with your son. It's very important."

"I'm afraid he's asleep."

"Please. It's urgent."

She hesitated a moment. She cleared her throat and then quietly shut the door. I glanced down at my nightdress. Speckles of blood were splattered down the front. I had dashed out of the room so quickly, I had no undergarments on. Because I was sweating profusely, my stained gown was matted to my skin. I could only imagine what I looked like to her and anyone else that happened upon me, including that officer of the ship.

I was about to knock again until the door creaked opened. "Christopher!" I said. "I need your help."

I was disappointed when Mrs. Smith, not Christopher, appeared at the door once again. "I'm sorry, but he's fast asleep. Maybe you could come back tomorrow?"

"Please."

"Mother?" Christopher called from the background. "Who is that? Is that Corinne?"

"Yes," I yelled past his mother. "I need to speak with you. It's urgent." I looked at Mrs. Smith. "I'm really sorry to disturb you, but I do need his assistance with an urgent matter."

"Christopher," his mother began, "I'm sure everything is fine. Go back to bed. Whatever she needs can be obtained from the ship's steward." She looked down at me. "Or the ship's doctor."

"What is it?" he asked, ignoring his mother.

"I need help."

"Of course, Corinne."

In his night attire, Christopher shoved his way out the door. He took me by the elbow and led me down the hall. In the background, his mother yelled, "Christopher, are you bloody mad? You cannot go out like that!" He ignored her as we rushed down the hall.

We turned a corner and headed down a hallway until I saw Officer LaPierre, the same officer I had seen moments earlier. I grabbed Christopher's arm and pulled him around the corner.

"What is it? Has something happened?" he asked.

"Shhhh," I told him.

He was standing outside of the room of the old lady that had needed his assistance with her safe. After exchanging a few pleasantries with some of the other passengers, Officer LaPierre disappeared around the corner.

I took Christopher's arm once more and led him toward my stateroom. "We have to get back to my room right away."

When we reached my cabin, I opened the door. This time Astrid lay crumpled up on the floor by the foot of her bed.

"She must have tried to get up," I said, rushing over to her.

"What happened?" He scooped her up into his arms and gently placed her onto the bed. When he saw the blood-stained sheets, he questioned, "What in the world happened, Corinne?"

I shook my head. "I don't know. You've got to help us."

"Where is your father?"

"I can't tell him."

"Your mother?"

I shook my head. "She's not here on the ship."

He cocked his head to the side. "But I thought you said your family was moving back to Canada. I assumed—"

"She's not here," I told him again.

"You have to tell your father."

"I can't."

"Well then, how about the ship's doctor?" he asked. "Have you called upon him?"

"I can't," I said again. "There's a certain situation and—"

I looked down. Astrid moaned and her eyes rolled to the back of her head. I was really scared. "Christopher! Help me!"

Christopher grabbed my arms. "Listen to me. She will die if she doesn't see a doctor. Go to the bathroom, get a cool cloth and rub it gently on her head. I will go for the doctor." With that, he disappeared out the door.

I did exactly as he instructed—grabbed a cloth and ran it under water. When I returned to Astrid's bedside, she was mumbling incoherently. Her hair was matted down with sweat and her nightgown sopping with a combination of both perspiration and blood.

"Astrid," I said, "don't try to talk. Everything will be fine."

I gently wiped her forehead with the cloth as she slipped in and out of consciousness. *Why was it taking Christopher so long?*

Several minutes later, Astrid regained consciousness. At first she only stared at the ceiling, but eventually she slowly turned her head. When she saw me, she reached up and grabbed my arm, pulling me closer. She was struggling to say something. I leaned in, turning an ear to her dry, chapped lips. "Yes?"

She lifted her head and whispered, "Stop wiping my forehead, please. It's giving me a headache."

"Sorry," I told her, relieved to see life back in her again.

When I heard a knock at the door, I jumped up and opened it. The doctor nodded a quick greeting and then headed straight for Astrid. Christopher remained at the door's entranceway.

"I'm Doctor Wahlberg," he announced. He sat on the edge of her bed. "And what is her name?"

"Astrid," I told him.

Doctor Wahlberg was a tall, angular man with masses of curly black hair and a thick black mustache. His big hands and thin fingers wrapped around Astrid's neck, like he was choking her. He looked back and saw my concerned expression. "Just feeling the glands." He pulled down the sheet and observed her midsection. He took his abnormally long index finger and poked at various places on her stomach. She cringed with his last prod. "It's okay, dear," Dr. Wahlberg said. He examined her a few more minutes and then looked at Christopher. "How long has she been bleeding like this?"

Christopher turned and looked at me.

"At least an hour," I told the doctor. "She was fine when I came in. I didn't notice anything until after my bath." I glanced down, forgetting I was still in my nightdress. The towel that was wrapped around my hair had fallen somewhere between here and there. My hair was dried into a frizzy puff.

Dr. Wahlberg reached into his black medical bag. "Does Astrid have any medical conditions?"

"She, um—"

Both Christopher and Dr. Wahlberg turned, waiting for my answer.

"She's pregnant," I softly admitted.

The doctor's sudden hesitation made for an even more uncomfortable situation. Quickly, he regained composure. "I see." He pulled something from the bag and continued. I didn't look back at Christopher.

"Is there a parent or guardian on board?"

When I didn't answer, Dr. Wahlberg asked again. "I need parental consent. Is there a parent on board?"

Astrid had made me promise not to say anything. I wanted to keep that promise but not if it was a choice between life and death.

"I, uh—"

Astrid's groans interrupted me.

"I need to know now!" Dr. Wahlberg commanded.

"No," I said. "There is no parent or guardian aboard. If you need consent, I can give it to you."

Dr. Wahlberg nodded. "It might be better if the two of you leave the room."

Christopher grabbed my elbow and steered me out of the room.

"She's going to be all right, isn't she?" I asked Dr. Wahlberg.

He turned from Astrid's bed. "This is your sister, I gather?"

"Yes."

"I know you love your sister very much. Don't worry, she'll be fine." He smiled warmly. However minimal, his reassurance provided some comfort.

Christopher took my hand and led me out of the room and down the corridor. "Let me take you to my stateroom," he offered. "We need to get some clothes for you before you catch your death."

I glanced down. I was still wearing my nightdress. "I'm sorry you had to see me like this, but when I saw Astrid lying there, bleeding, without thinking, I ran off down the hall to find you."

"Considering the circumstances, I think I'll let you get away with it." He gave a reassuring grin, but tonight, I didn't feel much like smiling.

As we walked, every step was heavier than the one before. Suddenly, I stopped right there in the middle of the hall. With my back against the wall, I slid down to a sitting position and wrapped my arms around my knees. I inhaled deeply, taking in every breath as if it was my last.

"She's going to be fine," Christopher said, slumping down next to me. He put his arm around my shoulder. "You'll see."

I rested my head on his shoulder. I could hear him breathing.

"Is this what you meant on the deck, about not discussing certain aspects of your life?" he asked.

"This among others."

"I assume others include the whereabouts of your mother."

I took in a few more breaths, attempting to relax. It was no use. My heart continued to race. My head pounded. The blood running through my veins was like ice. My body felt completely limp.

"We really should get some clothes on you," he finally said. He stood up, offered a hand and helped me to my feet.

"Thank you," I whispered.

"No need to thank me. You'd do the same."

Halfway down the corridor he said, "Let's devise a plan here. First, we'll find you something to wear. Then we'll go back and check on your sister. If you're hungry, we can get something to eat and possibly bring something back for her—if the doctor says she's up to it. Once we see everything is fine, and it will be, you'll need some rest. I'll watch your sister while you sleep and if there is any problem—which I'm sure there won't be—I'll be there to call on the doctor. You'll see, Corinne, everything will be fine. There is no need to worry. I'll stay with you for as long as you need."

I managed a weak smile, appreciating, as well as being impressed with his assertion during such a delicate situation—especially for a person he barely knew.

I grabbed ahold of his hand. "I really would."

"Would what?"

"Do the same for you."

He grabbed my hand as we headed off down the hall.

·≈|18|≈·

"**A**re you sure your mother won't mind?" I asked. My mind jolted back to the expression on his mother's face when I had come knocking earlier. Somehow, I didn't think she would approve of me "borrowing" clothes. "I can always go back to my stateroom and get a dress."

He shook his head. "The doctor is busy. We'll get something quickly and then go back and wait outside your room for the doctor. Besides, you'll catch pneumonia dressed like that. What good would it do you to be sick as well?"

As we entered, the room was dark and quiet. When he flicked on the light, I almost toppled over in surprise. Although our second-class room was not shoebox-small, it was tiny in comparison to the immaculate, spacious room I was currently standing in.

First-class rooms most certainly reinforced their sense of entitlement with the flawless, expensive furnishings, which included an electric fireplace, writing table and a contained living room space located toward the back of the deep stateroom. The furnishings were made of expensive oak and the bed sheets were hand-woven burgundy silk. On the writing table were a few strategically placed reading books along with a squire's desk set complete with a wood handle pen and brass single inkwell. The carpeting was the same color as the silk sheets, but was stitched with tan and black nautical designs.

"Where is your mother?" I asked.

"She and my uncle stay in the next stateroom."

"This room is yours?" I asked incredulously.

Christopher nodded. "I stay with them sometimes."

"I can't believe it," I told him. "This is like four of our rooms."

He laughed. "If you can be patient, I'll get some clothes for you." He walked out, leaving me standing there, gawking.

From first entering the room, I wanted to roll around on the plush couch that sat next to the fireplace, but felt I was inappropriately dressed to even think about doing such a thing. I pictured women in stylish ball gowns and fancy hats with matching gloves sitting on these couches while drinking a "spot of tea."

I couldn't resist. I carefully sat on the tip of the right side cushion, hoping my weight wouldn't leave too much of a dent. The tips of my fingers brushed against its soft covering. The material was like butter. I hopped up and quickly brushed away any indentation my rear may have made.

Christopher returned with an arm full of clothes. He laid them down onto the bed and said, "Take your pick."

I rummaged through the stack, neatly picking up one or two pieces of garments. "These are beautiful," I said, looking at a smartly designed black chiffon and lace skirt set. "But I think these may be a little much for now."

"Sorry about that," he said, taking the dress from my hands. "I just grabbed a handful, hoping you could find something in the pile." He leaned over and picked up a jazzy pink, ruffled dress. "What about this one?"

The dress was even fancier than the first. Plus, it looked at least two sizes too small.

I reached down and picked up a white princess slip with a fitted waist and darts in the front. The scoop neckline was beautifully decorated with Broderie Anglaise and its bust was designed with floral embroidery. I held it close to my body to measure its fit. Christopher quickly turned away. "I don't mean to stare while you are getting dressed."

With no undergarments on, I promptly dropped my nightdress to my feet. I quickly pulled the slip over my head, figuring I could wear it under a simple dress. But the bust was way too small. I hadn't been that size since the sixth grade.

As fast as I stepped into it, I took it off and placed it back on the bed.

"You can go into the bathroom to change if you like," he said, his back still toward me.

"It's much quicker this way. Just keep your head turned."

Using one of the too-small dresses to shield the front portion of my nude body, I scanned the remaining laid-out garments. I spotted a very simple but elegant white tea-length, crisp linen gown. The back was lined with small mother-of-pearl buttons and the neckline was embroidered with roses. This time, it fit perfectly.

I turned around, gathered my hair in my hands and held it up. "Do you mind helping with the buttons?"

Starting from the small of my back, he slowly began fastening each button until reaching the last one at the nape of my neck.

I twirled around. "What do you think?"

He reached out and secured his arms around my waist, pulling me toward him. He leaned down and for the first time, his lips touched mine and lingered there for an eternity. I closed my eyes and let it happen.

When he finally pulled away, I held on to his arm for fear of floating up to the stars and never returning. Delicately, he stroked my cheek as he leaned down and pecked my forehead with his soft lips.

I exhaled. For a fraction of a second, all worries had been released. I couldn't have been more carefree than when walking through the dandelion fields, barefoot in the summertime back in Cherbourg. With his arms around me, I was safe.

"Do you realize that in a couple of days, we will step off of this ship and never see each other again?" I said, crashing back down to reality.

"That's not true," he protested.

"It is true. You'll go home, live your life and in ten years, you'll be married to that British Sophia and have four lovely kids that say, *cheerio and pip, pip* and drink tea every day at high noon."

With one brow raised, he stared at me. "British Sophia?"

I started laughing. "Yes. British Sophia."

He started laughing, too. For a good few minutes, both of us doubled over and busted out with laughter.

"I do have to say," Christopher said between the laughter, "calling her 'British Sophia' sounds quite strange, but for some bizarre reason, it fits...like French pastry."

"Or Swedish meatballs," I said.

"Or Scottish Terrier."

With that, we burst out laughing for another few minutes.

"And for the record," he added, "I hate tea."

Christopher placed his hands on my shoulders. The warmth of his palms pressed against his mother's borrowed dress. His expression became serious. "No matter what, I am so thankful that I met you."

Looking into his eyes, I knew he meant it. He softly caressed my face and then leaned down and kissed me again. It was definite. I really, really liked him. No matter what, I'd let things unfold as they might. Most often, three days was a speck in a person's life. With him, it changed what had started out terribly into something beautiful.

"I'm sorry, Corinne. I didn't mean to, especially with your sister not well. We should get back." He turned and headed for the door. I followed.

A crooked smile formed across my lips. With my index finger, I brushed over the exact spot his lips had touched. It tingled some. I didn't care if I sounded like a schoolchild after her first kiss ever from a boy, but in my mind, I never wanted the fluttering in my stomach to go away.

That feeling soon disappeared when, as we headed down the hall, Christopher suddenly pulled me in another direction and then backed me into a dark corner. "Officer Wiley," he whispered.

Puzzled, I looked at him, wondering why it was that he—the Captain's nephew—felt it necessary to hide.

"I know what you're thinking," he whispered. "But my mother has Officer Wiley on her personal payroll."

"Personal payroll?"

"She doesn't know that I know," he said, "but she pays him to keep an eye on me to make sure I'm not embarrassing her in any way." He looked at me. "You know how she is, Corinne. I don't feel like explaining why a girl was in my room at this late hour."

"Any girl or just me?"

I peered over his shoulder and watched as Officer Wiley casually whistled down the hall. I wanted so much to shout, *Why can't I go wherever I want, first-class, second-class, who cares?* Instead, I stood quietly with my back plastered against the wall like a criminal hiding from the authorities.

We waited a few moments before Christopher said, "I think he's gone."

Holding hands, we continued down the hall. It was at that exact moment, reality washed through me like a tsunami would a small town.

"Are you sure your mother won't be angry that we borrowed her dress?" I asked as we darted down the hall and toward my stateroom. A feeling of guilt swept over me, thinking about our kiss when my sister was not well. By the way he kept two steps ahead of me, he may have felt the same guilt.

"Mother doesn't wear any of those dresses anymore," he said. "She only keeps them around, claiming one day she'll wear them again. Believe me, you're doing me and my uncle a favor by getting rid of it."

When we reached the door, Christopher stood to the side while I quietly knocked.

"Come in," the doctor said. When I pushed open the door, I saw Dr. Wahlberg standing over Astrid, who was sleeping peacefully. With her arms folded across her chest like that, it almost looked like she had passed on.

"How is she?" I asked quickly.

When Dr. Wahlberg smiled, the veins in my neck relaxed. "She's fine, but I'm afraid she lost the baby."

My heart dropped. I was ashamed for not even thinking about the baby—not once.

"A strange thing happened," Dr. Wahlberg said casually. "A Negro man came knocking on the door, claiming he was your father."

I hesitated, deciding whether to cover up the lie with another one. "That was him."

Shock splashed across the doctor's face. "Oh, I had just assumed you girls were—well, uh," he cleared his throat, "I didn't realize you were a Negro." He whispered the word, *Negro*, as if it were profane.

This was the part Astrid and I loathed—when, unbeknownst to us, people assumed we were white. When they found out we weren't, attitudes changed. With Sophia, it had at least been somewhat amusing, but the seriousness of the situation at hand did now allow for amusement.

Dr. Wahlberg stood up and walked over to me. He placed his hand on my shoulder. "I should say that I do not agree with lying, but the good news is that your sister will be fine. Have her rest and then if she is able, she may slowly get out of bed for a few hours to keep her blood from clotting." He reached inside his bag and pulled out a rectangular shaped card and handed it to me. "If you need anything else, please call."

"What about my father?" I asked. "Where did he go?"

"Oh, I sent him to the kitchen for some ice. Please see that your sister sucks on that if her throat gets dry. I've given her some medicine that will help her sleep throughout the night, but it will make her mouth as dry as field cotton." His face flushed. "I mean, it will really make her mouth dry."

"Thank you," I said.

He gave a nod. "Again, if you need me, please don't hesitate." Dr. Wahlberg headed for the door. "Good night, dear."

"Wait," I called.

"Yes?"

"Does my father know about the baby?"

He shook his head. "I didn't think that was my place."

I breathed a sigh of relief. "You won't tell anyone, will you?"

He placed his hand on the doorknob, but hesitated before turning it. "It'll be our little secret, however, you may want to say something to your parents." With a frown and his brow crooked upward, he said, "I have a daughter your age." He turned the knob and headed out the door, pulling it closed behind him.

Christopher came over and squeezed my hand. "I'm glad everything is going to be fine."

"Christopher," I said, burying my head into his chest, "I have so much to tell you. I don't even know where to start."

He held me tighter. "There's so much I don't know about you, Corinne. You're like this deep well of secrets."

"You never questioned me as to why I lied about my father," I said. "Thank you for that."

"You had your reasons, like you have your reasons for not telling me where your mother is."

There was a soft tap on the door. The knob turned and in came Daddy with a bucketful of ice cubes. "What the hell is going on?"

APRIL 13

2:04 A.M.

"Who is this boy?" Daddy asked, laying the bucket on the nearest nightstand. "And where have you been all night?" The defined lines around the frown of his mouth were heavy.

"Daddy, this is Christopher."

"Hellò, sir." Christopher extended a hand, but it was met with an unwelcoming glare.

"Where were you all night?" Daddy had already turned his attention back to me, completely dismissing Christopher. Realizing the obvious disregard, Christopher withdrew his hand and took a step back.

I glanced back toward a resting Astrid. "Daddy, please lower your voice," I said in a tone barely above a whisper. "I was having dinner with Christopher and when I returned—"

"This is where you were all night," Daddy interrupted, "while your sister lay here sick? This was that something you had to do and couldn't go to dinner with your own family?"

"It's not like that."

"Who is this boy?" he asked again.

"I told you, his name is Christopher."

"Well," Daddy said, finally turning his attention to Christopher. "Thank you for occupying my daughter's time. Your services are no longer needed."

"Daddy!"

"It's all right, Corinne," Christopher said softly. "I think I'd better go."

Christopher turned to leave, but I grabbed his arm. "No. Stay." I turned to my father. "How is it that you could treat Christopher worse than a stray dog? Have you forgotten about those policemen back in Cherbourg already?"

Daddy's hand drew back and connected with the left side of my cheek. A stinging sensation traveled from the center of my chin way up to my temple. Immediately, I brought my hand to my face.

"Corinne, honey, I'm so sorry," he said.

"Corinne?" Christopher stepped up beside me. "Are you all right?"

Stunned and with my hand glued to the side of my cheek, I did the only thing I was capable of doing at that point—I nodded.

"Oh, Corinne." Daddy wrapped his arms around me. "Please forgive me." He then turned to Christopher. "Would you please excuse us? I need to talk to her—my family." This time Daddy asked as a gentleman rather than an angry father.

Demonstrating the same respect, Christopher turned to me. "If you say so, Corinne, I'll go, but only if you say so."

"I'm fine."

Christopher squeezed my shoulder and then turned to leave. Daddy and I stood, facing each other. As soon as the door closed behind Christopher, I turned and headed into the bathroom, shutting the door behind me. I leaned against the sink's porcelain rim for support. *Daddy had actually hit me.* The stinging sensation in my cheek reminded me over and over again of his sudden outburst of anger.

"Can I at least talk to you?" Daddy called from the other side of the bathroom door.

"I'll be right out." I took a cloth and held it under the cool, running water. With my head bowed, I tried hard not to look into the mirror. Never once had he even raised his voice to me, much less struck me in rage.

I wrung out the cloth and took a deep breath to calm myself. When I felt I would be able to successfully hold back the tears, I pulled open the door and headed straight for Astrid, who was still asleep. I sat on the edge of her bed and gently dabbed at her forehead.

Standing behind me, Daddy waited patiently as I took the cloth and ran it down her arms—first her left, then her right. The throbbing in my cheek felt more intense. To shut out the pain, I squeezed my eyes tightly and clamped my jaw closed.

"Corinne?"

"Yes, Daddy?" I asked, still dabbing at Astrid's forehead. My voice cracked and a single tear ran down my throbbing cheek.

He placed his hand on my shoulder and squeezed. "Corinne, I love you."

I hopped up from the bed and threw my arms around him. "Daddy, I'm sorry you don't like white people, but it's not Christopher's fault."

"Oh, no, honey," he said, squeezing me so tight, I could barely breathe. "I have nothing against that boy. I've just been under so much pressure lately."

"Pressure? How?"

He took a deep breath. "Corinne, I believe now may be the time to explain everything. No more secrets." He took my hand

and led me away from Astrid's bed, toward the door. "I wanted to tell you earlier but didn't want to overload you with too much."

"What is it, Daddy?"

"I love you girls so much and I hated having to lie to you, but it really was for the best."

My heart began beating faster. "What do you mean?"

"First, I need to say that you girls are my world. I love you more than anything. Everything I do is for the good of the family. You know that, right?"

"Of course."

"Then believe me when I tell you that the reason I lied was because I didn't want to hurt you."

"What are you talking about?" My heart jumped up to my throat, making it difficult to swallow. "I don't understand."

"Your mother is sick, Corinne. That's why she is not coming to Canada."

My mind flashed back to the last time I had seen her. She had kissed my forehead and said good-bye to me before leaving and I had wrapped my arms around her, feeling bones protruding from her back. Even then, I had thought she was paler and more tired than usual. When I had questioned her about it, she insisted it was a lingering cold.

"I don't understand. Sick how?"

"She's been ill for quite some time. Something is ravaging her body. The doctors aren't even sure, but they're doing all they can."

"What does that mean?"

"Don't worry. She'll be fine," he told me. His eyes were shifting back and forth and avoiding me. "Trust me on this, Corinne. But...that's not all."

"There's more?"

"You need to trust me on this."

"Trust you on what?"

His hesitation made me real nervous. It didn't help matters any when he began fidgeting with one of his cuff links. I thought I was going to bust when he took an extra moment to draw in a deep breath and rub the back of his neck.

Finally, he said, "Everything happened so suddenly, Corinne. We had to make quick decisions on what we thought was best for you and your sister. The doctors for your mother are so expensive." He scratched the top of his head and rubbed his chin as if buying time. Every movement seemed to be in slow motion.

"What quick decisions, Daddy? Tell me." It pained me to watch the strained effort it took for him to say what it was he had to tell me.

Finally, he threw his hands up in the air and blurted it out. "We're going back to Winnipeg because I promised you and your sister to a couple of gentlemen—wealthy men that can take care of you the way I won't be able to anymore. In fact, they'll be able to care for you girls better than I could ever hope to."

Daddy's mouth was moving, but I was no longer listening. Instead the words...*promised you and your sister to a couple of gentlemen*, echoed in my ear, over and over. *Your mother is sick*, beat into my brain like a drum. I stared down at the floor, shaking my head disbelievingly.

Slowly, the information began to process. I looked at Daddy. He was mid-sentence when I uttered one simple word. "*No.*"

With a perplexed expression, he paused. "Excuse me?"

I shook my head and then focused on his face. His faced appeared older. *Had he gotten grayer around the temples?* I looked him dead in the eyes. "No."

"Trust me, Corinne. It's for the best, for you and your sister."

"You're prostituting us off to men we've never met and you tell me that I should trust you? How much did you get for us?"

"What are you saying?"

"I'm not saying," I argued. "I'm asking how much you were paid for these strange men to take us off your hands? Did you get a bargain price for the both of us, or is one of us worth more than the other? Tell me, Daddy, how much did you pawn us off for?"

"Corinne!" Daddy said. "I will not have you speaking to me in such a manner."

"I'm curious," I said. "Were you going to introduce me to this stranger and then perhaps say, *Oh, by the way, Corinne, meet your new fiancé?*" My voice trembled with every word. I didn't know how much longer I would be able to hold it together.

"Please trust me, Corinne."

"No, Daddy! I will not! This is unbelievable. How could you possibly allow this to happen?"

He went to grab for my arm, but I pulled away.

"Corinne, please."

"Why would you do this to me? To our family?"

"It's for the best."

I covered my ears with my hands while frantically shaking my head back and forth. "Stop telling me that! I'm sick of hearing how everything is for the best." I shut my eyes, stomped my feet and yelled, "No! I will not. No! No! No!"

"Corinne, stop it!" Daddy commanded. "Why are you behaving like this?" He reached up and pulled my hands from my ears and forced them down to my side. "It's done, Corinne. When we get to Canada, you *will* be engaged and then married. That's final!"

Maybe Astrid was correct, there was no such thing as a God, for He surely wouldn't have laid all of this heartache and pain upon me.

·⟨ 20 ⟩·

APRIL 13
6:13 A.M.

Early the next morning, I sat at the foot of my bed in a trance-like state while squishing the plush carpet in between my toes. I had been awake since two in the morning and was only now feeling the fatigue. More so, I was tired of fighting life circumstances because of the sudden rupture in the blanket of security that, until recently, had kept my world protected.

It was difficult to believe that only three months ago I was at peace back in Cherbourg. It was only a few months ago that I was in love with Sébastien—at least I thought I was. During the days, I studied and worked hard on the farm. During the evenings, I would relax under the stars, inhaling the sweet aroma of Momma's freshly baked bread.

Three months ago felt like an eternity now.

Last evening, around nine o'clock, there was a knock at the stateroom door. When I didn't answer, Christopher's soft voice called from the other side. *"Corinne,"* he had whispered. *"Are you there?"* When I didn't respond, he called my name one last time. He had waited a few minutes before leaving.

For the remainder of the evening and well into the early morning hours, I had sat up in bed while occasionally peering down at Astrid, who had slept restlessly throughout the entire night. I didn't want to wake her, but every time I had adjusted to another position, my bed creaked loudly.

I jumped down from my bed with minimal noise. When I hopped back up, it creaked so loudly, I thought it was going to pop from its hinges. Astrid woke up immediately.

"It's not that bad." She grumbled so softly, I thought she was talking in her sleep. "Did you hear me?" she asked even softer.

"Astrid, are you awake?" I whispered, peering over the bed's edge.

She had propped herself up against the back wall of her bed. "Of course I'm awake. How could anyone sleep with all that creaking going on?"

"Sorry. How are you feeling?"

"I don't think I'll be dancing ragtime in the near future." She struggled to sit up further. I hopped down from my bed and quickly fluffed up one of her pillows, resting it behind her back.

"Do you need anything?" I asked, pulling up the blanket by her feet.

She shook her head. "I needed rest, but that didn't happen when you and Daddy decided to have that quiet, loving discussion last evening."

"I'm sorry. I guess we didn't realize how loud our conversation had gotten."

"Conversation?" She smirked. "Is that what you call it?"

I went to the bathroom, retrieved another wet cloth and returned to her bed, taking a seat on the edge. "The past few days have been such a nightmare, Astrid. I don't see how it can get any worse." I dabbed at her forehead with the wet cloth.

"He means well," Astrid said.

I reached over onto the nightstand and grabbed for a piece of ice. Astrid took it from my hand and jammed it into her mouth.

"Has he been by?" she asked with her mouth full.

I nodded. "Quite a few times last evening to check on you. I told him I'd call upon the doctor right away if there were any complications. I assume he was okay with that, considering he didn't come back."

"Does he know the truth?" she asked.

I shook my head. "The doctor said he would keep quiet as well. Daddy thinks you have a terrible case of motion sickness."

"That's the best you could come up with?"

"Would you have preferred that I tell him you have a dreadful case of leprosy?"

"I suppose if that's the best you could come up with, then that will have to do," she relented. "I hope he believes it."

"Don't worry about Daddy," I told her. "As long as you stay consistent with your caustic wit, then he'll be none the wiser."

She shot me a look as she once again adjusted herself.

"Astrid?"

"Yes?"

"Are you sorry that the baby is gone?"

She didn't answer right away.

"Corinne, get me a glass of water."

I didn't move.

She rolled her eyes. "Pretty, pretty, please with a mountain of sugar on top."

I stood up and grabbed a cup from the bathroom and ran some cold water into it. When I returned, she was lying on her side and her eyes were closed.

"Astrid?" I asked, alarmed.

"My head is throbbing." She sat up and took the water glass from my hand. After two giant gulps, she reached over and placed the empty glass back onto the nightstand. "I guess I am," she said, lying back down and rolling over on her side.

"Sorry about the baby?" I asked.

She nodded.

I reached over and took her hand. "Me too."

She looked up and gently ran her fingers down my bruised cheek. "That looks like it hurts." With her thumb and index finger, she grabbed my chin and turned it from side to side for full inspection. "Daddy was plenty angry, eh?"

"You heard?"

She nodded. "Third-class heard."

I felt helpless watching her struggle to find a comfortable position. Eventually, she decided on, once again, propping herself up against the back wall with a pillow supporting her lower back. "It really is for the best, Corinne."

"Him slapping me?"

"Don't be silly. I'm talking about your engagement." She placed a hand onto her lower abdomen as she struggled to draw in a deep breath.

"Are you sure you're all right?"

"Please stop asking me that," she complained. "I'll be fine. It only hurts every once and a while."

Astrid turned over on her back and rested her arms underneath her head. Now looking quite relaxed and comfortable, it was hard to tell that she had suffered a miscarriage less than twelve hours ago.

"Astrid?"

"Yes?"

"Did you know about Momma being sick?" I asked suspiciously.

"Daddy didn't tell me, if that's what you mean, but I figured something was wrong by her appearance."

My mind raced back to my dinner conversation with Daddy, when he alluded that Astrid was aware of *some* things. "What about the marriage arrangement?"

"You weren't supposed to know that until we got back to Canada," she said. "As for Momma, Daddy told me that she's going to be fine."

"You knew she was sick. Why didn't you tell me?"

"Oh, Corinne, for once stop making me the villain. Anyone with eyes could see Momma wasn't in the best of health. You were too busy following Sébastien around like a lovesick mule to notice." Once again, she adjusted positions. "Only when I questioned Daddy about her did he tell me not to worry or tell you. She was going to be fine."

"That's what he keeps telling me, too," I told her. "But something in his eyes says differently."

"The thing is," Astrid began, "he said that she's going to be fine, but I overheard them talking one night and they both don't think—"

I shook my head. "Stop it, Astrid. I don't want to hear it."

"You have to face it, Corinne."

"No, I won't listen to this."

"This is what I mean," Astrid began. "You say you're not a baby and want to know, but when I attempt to tell you, you kick and scream. You have to grow up and face it. Daddy ain't fit to take care of us alone, so he is marrying us off to someone who can. Momma agreed."

"How long have you known about the marriages?"

"Before we left, Momma did confide in me that she wants me to keep an eye on my little sister always. She said I was the strong one, which is why she decided to tell me the truth—about the arranged marriages anyway. You'd eventually find out, but you're more sensitive. Corinne, if you only knew how much Momma loves you. She even loves you more than she loves me. But I don't care much," she said with a simple shrug of her shoulders. "I know you two had some special bond. I'm not jealous of that." Her lashes fluttered back and forth as if she was in a dust storm— her telltale sign that she was not telling the complete truth. "Momma cried so hard when she told me how much she was going to miss you. I don't suppose she cried that hard for me, but as I've said, that's fine with me. I'm not a little girl like you." Her lashes flickered so fast, she was about to take flight.

"Astrid?" I asked, my heart weighing down my chest. "Do you think we'll ever see her again?"

"Of course we will." She reached up and hugged me. I threw my arms around her, hanging on for dear life. "They will see to it."

I held onto Astrid as she gently stroked my hair. "That's enough of that," she said, "before you darn near crush me to death." She smiled. "Everything's going to be fine. You'll see."

"Is that why you were going to New York?" I asked.

She looked down at her stomach. "Not really, but since there is no reason to go to New York now, I guess I'll head back to Canada and get married," she said matter-of-factly.

"It doesn't bother you that you're going to marry a complete stranger?"

"It will bother me if he is so yellow, we'll have bright, white babies walking around."

I laughed. "I can't even imagine who my husband will be." The words, *my husband*, sounded so strange coming from my lips.

"You're not marrying him, are you?" Astrid asked. "You can't."

"What are you talking about? Daddy says I have to and you told me he and Momma thought it was for the best. Not to mention *you* just said this whole engagement situation was a good thing."

"Forget what everyone else says—including me. What do *you* say?"

"What do you mean?"

"I'm talking about that boy, Charles," she said. "I may have been slightly drug-induced, but I saw the way he was looking at you and you at him. Something is going on there."

"You mean Christopher," I corrected. "And he's only someone I enjoy spending time with. Is there anything wrong with that?"

"If you say so."

"I only met him a couple of days ago," I argued. "Am I supposed to run off with him and live happily ever after?"

"You only knew Sébastien a few days before dating him," Astrid noted.

"Yes, and see how that turned out. And even if I did like him, what can I do about it? Am I supposed to go against Momma and Daddy's wishes?"

"All I'm saying is that marriage is for life, or at least supposed to be. Once you marry this boy, that's it. Can you seriously say you're prepared for that?"

"Can you?" I asked.

"I'm different," Astrid said. "Let's be honest, I could do a lot worse than be taken care of by a man."

"But—" I hesitated, while searching for the right words. "Astrid, you're like a free bird. You will be miserable if someone sticks you in a cage. You need to soar. It's in your blood."

"It doesn't matter anymore," she said. "You're the one that deserves to be free and go to school and be the first woman lawyer and stuff like that."

"Actually, Arabella Mansfield beat me to that title."

"You know what I mean, Miss Know-It-All," she said. "Don't do something simply because you're forced to, Corinne. Trust your heart."

"I understand that, but what should I do?"

"You are seriously asking me what to do with the rest of your life when I don't even know what I want for breakfast this morning?"

"Tell me something—anything." My pulse quickened with the mere thought of making such a decision. "I'm not even sure how Christopher feels.."

"Then that's a problem," she commented casually. "But easily fixable. Tell him your true feelings. If he feels the same, that's good. If not—not so good." When she saw the confused desperation in my eyes, she said, "Would it help if I told you your waiting fiancé is ugly with two front teeth as big as barn doors and is so skinny, he'd fit through that keyhole right there?"

We turned to look at the keyhole. At the same time we burst out laughing.

"At least tell Christopher how you feel. What do you have to lose?"

"I can't do that," I told her. "He'll think I'm insane."

"Why are we even having this conversation? You're either going to do it or you're not. What's there to discuss?" She adjusted the pillow behind her head and pulled up the sheet to her waist. "Is it cold in here or is it me?"

"But what should I say?"

Astrid shrugged. "Tell him how much you like him and let the conversation lead itself. He'll either say, 'Corinne, I like you, too' or 'You're bloody crazy, you Negro girl. Now fetch me my slippers.'" She laughed, but then winced. She wrapped her arms around her stomach. "That's what I deserve for making fun of people, eh?"

"Are you sure you're all right?"

"I told you to stop asking me that dreadful question. And yes, I'm fine." Her eyelashes fluttered once again.

Astrid laid her head on her pillow. As soon as I heard her snore, I hopped off the bed and ran for the door faster than a mutt chasing a jackrabbit. If I had thought about it anymore, I would probably have lost the nerve. As much as it hurt, if nothing else, I had to tell Christopher the truth about my impending marriage.

When I opened the stateroom door, I was completely surprised to see him standing there with his fist in the air, ready to knock.

·≈{ 21 }≈·

"Good. You're awake. I have a surprise for you," Christopher said. His eyes were bulged open wide with excitement.

"Christopher," I began, "I think we should talk. There's something I need to tell you and would like to do so before I lose my nerve."

He shook his head. "No serious talk this morning, my fair Corinne. This morning you are going to relax." He was practically jumping up and down with enthusiasm. I couldn't help but feel the excitement as well.

"What have you gone and done?" I asked, grinning.

"You shall soon find out. In the meantime, get into comfortable clothing and let's go before we're late."

"Late for what?"

He grabbed me by the shoulders and turned me around. Gently, he steered me back into my stateroom. "Go, go, go and do as I tell you."

Christopher impatiently waited outside the room, knocking every five minutes to hurry me along. I tiptoed around the cabin, trying to dress without waking Astrid. I went through my entire suitcase before finally settling on a casual linen skirt and matching blouse.

"Where are you going now?" Astrid had awakened, and through sleepy eyes was staring at me.

"I don't know. Christopher came by early this morning requesting that I dress in casual attire."

Astrid's face screwed up, so I added, "If that's all right with you, of course. Are you feeling better?"

"Again with that question." She sighed. "I'm fine I suppose, but I don't want to be cooped up in this room all day by myself. The doctor said I need to walk in order to prevent blood clots."

"How about we go to breakfast when I return?"

"You said that when you went to dinner and I never saw you until late."

I took my index finger and formed a cross against my chest. "I promise I will be back in time to take you to breakfast."

"You'd better," she warned. "Are you going to tell him how you feel or has your spine turned to jelly again?"

"I think I should wait." I had already lost the nerve. I felt her look of disapproval from across the room.

I glanced in the mirror one final time, deciding that casual could also mean wearing my hair up. Seeing as it was neatly resting on my shoulders for the first time since being on the ship, I decided to keep it down. When I felt appropriately dressed, I opened the door and spun around once for his inspection. "Is this all right?"

"Wonderful." He grabbed me by the arm and pulled me down the hall. "Remember, today is relax day. No more troublesome talk."

Suddenly, he stopped. He reached into his trouser pocket and pulled out a black band. "If you would be so kind as to please turn around. "He took the piece of cloth and tied it tightly over my eyes. "There. Now we're ready." He grabbed my elbow, and once again pulled me down the corridor. I laughed nervously all the way down the hall.

"Where are you taking me?" I asked.

"If I told you, it wouldn't be a surprise."

"How do I know you're not taking me to some dark, remote place on the ship?"

"You don't," he said, still pulling me along. "You'll have to trust me." Suddenly, he stopped in the middle of the corridor. "Do you trust me, Corinne?"

"Yes."

Still blindfolded, he placed his hands on my shoulders. He leaned in and softly whispered into my ear. "No, I mean do you *really* trust me?"

"I do."

He gently brushed his lips back and forth against mine. He kissed one cheek and then the other. Being blindfolded, I relied on my senses. I relaxed and puckered my mouth the minute I felt he was going to kiss my lips. His lips were warm and soft. Goosebumps ran down my arm.

"You can always trust me. I'll never let anything happen to you," he said.

I had no doubts.

"The gymnasium?" I asked when he removed the band.

"Yes!" he exclaimed. "It's the perfect way to release stress. I do it myself all the time."

"I wasn't even aware the ship had a gymnasium." He had tried so hard to impress me, I attempted to hide my disappointment. The truth was, other than running after chickens on the farm, formal exercise was not part of my daily routine—yearly either.

"For first-class passengers only. Are you surprised?"

"Quite."

"Good."

The Titanic's gymnasium was well-equipped. Through the glass doors, I saw an electric camel, several stationary bicycles, a rowing machine and other apparatuses I didn't recognize.

"Am I even allowed in here?" I asked. "I'm not in first-class."

"My uncle is the Captain of the ship, Corinne. You are allowed in here. The best part is, you won't have to exercise alone. You see, I felt guilty for having to help my uncle this morning and not being able to spend more time with you, so I made sure you'll have company while exercising."

"You won't be with me?"

"No. Like I said, I have to help my uncle. Besides, nine until noon is ladies' hour."

I glanced around the empty room. "Who is the company?"

"Christopher, dear, what are you doing here?" Mrs. Smith and Sophia approached us.

"Mother, Sophia," Christopher began, "I knew you were coming down here this morning, so I invited Corinne to join you. Perhaps the three of you could have some breakfast afterward."

Mrs. Smith smiled graciously at her son. "Dear, I do wish you would have informed me, seeing as I'm not appropriately dressed for company."

Christopher laughed. "It's only exercising, Mother. You don't need to look like the Queen of England."

Sophia glared at me from every possible angle, starting with my shoes and working her way up to my face and hair.

"Enjoy yourselves, ladies," Christopher said. He turned to me. "Will I see you later?"

With a polite smile, I nodded.

"Wait, son," Mrs. Smith called. "You did remember that you and Sophia are to have lunch today. You promised, seeing as you barely spent any time with her."

"Mother, I don't know how busy I will be."

"But you two always have lunch."

"We did one time on the Olympic," Christopher said. "That hardly constitutes as always. Now if you ladies will excuse me, I have a tour to give." His irate tone was unmistakable.

Christopher disappeared around the corner, leaving me with the both of them. Mrs. Smith patted down her coiffed hairdo and said, "Well, I suppose we should go in then."

As soon as she opened the glass doors, I headed for the rowing machine. Mrs. Smith and Sophia turned their attentions toward the stationary bicycles.

From across the room, Mrs. Smith asked, "So, Corinne, exercise is a regular thing for you?"

"I would love to say yes," I told her. "But unfortunately it is not."

"Really?" Sophia said. "I would assume you would have to be in some sort of shape to work that farm and those pigs. Not to mention, those cows need a milkin' too."

Mrs. Smith quickly cleared her throat. "Yes. I do suppose it would be busy on a farm. So, that's what keeps your body sturdy and healthy?"

Sophia chuckled.

"Yes, Mrs. Smith," I said. "The farm does keep me busy…or at least it did."

"This machine must be set on difficult," Mrs. Smith commented. "I can barely pedal the thing."

"Here, let me help you," I offered.

"Oh, no dear," Mrs. Smith said quickly. "The darn thing is probably broken. I'll try another one."

Sophia stopped mid-pedal. "Let's stop skirting around the issue and be honest, shall we? You and Christopher are extreme opposites. You're from two different worlds. We're from the privileged world and you're…well…you're not."

"Sophia, please," Mrs. Smith said. "This isn't the appropriate time."

"I need to be frank," Sophia continued, glaring at me. "I don't understand why you're wasting your time with Christopher. There are plenty of good Black boys for you. And you'd have much more in common."

"Christopher and I are friends," I told her. "Nothing more. I don't understand why you feel so threatened."

She laughed. "*Threatened?* Who told you I felt *threatened?*" Her voice had risen two octaves. "*Sorry* is a more appropriate word. You're making a complete fool out of yourself and it would seem everyone aside from you knows it."

"Ladies," Mrs. Smith said, "please." She turned to Sophia. "Perhaps it would be best if we conditioned another time. We don't want to miss the dining hall breakfast this morning. Besides, today Christopher takes you on that special tour of the ship, so you may want to prepare for that as well."

"I don't suppose you will be mooching off the first-class this evening again," Sophia said. "Doesn't charity get a little wearisome?"

Mrs. Smith stepped up. "Oh no, Sophia dear. That was only a one-time occurrence. I'm sure she would like to spend a little more time with her own family. Our inane chatter probably bores the poor girl to death." And then she added, "But it was nice dining with you last evening." She turned back to Sophia. "I think we should go."

Sophia hopped off the bicycle and sashayed past me. Behind her, Mrs. Smith followed. Without making eye contact, Mrs. Smith passed and said, "Have a good day, Karen."

·❧{ 22 }❧·

April 13
10:22 A.M.

I looked down at Astrid's way-too-fancy-for-breakfast shoes and then my gaze traveled up to the hat she had saved six months' worth of wages from Jor'dan's bakery to buy. "We're only getting breakfast and then taking it back to the room," I reminded her. There was no need to doll herself up, especially with the dainty pearls hanging from her neck.

"This is the first time I've been out of that room since that entire situation," she said.

It was that understanding that kept me from lugging her and her theatrical attire back to the stateroom faster than a flashing lightning bolt.

"Anyway," she began, "I'm ready to find some rich gent like my little sister did. Is it wrong to dream for such?"

"What about the man you've been promised to?"

"Wasn't it you who said I could do better than be a broken-down housewife for some old coot?"

"This isn't want I meant," I told her. "What I meant was—"

"Speaking of old coots, why aren't we going to the dining hall with your newfound rich friends?"

"They are hardly my friends. And besides, I'd rather spend time with *my* family. We'll get breakfast on the deck and then take it back to the room. You need to rest. Are you sure you're even up to breakfast this morning?"

"Would you please stop asking me that, for God's sake?" she said, with a dismissive wave of her hand. "Doctor Wahlberg said I was fine."

"He also said to take caution," I reminded.

When I pushed open the glass doors onto the deck, the brand-new morning burst through brilliantly. The blue cloudless sky hovered above like a scene created from the heavens.

Astrid shielded her eyes with her hand. "Does there have to be so much sun? And those obscene birds are making too much noise."

One of those obscene birds, as she called it, flew a little too closely. Astrid snatched off her wide-brimmed hat and swatted at the helpless thing.

I grabbed her arm. "Would you please stop that?"

Reluctantly, she placed the garish headdress back onto her head. "I am completely famished." She held up the back of her hand to her forehead, letting out a loud sigh.

"What are you doing?" I asked, horrified at her theatrics. "Why are you acting like that?"

"Corinne, darling, you have to act rich if you want people to think you're rich. Money attracts money. It's the way of the world."

Realization swooped down on me like one of those birds. Astrid was going to cause a scene. In the privacy of our stateroom was one thing, but now she was taking her show on the road.

"Stop it, Astrid," I said. "You don't have to pretend to be something you're not."

"I'm just trying to fit in," she sighed. "Don't you get tired of sticking out like a sore thumb all the time?"

I understood what she meant. The stares of those who realized we were Black were quite annoying, to say the very least. However, even those stares didn't warrant pretending to be another person. I wasn't changing who I was for anyone. I only wished she felt the same.

A neatly displayed food table was situated toward the end of the deck. Quickly, I grabbed Astrid's arm and pulled her toward the delicacies. "Get what you like and then we're leaving."

She picked up a plate and then with her fork, stabbed a plump strawberry. She didn't put it on her plate. Instead she stood there, inspecting it. I thought I would crawl under the table when she held it to her nose, decided she didn't want it and then placed it back into the bowl. "Is this the best fruit they have?" she complained loudly.

"Corinne?"

Startled, I turned. "Christopher? What are you doing here?"

"Um, I'm pretty much everywhere on this ship."

I laughed nervously. "Yes, of course you are, being the Captain's nephew and all."

He looked at Astrid. "I'm glad to see you are feeling much better."

"Thank you," Astrid said and held up her hand.

Christopher looked at me.

"Stop it, Astrid!" I commanded, smacking her hand down.

"Uh, so, how was the exercise?" Christopher asked. "My mother said she had never felt so refreshed before."

"Fine," I told him. "And what did Sophia have to say?"

"Sophia?" he asked. "I don't know. I didn't ask her. Should I?"

"You went to exercise?" Astrid asked. "I can't recall the last time you exercised. In fact, I don't think you've ever—"

"Okay, Astrid," I said, feeling the rising heat burn my ears. "I think we understand."

"Is the food okay?" Christopher asked.

"Glad you asked," Astrid said. "Actually, the bread is stale and the—"

"It's delicious," I interrupted.

"Wonderful. I would love for you both to join us for breakfast."

"We won't be staying," I told him.

"I would love to," Astrid chimed in.

Both Astrid and I followed the direction of Christopher's extended finger. She beamed. I winced. Aside from Captain Smith, the entire table from the other night was there, including Sophia.

"Wow, so the rich eat. Will wonders never cease?" Astrid said.

"Uh—" Christopher was rendered speechless.

"In any case," Astrid said, grabbing ahold of my arm, "we would love to, wouldn't we?"

I forced a smile. "I thought they were dining in the hall this morning."

Astrid tugged my arm. "Apparently, they've changed their minds. So what? Let's go."

With Christopher leading the way, we headed toward the table. Astrid leaned over and whispered, "He is adorable. You will see if he has a friend for me, won't you? I don't suppose he has any well-to-do, Black-American acquaintances." She laughed.

"Astrid, please," I begged. "Don't embarrass me."

She stopped in her tracks and looked at me. "You think I'm embarrassing?"

"No," I began. "It's just that...sometimes you have a way of being—"

"I'm sorry I'm such an embarrassment to you. I'll try harder not to be."

I thought this was another one of her sarcastic moments, however, this time I was wrong. Her expression was sullen and she even looked slightly humiliated. I had clipped the wings from a proud, beautifully creative free bird.

"It's Karen, isn't it?" Christopher's mother said.

"Corinne," I corrected.

"Do forgive me. I'm horrible with names."

Most of the faces at the table were friendly, except for one.

"Christopher," Sophia called out, "I'm afraid I've only saved a seat for you. I wasn't aware you were bringing guests…again." The tension hung in the air like London fog as she looked from me to Astrid. "I'm afraid I don't know this one."

Molly Brown, who up until then had been quietly stuffing flapjacks into her mouth, looked up. "*This one?* My, that's kind of harsh, don't you think?"

"*This one,*" I said directly to Sophia, "is Astrid, my sister."

"Well, I'd ask the ladies to have a seat," his mother said, "but I'm afraid the table is full. Perhaps we'll meet up sometime this afternoon."

Molly gulped down a glass of orange juice. "No problem. I can scoot down a bit and if Angie here would kindly remove her overblown hat from the chair, we'd have plenty of room."

"That won't be necessary," Mr. Harland chimed in, standing to his feet. "I'm sure I've had my fill of food for the morning," he said, patting his protruding belly. "Take my seat. My wife was just finishing her pastry, weren't you, dear?"

"I was not," Mrs. Harland said.

Ignoring her, he reached down, grabbed his wife by the elbow and gently lifted up a surprised Mrs. Harland. "What are you—"

Molly leaned over and whispered, "You've just provided old

Harley here with an excuse to leave the table. If the missus had it her way, she'd eat and gossip all day long, which personally I can't say is a bad way to live."

"Well, then," Mrs. Smith, said, "I suppose we've hit upon a bit of luck, haven't we? Do sit down."

"I would love to," Astrid said, taking the seat previously occupied by Mrs. Harland.

I supposed having remembered me from the night before allowed for some familiarity amongst the guests at the table. This time, all eyes focused on Astrid and her choice of attire.

"Christopher?" Mrs. Smith called. "Could you please fetch some freshly squeezed orange juice for the table?"

"Of course," he said. "Excuse me, please," he announced to the table. He stood up and headed toward the food display.

"I must say, I don't see the sibling resemblance," Sophia said, studying Astrid. "The style of dress may be the same, but as for physical features, I'm not seeing it."

"What do you mean?" Astrid asked cautiously.

"Don't be offended," Sophia said. "I'm only trying to say that with Karen—"

"Corinne," I corrected again.

"Oh yes. What I was trying to say was that with your sister, now that she has pointed it out, I do see the colored in her. With you, not so much. Of course with the exception of the chosen clothing style."

"Sophia," Mrs. Smith said from across the table, "perhaps we can move the topic to a different discussion."

"I'm not trying to be offensive," Sophia told Mrs. Smith. "I just find it quite uncanny that you two look almost nothing alike. Different fathers, perhaps?"

From under the table, Astrid balled up her hands into two solid fists. Her eyes formed into two slits and the tiny vein in her forehead throbbed. Sophia had just told her she looked white, and for Astrid that was the biggest insult anyone could give.

Quickly, I grabbed my sister's wrist and pulled her from the table. "I'm afraid we won't be able to stay," I said politely. "However, I'm sure we'll see you this afternoon."

Sophia sighed as she dug her fork into her pastry and nibbled on the bite. "I'd be willing to bet on it."

The veins in Astrid's neck pulsated along with the tiny one in her forehead. She clenched her teeth. She was trying to respect my wishes and not embarrass me.

"Is your sister all right, Karen?" Mrs. Smith asked.

"Her name is Corinne," Astrid said through still-clenched teeth. "What is so hard about that?"

"Yes, yes, I do apologize…Corinne," Mrs. Smith corrected.

"She's fine," I said. "I'm fine. Everyone is fine."

"Maybe *Corinne* was out late last night on the deck doing Lord knows what." Sophia spat out my name like she had just tasted a pot of sour okra. "But then again, that wouldn't be appropriate for any young lady. Would it, *Corinne*?"

"What's that supposed to mean?" Astrid asked. "Are you implying my sister is a slut?"

Mrs. Smith and a few other women choked back their shock at the turn the conversation had taken.

"I think it's best we left," I told Mrs. Smith.

Before Astrid had the chance to reach across the table and expose Sophia's insides, I rushed her out of there like a tornado.

As we exited the deck, Christopher returned with a glass pitcher filled with orange juice. "Where are you going?" he called. "Will you be back?"

"I don't think so," I said, rushing Astrid through the exit.

Thankfully, we were through the doors before Astrid took a deep breath and screamed out loud, "Who does that witch think she is? I'm sorry, Corinne, I tried to keep my mouth shut, but she kept insulting and wouldn't stop. I don't understand how someone can seriously believe they are so much better than anyone else. It's ridiculous how they—"

"Astrid," I said calmly.

"No, Corinne!" Astrid yelled. "I tried so hard not to embarrass you and I'm sorry, but I refuse to allow—"

"Astrid," I said, attempting to interrupt her rant again.

"I'm sorry," she said. "but I don't take people insulting me or my family too well. I tried, I really did, Corinne, but I suppose I messed up again."

"No, you didn't," I told her. "In fact, I'm proud of you. I should've never said you embarrassed me. The fact is you stand up for yourself and even for others. You have absolutely nothing to be sorry for."

"You're not mad?"

"Mad? I only wished you reached across the table and punched the little snot right in the nose."

We both laughed.

"What I don't understand," Astrid began, "is how she can believe she's better than everyone else when she looks like Jacky boy."

"Jacky boy, our pig back on the farm?"

Astrid nodded. "Yes! Her nostrils look just like Jack, don't they? Hers flare in the corner, too."

I laughed. As far as pig noses went, Jacky boy did have an extra-round snout with flaring nostrils.

"C'mon," she said, "let's go eat somewhere we're wanted."

"I agree."

She held out her hand and I took it, and then off we strolled, down the hall.

❖[23]❖

With his mother's borrowed dress slung over my shoulder, I hurried down the hall, heading toward Christopher's room.

Before breakfast, Astrid had talked me into telling him my true feelings. Even after breakfast, those feelings hadn't changed. His family, however, placed a new twist on things. I had dealt with girls like Sophia before. Normally, I could ignore animosity toward me, toward my family, but this was different. Sophia's outward comments may have been exactly what the others were thinking but dared not say. Regardless of how dismissive Astrid pretended to be about such prejudices, her angry actions only reinforced the fact that hatred hurt.

Three times I hesitated in the hall, changing pathways and headed back toward my stateroom.

I was halfway back to my cabin when I saw a handwritten sign with an arrow pointing to the right that read, *Chapel this way*. I headed down that hall and was a quarter of the way when I spotted the beautiful stained-glass double door with gold crosses etched in the center. I gently pushed the doors open and peeked inside. It was empty.

Feeling slightly like an intruder, I tiptoed inside. I headed straight for the high-rise altar and knelt down. With my hands neatly folded and resting on the soft leather of the altar, I bowed and silently prayed. I closed my eyes, but soon realized I had no idea what I was praying for.

As children, Momma used to drag Astrid and me to church. When Daddy wasn't working, he would attend. For all appearances, we might have been deeply religious, but truthfully, we really weren't. Most of our church time was spent sitting in the back pew daydreaming our way through the sermon while Reverend Cobb would remind us of what sinners we were. At least that was my eight-year-old interpretation of theology.

I shut my eyes even tighter and saw Momma's face floating through my mind. I began to pray for her to have strength against the sickness that ailed her. I prayed that Astrid would take better care of herself. I prayed for the baby she had lost and even gave it a name. I pictured the baby as a girl that I named Camille. I prayed that she would rest peacefully in heaven. I thought about Daddy and how much I loved him, even though lately we disagreed most times. I prayed that through all those disagreements, I would always understand him as a man who loved his family dearly and only wanted the best for us. I also prayed that he would one day think of me as an adult and trust my decisions.

Then there was Christopher. But what about him?

Through my time of turmoil, Christopher had been so courageous and strong when he didn't have to be. Who was I to him but some girl he had only met two days ago, boarding the ship?

Instead of praying for everything to be perfect, I prayed for life to happen as it should, trusting that God would take care of us. I strongly believed that the universe would always balance out. When I was done praying, I stood up and quietly exited.

I continued on to Christopher's room, but my feet were moving slower than a salted snail on a sunny day. Upon each corner turned, I peered down the hallway to be certain I would not be caught roaming the first-class corridors again. When I turned down the passageway of the last hall, I hesitated. The ship would be docking soon and I would be heading back to Canada to get married. Would telling him now really make a difference?

I went back and forth for several minutes, trying to decide what exactly I should tell Christopher or even *if* I should tell him. The simple thing to do would be, when the ship docked, to go our separate ways. But I couldn't do that.

Or could I?

I glanced down at his mother's dress slung over my forearm, deciding the dress would be the priority for my unexpected visit. If we happened to discuss the future—if there was one—then I'd deal with that as it unfolded.

I forced myself to continue down the hall. When I reached his door, I raised my hand to knock but stopped when I heard voices in the room. I recognized Christopher's voice. The other was unfamiliar. However, the higher pitch identified the other person as a woman. With my hand still in mid-knock, I checked the room number to make sure I hadn't made the calamitous mistake of coming to his mother's room.

I hadn't. It was definitely Christopher's room.

I placed my ear to the door to listen closer, but the voices were too muffled to understand. As soon as I pulled back, deciding perhaps now was not the best time, the neighboring door—his mother's door—slowly began to open.

I had been caught again.

Fear rightfully took its place in the pit of my stomach as the cotton wad in my throat grew to immense proportions. There was absolutely no possible way to explain momentary eavesdropping on her son to a mother, so there I stood, waiting.

Instinct took over. I began running down the hall. Not realizing the lace of my boot was untied, I tripped and in slow motion saw myself falling to the ground.

I stumbled onto one knee, and the dress dropped out of my hand and onto the floor.

"My goodness, are you all right?" I looked up. As soon as I saw the cabin attendant emerging from the room, I breathed a sigh of relief. When the attendant saw me, he immediately dropped the stack of white towels from under his arm and extended his hand. "Are you hurt, miss?"

I slowly stood to my feet. "I'm fine, thank you." As the helpful cabin attendant headed down the hall, I brushed off my dress and patted down my hair.

When the embarrassment drained from my face, I once again lifted my hand to knock. Before I could, the door thrust open and there stood British Sophia. With her two-inch, laced-up boots, she still stood at least four inches shorter than me. Her hair was all pinned up at the top of her head and her makeup—as usual— was in excess and not particularly flattering for her alabaster skin tone. The scent of her excessive perfume pierced my nostrils.

When her initial shock wore off, she asked rather snottily, "What are you doing here…once again?"

"What are *you* doing here?" I asked.

A sly smile formed across her thin lips. She turned her head and called, "Christopher, your little servant girl is here."

I took a step toward her, ready to pounce like a wild cat would a mouse. Christopher quickly stepped in between us. "Just go, Sophia," he told her.

She frowned as she narrowly inched past my steadfast frame fixed in the doorway.

As she passed, she looked down and saw the gown that was still lying on the hallway floor. She bent down and picked it up. "This must be yours." She wiped her hands on it and then threw it at my feet. *"Cette robe est si vilaine!"*

I smiled. "I'll be sure to tell Mrs. Smith that you think her dress is hideous."

British Sophia huffed off. Christopher and I watched after her until she stomped off around the corner.

"Corinne, I'm glad you came," he said. He went to hug me, but I pulled away.

"Are you glad, Christopher? Or maybe I interrupted a cozy conversation between you and your intended future wife." The entire scenario played out like a page from the Sébastien and Claudette story, in which I was the main protagonist—the letdown, passed-over, silly protagonist.

"What are you talking about, Corinne?"

"I'm talking about Sophia in your stateroom," I said. "I'm sorry for the interruption. And don't forget the romantic tour you are to take her on. Will that be before or after your special lunch? Don't think I didn't hear your mother remind you at the gymnasium while I was standing there looking like a complete fool."

"Corinne—"

"Stop," I interrupted. "I don't want to hear any more excuses from you or any other boy whom I have the misfortune of caring about. If you want her, go to her." I took his mother's dress and hurled it at him. "And take your mother's ugly dress back, too!"

I turned and stomped off down the hall, taking the same path Sophia had taken moments earlier. Halfway down the hall, Christopher darted after me and grabbed my elbow. "Corinne, please. It's not like that. My mother has been driving me bloody mad trying to push Sophia and me together. She will never understand that I don't love her. I barely even like her." He was breathing heavy and his hands were shaking. "Corinne, please understand that it's you that I've been thinking about. Please, Corinne."

"What have you been thinking, Christopher?" Beads of sweat gathered on his forehead and his breathing came in rapid, short bursts. "What's wrong? Why are you so nervous?"

"There's absolutely nothing wrong. In fact, it's the opposite. For the first time in my life, I'm making a decision for myself without mother's interference."

"I don't understand—"

He took a minute to catch his breath. With the dress still in his hand, he wiped at the sweat that had begun to roll down his flushed face. "I have to tell you this, so please let me do so." He paused for a minute, and in that brief moment, I assumed he had changed his mind, but then he said, "Corinne, I care about you so much. I need you. I don't want to ever be without you."

As quickly as it had surfaced, the welled-up anger drained right out of me, leaving both feelings of relief and confusion. I was left speechless.

"But—," I began. "After this voyage, we'll probably never see each other again." My heart pounded through my chest.

He threw his hands up in the air as he wildly paced back and forth. The sweat had come full force now and his face was completely flushed. "I know, Corinne. I understand that, but—" He grabbed me and pulled me close. "Don't you see? I don't want to be without you. I want us to be together."

"What are you saying?"

"I don't know what I'm saying. No wait, yes I do." He drew in a deep breath as he looked down at the carpeted hallway floor. He pulled me in even closer, holding onto me for a few seconds. I desperately clung to him, never wanting to let go. Through our clothing, I could feel both heartbeats pumping, synchronizing with one another.

He gently placed his hand on the back of my head and pulled me to him. His soft lips tickled my ear. I thought I was dreaming when he whispered, "Marry me, Corinne."

·❦ 24 ❦·

While Christopher slept, I kissed the tip of his nose. He rustled about and then fell back to sleep. With the slight smile on his lips, he finally looked at peace. The silk sheet rested at his bare waist. My side was pulled up to my chin. The one time I had been with Sébastien was so different. That particular time I had snuck into the barn after everyone had fallen asleep. On a horse blanket in the middle of fall, Sébastien had plowed into me with such force, I was sore days after. That was partly the reason I had been so hesitant to give myself to him a second time.

This was the complete opposite.

Christopher had taken the time to caress and hold me, making sure I was all right with what was about to happen. When it was all over, unlike Sébastien, who zipped up and left, Christopher had gently stroked my hair, until both of us fell into a deep, peaceful sleep.

Holding the sheet close to my chest, I sat up in the bed. Christopher stirred, rolled over and then commenced snoring. I glanced around, remembering how the room appeared to me that first time I had visited. I had felt like an intruder who didn't belong. One day later, the mood was completely different.

The scent of his room struck me as odd—not in a bad way, more like a strange way for the room of a boy to smell. It reminded me of summers in Cherbourg when the honeysuckle tree shed its delicate petals and fell to the dirt. My bare foot would crush those tiny petals and carry the scent all the way home. For the rest of the afternoon, I'd smell honeysuckle until bathing later that evening. That was how his room smelled—like crushed honey-suckles.

The ship must have crashed against a strong wave because I felt the floor rock back and forth beneath my feet. It was barely noticeable, but if you stood still for a few moments, you could feel the unsteadiness. Christopher only stirred and turned over on his side. Never once did his eyes open.

I reached over, grabbed one of his white silk shirts strewn over the decorative armoire, and wrapped it around me. When I went to get up, the wooden bed frame creaked. I looked down to make sure I hadn't awakened him. He was still fast asleep. I slowly stood up, but the bed creaked again. Christopher flung his arm to my side of the bed, felt around and then went back to snor-ing—this time much louder.

I tiptoed over to the sitting area. With each step, the plush carpet left a subtle footprint. The floor beneath me rocked and I lost my footing. When it stopped, I continued over to the sitting area.

The other evening I had seen photographs encased in beautiful, silver frames. I picked up the first frame, careful not to smudge it. The image was his mother at least twenty years ago. She looked the same except for a few less lines around her mouth and the corners of her eyes. Her hair was dark brown and hung loosely around her shoulders. She didn't smile. Surprisingly though, the edges of her thin lips did curve upward a bit. The second picture was of the entire family on some sort of vacation with a large, woodsy lake in the backdrop. A scrawny, black-haired thirteen- or fourteen-year-old Christopher stood in the foreground while his mother and uncle stood behind him. That made me wonder about the whereabouts of his father.

The next picture, another one at the same lake, was more recent. His mother's strict bun was completely gray as was Captain Smith's full beard. Mrs. Smith's cheerful expression appeared fake. It looked like she had just swallowed a lazy stink bug on a hot summer afternoon. Captain Smith stood tall with his shoulders thrust back and his head held high. He was in full uniform with his decorated Captain's hat in his hand. Christopher, wearing his swimming trunks, was the only one dressed appropriately for a vacation.

I picked up another picture. This one was of Christopher as a boy of about seven or eight. He was sitting in a pile of dirt next to a dark-haired little girl with chubby legs. Her pink and white socks strangled her ankles and her mouth hung open as tears streamed down her plump red cheeks. I couldn't remember even one photograph of myself where I wasn't smiling. Momma always told me I was a happy baby and God's sunshine always smiled down on me. Astrid was a bit more ornery and, as Momma had put it, was forever blessed with God's clouds. To this day, I wasn't sure what that meant.

Christopher sat up in bed and stretched. "How long have you been awake?"

"Not long," I said, skipping back to the bed. I sat on the edge and strategically placed a peck on the tip of his nose. "I feel won-derful."

"While you were resting," he said, "I went down to the kitchen and asked them to bring us some lunch. Is that all right with you?"

"*C'est magnifique!*" I exclaimed with a quick pat of my stomach. "But could we take something to Astrid? I need to check on her to make sure she's well."

"I think that'd be good."

I leaned over and showed him the picture of him and the pudgy, crying girl. "Who is this?"

"That's me."

"Of course that's you, silly. Who is the girl?"

He thought a moment. "Oh, that's Sophia. I believe we were six in that picture."

"You've known her that long? I had no idea."

He nodded. "You hungry yet? I can get the food."

The one thing Momma always told me was that a lady should never ask a question she really didn't want the answer to. In this case, it couldn't be helped. "Why haven't you ever dated Sophia?"

"Who says I haven't?"

"So, you two have been together *together*?"

"Is my princess jealous?" he asked with a sly grin.

"Stop that, Christopher. I'm serious."

With a mile-wide smile, he reached over and grabbed me. "At this point, does it matter?"

"Am I your first?" I asked, then quickly added, "Never mind."

He reached over and with his index finger, jabbed at my side. "Am I *your* first?"

"Does it matter?" I mocked.

He grabbed my arm and wrestled me down to the bed. He pinned me down, threw himself on top of me and tickled me until tears ran from my eyes. "Just admit it," he said. "You're jealous. Say it."

"I will not!"

He poked at my sides and tickled me until I thought I would explode.

"Please stop," I said, laughing.

"Admit it!" he commanded. "If you say you're jealous, I'll stop."

"Ok, I'm—"

"I told you!"

"You didn't let me finish," I yelled over him. "I was going to say, I am most certainly *not* jealous!"

He rolled off me. "You're hopeless."

"Why don't you like her?" I asked, sitting up. "She's attractive and she's from the right family. Your mother adores her. Why is it that you have no interest?"

"Now you're sounding like Mother," he said. "Do you really want to know why I don't care for Sophia?"

"Only if you want to tell me."

He plopped down on the bed. "A year ago I found out my mother and Sophia were secretly planning a wedding, my wedding.."

"Really?"

He nodded. "They even went as far as to reserve Westminster Cathedral for May of next year. The menu was going to be roast duck in an orange glaze with garlic potatoes."

"Really?" I asked. "I suppose we have a lot more in common than I thought."

"What do you mean by that?"

"Never mind," I told him. "Go on."

"That's basically it. They've been pressuring me to marry her, but lucky for me, I found someone better." He kissed my cheek. "Much better."

"I wonder how big this ship is," I said, looking around. I had grown weary of having the topic of Sophia dominate our conversation.

"Colossal," he told me. "Why don't I get the food? I'm starved."

"Seriously, how big is the *colossal* Titanic?"

He hesitated a second and then said, "The ship is eight hundred eighty-two feet, eight inches long, ninety-two feet, six inches wide and one hundred-four feet high with nine decks and boiler rooms and weighs forty-six thousand, two hundred thity-eight tons. On board are one thousand, three-hundred sixteen passengers, but with staff on board, the figure during this maiden voyage is more like two thousand, two hundred twenty-eight people. It has twenty life boats designed to accommodate a maximum rate of one thousand, one hundred seventy-eight people."

"You have all that memorized?" I asked, amazed.

"Have to. It's for the tour...except the part about the lifeboats, of course."

"So, twenty lifeboats?" I questioned. "With two thousand, two hundred twenty-eight people aboard and only enough lifeboats to accommodate only about half of the passengers? What would happen if the ship sank?"

"It's unsinkable, hence its nickname," he said, grabbing my waist. "Just like us."

"Really? And how do you know that?"

"I just do."

"This ship is fascinating," I said. "Tell me more."

He sighed. "I don't want to talk about this ship. I'd rather talk about us."

"Please," I begged.

"How about this?" he began. "After lunch, I can take you on an in-depth tour if you'd like. If you are going to be my wife, I have to get you familiar with this ship anyway. By the end of this voyage, you will never want to hear another measurement again."

My expression turned somber yet hopeful. I thought about Momma, wishing I could share all that has happened to me in the past few days. "Christopher, are you sure this is what you want?" I asked. I felt my heart skipping inside my chest. My eyes shifted downward to the silk bed sheet and away from his gaze.

"I want nothing more," he whispered. He reached over into the top drawer of the nightstand and pulled out a long, brown cigar. He yanked off its golden band. "Why are you looking at me like that?" he asked, peering down at his hands. "Ohh, this cigar isn't mine. It's my uncle's and even he doesn't really smoke. He keeps them for special occasions." He grabbed my left hand. "Is this the correct hand?" His voice was trembling.

"I don't know," I said, just as nervous. "It's not like I get engaged every other weekend." As soon as I said it, I realized the irony.

With fumbling fingers, he slid the band down around my third finger, forcing it over my knuckle. "Will you marry me, Corinne?"

I wrapped my arms around him, squeezing tightly. "Yes." I looked down at the band. It was as beautiful as any five-carat diamond ring. "It is now official," I said. "I am going to be Mrs. Christopher—" I stopped. "Adam? I just realized I don't even know your middle name."

"Why would you think Adam?" he asked.

"That first evening in the hall you gave me your handkerchief—the one with the crest on it—and it had the initials *CAS*."

"Oh. It's actually Andrew. And yours?"

"Alexandra."

"That's beautiful."

"Anyway," I continued, "I am going to be Mrs. Christopher Andrew Smith. It has a nice ring to it, doesn't it?"

"That it does." He looked into my eyes and with the softest voice, said, "I'm not sure how you're going to feel about this, but—"

"What is it, Christopher?"

"I need to go to your parents and ask for your hand properly. It is the gentleman's way."

⋯❧[25]❧⋯

APRIL 13

"There are things you don't know about me." I was afraid his feelings would change if he knew the truth, but I had to tell him before it was too late. "My mother is back in Cherbourg." The thought made my heart drop into the pit of my stomach. "She's not well, Christopher."

"But she'll be fine, right?" he asked.

I shook my head. "I don't know. Daddy tells me one thing and Astrid believes another. In any case, no matter where I am, I've always planned to go back and see her. I'll never leave her, Christopher. *Never*."

"I understand. We can go back anytime you want."

"I miss her so much. It really hurts that she didn't tell me the truth. No one did. Daddy didn't. Astrid didn't. Why would they do something like that?"

"I don't know, Corinne," Christopher admitted. "But your family loves you very much, so I'm sure it was for a good reason. Whatever the reason, it doesn't matter. We will go back and see her."

"I do think she'll adore you."

"I think she will, too," he agreed. "In fact, I *know* she will."

I laid my head on his shoulder while he softly patted my hair. I snuggled in closer, wanting to stay with him forever.

"What was the other thing you needed to tell me?" he asked.

"Other thing?"

"You said there are *things* I didn't know about you. What other things are you referring to?"

This was my opportunity to mention that I was to be in a pre-arranged marriage— and until Daddy knew about Christopher and me—still was. I had a decision to make, be honest or continue keeping secrets.

"That was it. I don't have anything else to tell you," I lied. Then another thought occurred to me. "Christopher, you do under-stand that some people won't want to see us together?"

He nodded. "My mother will have to accept it. She has no choice."

"But will we live in England? Somehow I doubt that your mother is going to welcome the likes of me into her home, unless I'm holding a broom. I bet she even has slaves," I said, thinking of her earlier conversation regarding Millie, Sophia's servant.

"They're not slaves," he defended. "They're people that work for us. They're like extended family."

"Are you serious?" I asked, offended. "Are those extended family members out there picking cotton in the fields in the hot sun, too?"

"Corinne, it's not like that. These are people that have worked for us for years. They depend on the money to feed their families."

My voice softened. "I understand that, but can you at least see this from my point of view?"

"I do." He spoke slowly and carefully. "I don't know exactly what we're going to do, but don't worry, we'll figure it out."

There was a knock at the door, startling both of us.

"Must be the food," he announced. "And right on time, too. I'm starved."

"I'll get it," I said, jumping up.

Christopher quickly grabbed my arm. "Don't, Corinne. My uncle knows the crew personally. I don't want the news getting back to him before I have the chance to tell him about us."

I flopped back down onto the bed. "Sorry, I forgot."

Christopher stood up. With the satin sheet still wrapped around his waist, he dragged it all the way to the door. When he opened up the door, I heard a voice, but it definitely was not a ship steward. I tried to duck out of the way, but it was too late. Sophia barged past Christopher and stepped into the stateroom. She was barely in the room, but stepped in enough to clearly see me sitting on the edge of Christopher's bed wearing nothing more his nightshirt.

Sophia's eyes formed into tiny slits that were so cold, I felt the ice right through his white, silk nightshirt. Normally, I would stand up to her, but being half-dressed, I was in a compromising position. Her glare began at my naked feet, headed up to my knees and finally rested on my wild, unruly mane. As if it made much of a difference, I reached up and patted down the scraggly strands at the crown of my head.

I glanced over at Christopher. He had the same defeated look on his face that undoubtedly was on mine. The deafening silence seemed to go on for hours. Finally, without saying a word, British Sophia turned and quietly walked out. I'd bet the farm that she was headed straight for Christopher's mother.

After she made her hasty exit, Christopher shut the door behind her. "What do you think?" he asked.

I reached for my crumpled corset at the foot of the bed. "I think we'd better get dressed."

❧[26]❧

"Are you absolutely mad?" Astrid asked. She was sitting up in bed and meticulously brushing her hair. She leaned over, reached for a gold barrette on the nightstand and poked it into the top of her hair. She picked up the portable mirror resting on the bed by her side and inspected herself for a good minute. She gently rested the mirror back onto the bed, looked at both of us and said again, "Seriously, are you completely mad?"

As soon as we had come to the room, Astrid furrowed her brow and inspected every inch of Christopher and me. I assumed it was our disheveled clothing that gave us away. Astrid had stared into our eyes, searching for any telltale hint. It took her less than three minutes to realize our big secret. "My sister is no longer a virgin!" she had announced at the top of her lungs. Astrid had no idea about the one time with Sébastien and, if I could help it, never would.

Christopher's face turned bright red while I fruitlessly attempted to deny her allegations. Regardless, she didn't believe my emphatic denials. Each time I tried to tell her what had happened—minus the intimate parts, of course—Astrid smirked and interrupted me, causing me to have to start from the very beginning of the story.

I folded my arms across my chest. "You're the one who told me to tell Christopher how I feel."

"I said *tell*, not show."

"I never set out to do this," I told her. "It just happened."

"Giving yourself to a boy doesn't just happen. And what if Daddy finds out?"

"How would he?"

"Did you not say his girlfriend, Miss Snooty, caught the two of you?"

"She's not his girlfriend," I corrected. "Besides, do you think Sophia will tell?"

Astrid laughed. "Of course she will. She is a scorned woman. Plus, she's a witch. The entire ship probably knows."

Astrid was right. We had to inform our families before Sophia had that chance.

"Well, Corinne," she said, "I guess you don't need to worry about whether or not he has feelings for you. Apparently, that's been answered. And from the looks of you both, quite a few times this afternoon."

I blushed.

"Do you regret any of what happened?" Astrid asked.

I looked back at Christopher. Even if he *wasn't* in the room, the answer was the same. "No, not in the least."

"That's good." She shrugged, then added, "Doesn't make it right, though."

"I'm not asking if it's right," I said. "What should we do?"

"There's only one answer to that question," she told me. "Tell Daddy before that witch has the chance to." She picked up the mirror and once again began admiring her reflection. "I'm just shocked it isn't me at the center of all this mess."

I turned to Christopher, who stood back in the corner of the room. I had asked him to come along, but he told me he didn't feel right about—in his words—interfering when two sisters were having such a talk. Nonetheless, he agreed he would be there, at a distance, for support.

"So, what are you going to tell dear ol' Daddy?" Astrid asked.

"The truth: Christopher and I will be married. There's nothing Daddy or anyone else can say to make us change our minds."

Astrid took the focus off the mirror long enough to glance over at Christopher. She rested the mirror back onto the bed and began furiously clapping her hands. I looked back at Christopher. He was as confused as I was.

"Good for you, little sister," she said, still clapping. "Somehow Christopher provided you with a spine. Any boy that can do that, I respect."

"What is that supposed to mean?" I asked angrily.

Finally, Christopher called out from the corner, "Corinne, I believe your sister is giving you a compliment. I don't think she meant—"

"Oh yes she did," I told him. "She has always considered me weak. I'm sick of it. Simply because I'm not a rebel that causes trouble every chance I get, does not mean that I don't have a backbone. Is there harm in choosing my battles rather than arguing every point?"

"Oh, please," Astrid said, smoothing down her hair. "When have you ever caused trouble?"

"There was the time back in Cherbourg with Claudette Beauchamp and—" I stopped suddenly when I realized where the conversation was headed. "*J'ai vu Claudette au magasin avec*

Sébastian. Nous nous sommes battus jusqu'à l'arrêt par le gestionnaire!"

I was glad to finally confide in her regarding the Claudette incident, even though at the time, I had vowed to take that regrettable incident to my grave.

"If that's so, why have you never told me?" Astrid questioned. "And why would you go after her? Sébastien was the jerk. He should have been the one to have his head smashed in dirt."

"Believe me, he was next," I said, glancing over my shoulder at Christopher. "Oh, never mind. My point is, we're getting married and there is nothing Daddy or anyone else can say or do about that. That proves I'm not weak!"

"And my point is, good for you, Corinne. I'm glad to see you finally doing what you want, instead of what everyone else expects of you." Her lips turned upward and her eyes softened. "Now hurry and tell Daddy, so he can stop asking so many questions about me. The seasick excuse is beginning to wear thin. Eventually, he's going to suspect something." She grinned as she smoothed out the hem of my skirt. "If this is really what you want, then I'm happy for you." She turned to Christopher. "For both of you."

"Thank you, Astrid. We'll be off to find Daddy and then Christopher's mother," I told her. "Is there anything you need?"

"I've been fine for at least a day now," she said. "It's that darned doctor that won't let me on my feet. I wouldn't be surprised if he enjoyed coming to see me."

I sighed. "Good-bye, Astrid. I should be back soon if you need anything."

I took Christopher's hand and we headed out the door to find either Daddy or Christopher's mother. Either way, I wasn't looking forward to either of the conversations that needed to take place.

"What did you tell your sister in there?" he asked. "Who is Sébastien?"

"Oh, that," I said. "That was nothing."

As Momma used to say, some things the lips need not say. My addendum to that was, some things the lips need not say *unless in another language*.

Our fingers were intertwined as we walked down the corridor. Calmer than expected, I rested my head on his shoulder.

"Take a look down the hall," Christopher said. "What do you see?"

I glanced down the corridor. "A chair, doors, numbers, the doors leading to the deck."

"No," he said. "This is our wedding aisle. We'll stroll down this hall and toward the awaiting priest, who, after our sacred vows, will call you my wife."

He squeezed my hand and marched me down our pretend aisle. "After we are married, I will pick you up and carry you to our bedroom where we will make love all night long." He bent down and swooped me off my feet. "Just like this." He pushed open the doors to the outside deck and carried me through.

"My, what a lovely couple." A toothy Percy Harland smiled at us.

Startled, Christopher quickly set me down.

Mr. Harland was spruced up in a tuxedo with a top hat, bobbling back and forth on his head. In his left hand, he carried a silver-plated governor walking stick, and in his right, a copy of *The Hound of the Baskervilles* by Arthur Conan Doyle.

"From the moment I saw such beauty, I realized that this young lady was the right one for you," he said, tipping his hat. "Don't ever let anyone tell you otherwise."

"Thank you, Mr. Harland," Christopher said. He squeezed my hand and smiled.

Mr. Harland looked up at the moon. "Beautiful evening, isn't it? Reminds me of this farm I used to work on when I was a lad. Had these chickens, it did. Every night those things would squawk and cackle about." He looked at Christopher and whispered, "kind of like your mother and my wife. No offense, my good man."

"None taken."

"Those chickens were huge birds with a wing span from here to eternity." He lifted his arms and started flapping. "You know the ones I'm talking about. Their noses are about this long and they spend the days cawing at everything that moves."

Christopher and I stifled a laugh. Mr. Harland was so animated with his flapping arms I thought he may take flight at any moment. The fat on his chin waddled as his neck dipped back and forth. Approaching passengers quickly turned and headed in the opposite direction.

"Well, you kids have a good night. I suppose I'll see you later this evening, perhaps?"

"Before you go, sir," Christopher said, "do you have the time?"

"Of course I do, young man." Mr. Harland reached down to his side for the gold-toned men's filigree watch hanging from his trouser pocket. He reached into his other pocket and pulled out a glass monocle attached to a chain. "I apologize, my good man, but I do believe my watch has stopped." He looked up at the full moon. "Hmmm, by the placement of the stars, it must be between the hours of eight and eleven in the evening."

Christopher gave a nod as Mr. Harland headed off. "Thank you, sir." After Mr. Harland was out of earshot, he turned back to me. "Didn't I tell you he was peculiar? Nevertheless, he is a good man."

"Has he been drinking?" I asked.

"No. That's his way. He's a shrewd businessman and that's why I think everyone puts up with him. Other than that, they treat him like he's less, which is a shame."

"I can relate," I told him. "Sometimes I feel as though your mother views me as less."

"That's not fair, Corinne," Christopher said defensively. "She's never said that and if that's how she comes across, she's misunderstood. All she wants is the best for me."

"Oh, honestly, Christopher. You haven't noticed how differently she treats me after finding out I'm not in first-class?"

"No, I haven't noticed."

"What about the way she's acted after finding out I was Black?"

"That may have been a shock to her, but that's only because she assumed you were white."

I sighed. "What about her running your life? How are you able to deal with that?"

"What about you?" he responded. "Didn't you tell me your father decided that your family was going back to Canada without even asking what you thought?"

"That's different," I said, glad for not mentioning the prearranged marriage earlier.

"How is it different?"

"It just is. He's family. He wants the best for us."

"Precisely! The same could be said for Mother."

"What about Sophia? She's rude and ill-mannered."

"You're exaggerating. She's not that bad. She may be rude at times, but she can be a good person."

"You can't be serious?" I asked, surprised at his defense of her. "Next you'll tell me Attila the Hun was a man of honor."

"Some may think so."

His lighthearted tone made me angrier. "Oh, please."

"You're judging Sophia like you claim she's judging you."

"Claim?" The blood in my veins was boiling. "You have absolutely no idea. She's done nothing short of look down on me since our first meeting."

"You can't blame her for that. That's her upbringing."

"So, I'm supposed to excuse that? And is it her upbringing that allows her to talk to people in such a rude and disgusting manner?"

"Corinne—," he said, grabbing for my arm. "Why are we even arguing about this?"

I snatched my arm away. "Since you're so fond of her and her upbringing, why don't you go be with her?" I stormed off, leaving a perplexed Christopher standing in the middle of the hallway.

"Corinne!" he called after me. "Corinne, *please!*"

I turned the corner and ran off down the hall.

The Sinking Ship

꩜ 16½ hours until... ꩜

·◦[27]◦·

"What did I miss?" Astrid asked. "When you left here yesterday evening, you were going to tell Daddy and Christopher's mother everything. You came back here mad at the world. Then you huff off to bed and toss and turn all night. Now you're sitting on the edge of your bed with your arms folded across your chest, kicking your feet like a two-year-old."

"I don't want to talk about it," I told her.

"Fine." She slowly lifted herself out of the bed and walked to the bathroom, locking the door behind her.

While she was washing up, I remained on the edge of the bed, waiting for her to finish, so I could be angry with her for not insisting on the full story.

Minutes later, she emerged. "It's really strange, but I feel good today. Perhaps I'll have breakfast in the dining hall this morning."

"Do you not even care what happened last evening?"

"You said you didn't want to discuss it. I'm not going to press you." She casually strolled over to the suitcase at the foot of her bed and rummaged through it. "Have you seen my brush?"

"I would never marry a boy like that," I told her.

She poked around the suitcase a few more minutes before giving me her full attention. "Fine. What happened?"

"First," I began, "he had the nerve to insist that Attila the Hun was a great dictator. He was a murderer, for God's sake."

"Who cares?"

"What kind of person thinks that?" I jumped off the bed. "Seriously, Astrid. What kind of person thinks that a man who killed so many people is decent? I'll tell you. None! None that are rational-thinking people, that's who."

Astrid sighed. "Are you joining me for breakfast or do I have to drag Daddy along?"

"Then," I said, knowing she would most certainly agree on this point, "he had the audacity to say that Sophia isn't a bad person. According to him, her rudeness is only a part of her upbringing. Can you believe that?"

Astrid shrugged. "It's what they know, Corinne. If I cared enough, I'd probably say the same thing. If I were you, I'd get used to that type of snobbery. Do you honestly expect to go to England, marry into a wealthy family and have no one look at you from the corner of their eye?"

She pulled a pale-pink dress from the closet. "Do you want my honest opinion? I think you're purposely picking an argument."

"That's ridiculous. Why would I do such a thing?"

"That girl, Sophia, is a witch and Christopher's mother is a persnickety snob. You already know that. You don't need him to verify that for you." She held up the dress, inspecting it for imperfections. "I don't like this one. Do you? It reminds me of salmon and I hate fish."

"Why would you say I'm making more of this than needed?"

"Isn't it obvious?" she asked, poking around in her suitcase. "You're scared."

"Of?"

She pulled out a pale-green dress and held it up. "This is the one."

"You were saying?" I was becoming annoyed with her flippant attitude.

"What was I saying?"

I sighed. "You said I was scared."

"Oh, right," she said. "You're scared of the decisions you've made. Maybe you think you're only marrying him because of the alternative—maybe not. Who knows?" She stood up and quickly pulled the pale-green dress over her head. With the palms of her hands, she smoothed out its full bodice. "You can stay here and sulk all you want. I'm going to breakfast."

"I'm sorry, miss," the suited man said. "The ten-thirty church service is specifically for first-class. There is another service in an hour."

At first, when Astrid had insisted that I may actually be afraid of my decision, I was angry. Then I thought about it and was angry at her for her keen perception. As soon as she left to find Daddy for breakfast, I went to find Christopher.

"But I need to locate someone in there," I begged. "I'll only be a minute."

The man shook his head. "I'm sorry."

"Could I peek my head in? If he sees me, he'll come out."

"I'm sorry."

Disappointed, I turned to leave.

"Corinne?"

Christopher walked out of the double stained-glass doors. He was fully dressed in a navy suit with a white 'kerchief stuffed in his breast pocket. He looked quite distinguished with his dark hair slicked back. "What are you doing here?"

"How did you know I was out here?"

"When the door opened, I caught a glimpse of you. What are you doing here?" he asked again.

"I'm sorry, Christopher," I said, throwing my arms around him. I became worried when I didn't feel him return the embrace. "I don't know why I got so upset."

"That's all right," he said, wrapping his arms around me. "I would have invited you to the service but thought I'd give you time to miss me," he said, grinning. "I was going to come see you afterward."

"I did miss you." I leaned up and kissed him. The faint organ hymn, "Lead, Kindly Light," played softly in the background. The song made me happy and yet sad. It reminded me of Momma and our Sundays back in Cherbourg.

The uniformed man standing outside the chapel doors cleared his throat. Immediately, we broke apart.

"Are you ready to tell Mother?" he whispered.

"Are you sure this is what you want to do?"

"Of course, aren't you?"

It had only been a few hours, but I had missed his reassuring smile. "I suppose we have to at some point," I admitted. "However, I don't think we should disrupt her in service."

"She's not in there. She fell ill this morning and decided to remain in the stateroom to rest."

"Shall we go now?" I asked.

"I guess now is as good a time as any."

We headed off down the hall. With each step, I felt more uncomfortable with what we were about to do. When we reached the third-class corridor, he took my hand. By the second-class corridor, he wrapped his arm around my waist. At that point I felt as though everything was going to be fine. *It had to be.*

"This is it," he said when we reached the first-class hall. "There is no turning back after this."

I took a deep breath and cleared my throat. "I'm ready."

We continued down the hall toward his uncle's stateroom. When we reached the door, I tugged at his arm. "Christopher?"

"Everything will be fine," he reassured.

He reached down and took my hand. Our palms stuck together with sweaty moisture. Together, we drew in a deep breath.

"You ready?" he asked when he raised his fist to knock.

"Do I have a choice?" I asked with nervous laughter.

He pounded on the door with the side of his fist. Both of us stood strong, nervously awaiting the most uncomfortable conversation that was about to take place.

After the second knock, the queasiness in my stomach traveled its way to my throat. By the fourth knock, I was prepared to turn and run down the hall. After the fifth knock, my knees practically buckled from under me. I was slowly losing courage.

Sensing my hesitation, Christopher squeezed my hand. "Don't be nervous." He was only saying that to reassure me. His clammy hand indicated he was as scared as I was.

"I don't think she's here," I said.

"We can wait for her in my stateroom," he offered. "Wherever she went, she shouldn't be gone too long."

He opened the door to his cabin and led me in. I headed for the bed and sat down on the edge. "Maybe this is a sign," I said nervously. "Maybe your mother isn't there because God is trying to tell us that this is something we shouldn't be doing. What if this isn't right? What if this ends up being the biggest mistake of our lives?"

"Corinne—"

"This is all happening so fast," I said, out of breath. "What if we are not meant to be?"

"Corinne—"

"Christopher, this may be one big, huge—"

"Corinne!"

"Yes?"

"Take a deep breath," Christopher said. "You're nervous, that's all. How can you possibly say we weren't meant to be?" He sat down on the bed next to me. "We'll sit and wait. In the meantime, you should relax and take your mind off this."

"How am I supposed to do that?"

He lightly brushed the side of my cheek with his fingertips. "I can think of something." He gently kissed my cheek, his touch warm and soft. His lips slowly connected with mine and then worked their way down my neck. "You are so beautiful, Corinne." His fingers gently stroked the side of my arm and worked their way up to the zipper on my dress. He unbuttoned his shirt and pulled it off. My heart was racing. I loved his body. His broad shoulders and muscular arms overwhelmed me. He reached up and pulled my dress down around my waist while he tickled my ear with his lips. He lay on top of me and started kissing every inch of my body. He reached down and began unbuttoning his trousers. I closed my eyes, attempting to fall deeper into the moment, but instead, I found myself squirming restlessly under his body.

"What is it?" he asked. "Am I doing something wrong?"

"It's not you,"

"Then what?"

I sat up on the bed. "You don't think we're rushing into this marriage?"

He sat up alongside me. "No, do you?"

"From my standpoint, things have been happening so fast— my sister being pregnant, to losing the baby, from my parents' separation, to finding out Momma's sick...and now us. Aren't you afraid of being wrong?"

"Wrong about what? That I want you to be my wife? Honestly, Corinne, I don't think we were brought together by mistake. I truly want us to be happy and that's not going to happen if we're apart. Isn't that what you want, too?"

I thought a moment, afraid that he would think my hesitation was because I didn't care for him—which was untrue.

Concern washed over his face when I didn't answer. "Don't you, Corinne?"

"Yes, Christopher," I blurted out. "I do want us to be together."

He whispered, "I want to show you how much I want to be with you. You will never doubt us again."

Gently, he laid me down on the bed. There we stayed for the remainder of the morning and well into the afternoon hours. During those magical moments, every worry, every bit of nervous energy had floated from my body. In its place was sheer pleasure.

7 hours until...

·⋑{ 28 }⋐·

I stretched lazily from under the silk sheets. "I suppose I should go check on Astrid and see if she's all right."

"Don't go yet," Christopher said, grabbing for my arm. "Let's stay in bed another hour, then we'll go."

"What time is it?" I asked.

He reached over to the nightstand and grabbed his watch. "It's after four-thirty!" he exclaimed. "I had no idea it was that late."

I hopped out of bed. In a panic, I reached for my skirt, grabbed one of my boots lying on the floor by the door, and then got down on my hands and knees and frantically searched for the other boot. "You do realize that Sophia has probably already informed your mother of yesterday evening." I said, pulling up the dust ruffle and searching under the bed.

He scratched his head. "Which is why I'm confused she hasn't been pounding down my door." He jumped out of the bed and grabbed his shirt from the back of the chair. "We should go find our parents as soon as we can."

I scampered into my skirt and struggled with the buttons. "I'll check on Astrid first. Meet me at my stateroom in fifteen minutes, and then if Daddy's there, we'll tell him. If not, we'll look for your mother."

I darted for the door, but he grabbed my arm and pulled me back down onto the bed. "After that, we'll come back here and continue."

I pecked the tip of his nose as I scrambled from underneath him. Somehow I didn't believe either one of us would be in the lovemaking mood after telling our parents of our intentions.

Even with the urgent matter at hand, I smiled while strolling down the hall, feeling like a queen. Officer LaPierre, the man in uniform who had stopped me last time, stood at the end of the first-class corridor. I held my head high. This time I approached him with confidence. I was no longer just any girl roaming the halls. I was going to be Mrs. Christopher Andrew Smith.

He met me halfway up the hall. "Miss, I do believe I have told you that non-first-class passengers are not to be roaming these halls. I'm afraid I'll have to notify security if I see you again."

I walked right past him. "Yes, sir," I said, giving a playful mock salute. He didn't find that at all humorous, but I didn't care. I was going to be part of a family that was able to walk wherever they wanted, whenever they wanted. Next time we boarded the ship, I may have even seen to it that Officer LaPierre would get fired for so callously treating me the way he did.

I continued down the hall, fantasizing about all the fancy parties I would attend and all of the spectacular dinners we would have. The holidays would be festive with our families, sitting down at a table, enjoying a nice plump roast beast. And dare I think about our children that would run around the spacious corridors of our luxurious home? Definitely one of each—a beautiful little girl and a strong, handsome boy. I would make it a point to vacation at least twice a year while the children were on summer break from classes.

From under his breath, Officer LaPierre mumbled. By his furrowed brow, it was not something favorable.

"Excuse me?" I asked.

His eyes, cold and angry, focused on me. "You heard me. You coloreds don't belong in first-class, or anywhere on this ship, for that matter. Although it would be too much of a headache for me to report you at this current time, if I see your brown face around here again, I will have you thrown off of this ship to live with the bottom dwellers where you belong."

My eyes widened in disbelief. How could this man have so much hatred for someone who had never done him any wrong? Yes, I was definitely going to have him fired. "I'll have you know I was with a first-class passenger. You cannot speak to me in such a manner. I demand you apologize."

Officer LaPierre laughed. "Are you mad, girl? I don't bloody well care if you *are* sleeping with the Captain's nephew. You will never fit in. You're just a Negro."

I stood, with my mouth gaped open, appalled by his disgusting words. I turned and rushed down the hall. When I reached my cabin, I stood at the door and took a deep breath.

You will never fit in.

You're just a Negro.

As I turned the knob to go in, Sophia rounded the corner and barreled straight toward me. I sighed, not in the mood for another ugly confrontation.

"Who do you think you are?" she spat. There were deep frown lines around her mouth and hatred in her eyes.

She lifted her hand and pointed her thin, witchy finger within inches of my nose. "I know about your plans to marry Christopher. I know you were with him all afternoon as well as the evening before."

Officer LaPierre! He had said that he didn't care whether or not I was sleeping with Christopher. How would he know something like that? "You've been having us watched!" I exclaimed. "What is wrong with you?"

"What's wrong with *me?*" Sophia's cackling laugh echoed down the hall. "What's wrong with me is that I will not have some po' lil' Negro girl pushing her way into the family that I have worked so hard to get into. For God's sake, girl, yo' Daddy is a Negro farmer," she said in a belittling accent. "Do you think Mrs. Smith would allow such a thing?"

"I suppose you told her everything."

"Of course I did. She thinks this whole dreadful situation will simply disappear. I know better. I know how desirable a woman's nectar can be, and with your voodoo, I wouldn't be surprised if he actually thought he wanted to marry you. As soon as I go back and tell his mother where you were this afternoon, I'm sure she'll come to her senses and realize just how powerful your Negro black magic is. You...need...to...be...stopped."

"This is not a game. Christopher wants to marry me and I want to marry him."

"Christopher is mine!"

I looked at her in amazement. "Are you serious? He's not a possession. Why can't you accept the fact that he does not want to be with you. He wants me."

"Really?"

"Yes, really."

She stared at me with a contemptuous smile, attempting to find fear in my eyes, but I held her gaze. She took a step back. "You will never marry him. I will see to that."

"There's nothing you can do, Sophia."

"Think so?" She turned and headed off down the hall. Just then my stateroom door opened.

"What is going on out here?" Astrid asked.

"Nothing," I told her. "How are you feeling? Do you need anything?"

"Maybe earplugs. What the hell was all that noise about?"

"Nothing," I said, pushing her back into the room. "Has Daddy been by?"

"At least half a dozen times, looking for you. Where were you all afternoon?"

"I need to find Christopher He's supposed to meet me here, so if I miss him, send him back to his room and tell him I'll meet him there instead." I headed back out the door. When I turned the corner, I practically ran him over.

"What's wrong?" he asked.

"We need to find your mother right away. Sophia is set out to cause trouble and this time she means it."

❦ *3 1/2 hours until…* ❦

❧[29]❧

"I can't believe your mother has not returned yet," I told Christopher. He locked his stateroom door and then headed off to look for her once again. We had spent the remaining afternoon, well into the evening hours, in search of either his mother or my father to no avail.

"It's almost like they disappeared on this massive ship," I told him as we hurried down the hall.

"She missed dinner this evening. I hope everything is all right."

"Corinne!" From down the hall, my father headed toward us. He was frantically waving his arms in the air. There was something in his hand—a piece of paper of some sort.

Once he was upon us, I asked, "What are you doing here? Where were you all afternoon? We've been looking for you."

"I should say the same about you." He turned to Christopher, then gave a respectable gentleman's nod. "I must've missed you by seconds this morning, and then I received the most glorious tour of the inner workings of the ship by a fine gentleman by the name of Percy Hartford."

"Harland," I corrected.

"Yes, well, Mr. Harland is in the business of ships. He took me to lunch where we discussed possible future business plans. I apologize for not being around, but we lost track of time."

There was a light in his eyes that I hadn't seen in quite some time.

"That's great, Daddy," I said. "I'm glad you're here. I've been looking for you all day."

He pulled out a worn handkerchief and dabbed at beads of sweat forming on his forehead. I recognized the handkerchief as the one Astrid and I had bought him for his birthday years ago, when we were little girls. "Do you recognize this handkerchief?"

I nodded. "Yes, I do. Astrid and I saved up our chore money for a whole year. I thought you threw that ratty old thing out."

"You and your sister bought this for me when you were my little princesses," he said. "I carry it around to remind myself that you're not little girls anymore. You're mature young women." He paused. "Corinne?"

"Yes?"

"I'm so sorry for hitting you. It was just that I was feeling so—"

"I know, Daddy." He didn't need to finish the sentence. This was the first time I looked through his eyes and down to his soul and saw how truly scared he was.

"You never did tell me how you knew where to find us," I said.

"Your sister told me, so I thought I'd come find you." Daddy turned back to Christopher. "Your name is Christopher, correct?"

He nodded. "Yes, sir."

"Don't sound so formal."

"Sorry, sir."

Seeming unusually giddy this evening, Daddy chuckled. "That's okay, son. That means you were well-raised. In any case, formal or not, I'd like to invite both of you to dine with me tonight." He held up the tickets he had in his hand, waving them high like an auction paddle. "This is why I came to find you. Mr. Harland, the man I discussed business with, was generous enough to give me three tickets for the special feature this evening. These are not easy to come by, so a refusal will not be accepted."

With the excitement in Daddy's eyes, I didn't have the heart to tell him that being the Captain's nephew, Christopher could have obtained the same tickets just as easily.

"Sir, that's quite generous of you," Christopher began. "But—"

Daddy raised his brow. "I will consider it an insult if you don't let me take you to dinner." He turned to me. "After some coaxing, your sister finally told me everything that has happened these past few days. I would like to do this, son."

Christopher and I cautiously looked at each other. "She told you everything?" I asked, astonished.

"That, she did."

"Pardon me, sir," Christopher began, "but you seem to be taking this rather well."

"As I should. Why wouldn't I?"

Again, Christopher and I glanced at each other.

"Astrid told you everything?" I asked, again.

This time it was Daddy's turn to be confused. "Yes, I see no reason to hide the truth." He turned to Christopher and extended his free hand. "And I commend you for it."

Christopher hesitated, but eventually grabbed Daddy's extended hand. "Uh, sir," he stammered, mid-shake, "somehow I don't believe we are speaking on the same topic."

Daddy's face clouded over with confusion, but there was no time to question. Captain and Mrs. Smith rounded the corner, heading in our direction. Mrs. Smith wore a deep frown of discontent. His uncle was a little harder to read. His lips formed a perfect line, not turning upward or downward. Their pace was curt and immediate. Sophia was two steps behind them and unlike Christopher's family, Sophia's crimson lips wore her trademark mischievous smirk.

My heart pounded rapidly under my blouse, more from anticipation than fear.

"Christopher, dear," his mother said when she reached us. Her faded smile was joined by a worrisome crinkle in her forehead. "What is this marriage news we are hearing of?"

Christopher stepped up. He glared at Sophia. "We wanted to be the ones to tell you."

From behind me, Daddy questioned, "Marriage? Who said anything about marriage?"

Mrs. Smith's nervous chuckle carried down the hall. "Well, sir," she said to Daddy, "I do believe your daughter and my son have made plans for a union that apparently no one knows anything about." She turned back to Christopher. "Please tell me this isn't so."

"Mother, I—"

"Are you mad, Christopher?" Sophia interrupted, stepping from his mother's shadow. "There is absolutely no way you can marry *her*. Your mother and I will never allow such a thing."

"Excuse me?" Daddy reached for my arm and stepped up in front of me. "I kindly ask that you not speak about my daughter in that manner, young *lady*." His emphasis on the word *lady* indicated that he didn't think that of her at all.

"Ahhh!" Her painted-on brow arched as her voice softened the way cold butter does in hot a skillet before it pops and burns you. "And you must be her father. Can you not control your own children? Your daughter must be bloody insane if she thinks the Smith family would allow such a union to occur."

"Sophia." Mrs. Smith rested a hand on her shoulder. "Please, dear, I'm sure there is some explanation. I'll handle the situation."

"Surely, I have no idea what you are talking about," Daddy said, speaking directly to Sophia.

"I don't believe that. Isn't that why you're here?" Sophia questioned.

Daddy turned around. "Would someone please tell me what's going on?"

"Daddy," I began, "Christopher and I have decided to get married."

Mrs. Smith turned to her up-to-then reticent brother. "E.J., would you please speak to your nephew? Apparently, he is not hearing one single word coming from me. Maybe he'll listen to you."

"Christopher," Captain Smith began, "you are far too young for marriage."

"Too young?" Sophia spat. "Age has nothing to do with it. She's a second-class citizen for God's sake. She is the daughter of a farmer. What kind of union would that make?"

"Please, Sophia," his mother finally said, "I can handle this." She turned back to Christopher. "Son, may I have a word with you?" She grabbed his elbow and hurried him down the hall.

Daddy looked at Sophia. "Young lady, out of respect, please refrain from insulting my family."

Sophia cackled. "Respect for whom?"

"Sophia, please," Captain Smith said with an exasperated sigh. "I'm sure this will all be resolved soon."

I looked down the hall and toward the intense discussion between Christopher and his mother. I watched helplessly as Christopher's arms flailed about in frustration. On several occasions, his mother hushed him, but the more she attempted to quiet him, the louder he became, forcing her to match his tone. From down the hall, the two could be heard quite clearly.

"Christopher, I forbid this union. If you won't think of our family, think of the children you may someday have with her. I cannot allow that."

"Mother, please. The decision has been made and there's nothing you can say or do."

"Christopher," his mother pleaded, her voice rising, "you are doing this to spite me. Do not think for one moment I will have Black grandchildren running around my house."

As soon as the words were said, she turned back toward us. "I-I, simply meant that this type of union…well, it would not be beneficial to all parties involved, including small children."

"Christopher," I said, taking a step toward them, "maybe this isn't the best time to discuss this."

"Oh yes, perhaps you'd like to return to his room and lay down with him once again," Sophia spat.

Quickly, I turned to Daddy. His expression was more hurt than shocked. "Corinne?"

"Daddy," I said, "I didn't want you to find out like this."

"He can't be surprised that you're sleeping about," Sophia said. "This type of behavior is expected from someone like you."

Daddy stepped up. I thought he was about to haul off and slap the white clean off Sophia's overly painted face. Instead, looking dead in her eyes, he calmly responded, "When you insult my daughter, you insult me as well, implying her mother and I have not raised her properly. I do understand your hatred, young lady. It's something that has been embedded within your family for generations. I understand that. What I don't understand is how you, a well-bred young woman, do not respect another human being."

He took my arm. "Come, Corinne. I will no longer listen to these insults."

Sophia looked at both of us, lifted her nose to the ceiling and said, very calmly, "Niggers."

"Excuse me?" I stepped up, preparing to make her regret uttering such a word, but Christopher blocked me from her path.

"See? Look at her!" she said, pointing her haughty finger at me. "She's ready to fight like an alley cat in heat."

"That's quite enough, Sophia!" Captain Smith exclaimed.

Sophia rested her hands on her tiny hips. "With much respect, Captain, do you want your only nephew to marry *her*?"

Daddy, who had been relatively calm up until this point, slowly stepped up, this time standing inches from Sophia's pointy, up-turned nose. "With respect, young lady, this is none of your business. Leave this to the families involved."

Hatred must've gone off and given Sophia a lethal combination of courage and stupidity because she stood her ground. She stared at Daddy. "No offense to you, *sir*." She emphasized the word *sir* in the same distasteful manner Daddy had *lady*. "But I am and will always be involved."

I grabbed Daddy's elbow to make a hasty retreat. I didn't want to reach a point we all might have regretted. I tugged twice, but Daddy wouldn't budge. "Let's go, Daddy, please," I begged. "She's only trying to goad you."

"Corinne, wait!" Christopher called out.

Finally, I was able to coax Daddy into walking away. When he did, Sophia reached out and grabbed his arm. Her colorful nails dug into his skin. "How dare you turn your back to me!"

Daddy snatched his arm away and continued walking. There was a big thud as Sophia slammed back against the corridor wall. Slowly, she fell to the ground.

"Sophia!" Christopher yelled.

Captain Smith reached out to grab her, but it was too late. She slid down the wall with her rear end landing on the ground in a hard clunk.

Her eyelids fluttered as her hand reached up to her chest. Like a fish squirming on the shore before taking its last breaths, Sophia frantically inhaled and exhaled. She threw her head back and muttered, "Dear Lord, someone please help me." The sight lasted less than a few seconds, but the entire scene was quite theatrical.

"Fetch Doctor Wahlberg!" Captain Smith yelled into the crowd that had gathered in the hall.

A woman carrying a crying baby stood over Sophia. "Is she dying?" A man stepped up behind her, scolded her for allowing a child to witness such a scene, and then brusquely steered the woman back toward her stateroom. The entire time, the baby wailed at the top of its lungs.

Concerned, I took a step toward Sophia lying on the ground, gasping for breath. When she saw me standing over her, miraculously she was able to speak. "Get this…this person away from me."

Daddy and I stood in utter disbelief as onlookers gathered in closer, eventually forcing us back farther until Christopher and his family disappeared within the growing crowd. We were left with the sight of the back of the crowd's heads.

Daddy reached down and grabbed my arm. "Come on, Corinne."

"Where are we going? We have to help her."

"There's nothing more we can do," he said. "We can't stay here."

"But, Daddy— "

"Let's go…*Now!*"

Just then, a man from the center of the commotion jerked up and looked around. When he saw Daddy and me, he pointed and yelled, "Arrest that man for attempted murder!"

❧ 1 1/2 hours until... ❧

·❧[30]❧·

*T*wo very large uniformed men quickly raced toward Daddy and me. One grabbed Daddy's arm and twisted it behind his back. The other tackled him to the ground like a rabid street dog. The three fell to the ground in a hard thump with Daddy on the bottom of the mammoth pile.

"Daddy!" I screamed, darting toward them. I tried pulling one of the men off Daddy, but he was too big. In the midst of their tousling, the other large man elbowed me right in the face and I fell backward onto the ground. "Somebody, help my father!" I yelled into the crowd. *"Please!"*

Most of the mob was still gathered around Sophia and hadn't even witnessed what was happening behind them. From the corner of my eye, I saw Dr. Wahlberg racing down the hall, heading for the crowd's center.

"Doctor," I called. "Please help me. These men are hurting my father."

The doctor wasn't a large man, but he was tall and lean enough to make up for his lack of girth. He stopped abruptly, unsure of how to proceed. After a short pause, he dropped his black medical bag and ran toward Daddy. He reached out to one of the men, placed his large hand on his shoulder and pushed him down to the ground. The other man picked up Daddy by the collar of his shirt and slammed him against the wall. Blood gushed from a gash on Daddy's forehead.

"Everything is fine now, sir," the man holding Daddy said to the doctor.

"Doctor!" Mrs. Smith called. "We need you now."

When Dr. Wahlberg saw the situation was calming, he raced over toward Sophia, who by this time, was lying on her back but breathing much easier.

The second ruffian Dr. Wahlberg had successfully pushed away stood up and took Daddy's other arm. As the men began walking him down the hall, I peeked over the tops of several heads to see Mrs. Smith leaning over Sophia, holding her hand. Dr. Wahlberg placed a pillow underneath Sophia's head as Captain Smith positioned another one beneath her shoeless feet. I turned and followed Daddy and the two men.

"You are not allowed. This is official business," the bigger of the two ruffians said to me in a baritone voice. He clomped his large, gorilla-like paw on my shoulder and held me back like a rag doll. The other slightly smaller man continued to escort Daddy down the hall.

"Daddy!" I screamed after him.

Daddy struggled to turn around. His eye was beginning to swell shut and the blood from the cut on his forehead trickled down his cheek. "Don't worry, honey," he told me. "You stay here and look after things. I'll be back."

The two men dragged him down the hall and around the corner. I turned back to the crowd and pushed my way through.

"She'll be fine," I heard Dr. Wahlberg saying. There was a collective sigh throughout the crowd as a few onlookers began to disperse. "She'll need some rest tonight. I'll have a stretcher brought down to take her to her room."

"No need," Captain Smith said. "Her stateroom is right here with us." He scooped up Sophia and slowly carried her through the scant crowd and to her room. The entire time, she had her hand on her head and was repeatedly saying, "That big Black man was so frightening. I didn't know what to do."

When there were fewer people in the halls, Christopher went to enter his mother's stateroom. "Christopher?" I called out. He didn't turn around. "Christopher?" I called again. This time he turned and looked, but continued into the stateroom behind Captain Smith and Sophia. The door shut and I was left standing alone in the hall, wondering how to get to my father.

"Oh my, are you all right?" Dr. Wahlberg asked, placing a gentle finger under my throbbing, bruised eye.

I shook my head and the throbbing increased times ten. "No, I don't know where they have taken my father."

"I think I can help you with that. Let me knock and ask Captain Smith where they take crimin—uh, I mean, those persons under arrest." He cleared his throat and headed toward the room. "I'm sorry, dear. I'll only be a moment."

The doctor entered into the room and closed the door behind him. I leaned back against the wall and touched my smarting left cheek. Up until this moment, I hadn't noticed that elbow to the face gave me quite a bruise.

I took a deep breath, patiently waiting for the doctor to return. When he hadn't returned fifteen minutes later, I worried. I went to the door, lifted my hand to knock, but thought better of it. I plopped back down and sat in the hallway outside of the door, watching people casually stroll past. Minutes later, the door creaked open. I jumped back, expecting Dr. Wahlberg to exit. Instead, it was Christopher.

"What are you doing out here?" he whispered.

"I don't know where—" I took in a deep breath, deciding now may not have been an appropriate time. "How's Sophia?"

He took a step out the door and gently closed it behind him. "She'll be fine. She's resting."

"Good," I said, expecting him to spit on me after what had happened. Instead, he gently raised his hand to my swollen cheek. "Are *you* all right is a more appropriate question. What happened?"

"That's why I'm still here, waiting. Otherwise, I'd let you tend to your family, but I need to know where they took Daddy."

"Who took your father?" he questioned.

"The two men who wrestled him to the ground."

By his puzzled expression, he had no idea what I was talking about. "My father was forced down the hall by two big goons," I explained curtly.

"What for?"

"For striking Sophia."

"That was an accident."

"I know," I said. "But they still took him and I don't know where."

Christopher took my arm. "Come on. I think I know where he is." As we headed down the hall, the stateroom door opened. Mrs. Smith poked out her head.

"Christopher, where are you going?" she called after us.

"Tell Uncle Edward I'll be back soon," he said, rushing me down the hall.

As we turned the corner, in frustration, Mrs. Smith yelled after us, "Don't think for one moment our conversation is finished!"

❦ *1 hour until...* ❦

·•❧❩ 31 ❨❧•·

"They won't hurt him, will they?" I asked.

He took my hand and pulled me down the corridor. "Christopher," I said, "I can't keep up. Please slow down."

"We don't have time, Corinne."

"What's wrong? Do you think they'll harm him?" I asked again.

As he hurried me down the hall, we passed a clock. It was almost eleven in the evening. We turned down one corridor, almost colliding into a man and his wife. The young woman turned and gave an irate expression.

"I'm so sorr—"

Christopher quickly pulled me down the hall and around the corner. I struggled to keep up his pace.

"Where are we going?" I asked, out of breath.

"There's a wing still under construction," he said. "I'm assuming they took him there."

We headed down another hall and down a four-step flight of stairs, eventually ending up in a dark and dank corridor. The smell reminded me of the tiny wooden schoolhouse back in Cherbourg when it rained heavily for days straight and all windows were sealed tight to avoid mold infestation.

The hall carpeting was frayed and torn with dirt stains, but it wasn't like you could see it clearly anyway. The lighting was so dim, at one point, I had to reach out and feel for the wall to make sure I didn't ram into something.

"Where exactly are we going?" I questioned again. He didn't answer, only kept pulling me. Finally, I stopped in the middle of the hall and snatched back my arm. "Christopher! What is wrong? Is my father in danger?"

He shook his head. "Corinne, I don't know, but you're telling me that two big men took him—a Black man—away with claims that he struck a white woman. What does that mean to you?"

"Are you telling me something bad might happen?"

"I'm telling you they took him away by force. Something bad has already happened. I'm trying to keep it from getting any worse."

My heart raced inside my chest. "Christopher, you're scaring me."

"It's right around the corner. Everything will be fine." His voice was shaking as he reached down and grabbed my hand. "Right around the corner," he repeated, drawing me farther down the hall.

When we reached the door, Christopher quickly dropped my hand and knocked. The slightly ajar door pushed open. He peeked his head in. "Hello? Is anyone in here?"

We waited for a response. As I struggled to look over his shoulder, a tiny trickle of sweat made its way down the side of my face.

"Hello?" he called.

There was no response.

Christopher pushed the door open further and stepped inside. I followed closely behind.

The empty room was small—way too tiny to be a stateroom— and had exposed pipes hanging above our heads. The gray carpet contained several water stains as did the gray painted walls. In the dead center of the back wall was a circular-shaped window. The only light in that room came from the full moon that shone between the planks and through that window.

On the left side, I spotted a closed door. Christopher glanced back at me before proceeding. "Maybe you should stay here," he warned.

I shook my head. "I'm coming."

Carefully, he took the knob and turned. He pushed the door open. Aside from a broom and a few cleaning supplies, it was empty.

"Christopher!" boomed a voice behind us.

Startled, we both turned and saw the silhouette of a man standing tall in the doorway of the small room. "What in the world are you doing in here? This part of the ship is off-limits. You know it's dangerous in this area."

"First Officer Murdoch, sir, we were looking for Mr. LaRoche," Christopher said. "Have you seen him?"

Officer Murdoch raised his chin. "I can assure you, Mr. Smith, he's not in here. However, I can take you to him."

"He's not hurt, is he?" I asked, following First Officer Murdoch out of the room. Christopher followed behind both of us.

"He's fine," Officer Murdoch said. "He's been taken into custody because of his actions."

"But he did nothing wrong," I protested. "It was an accident."

"I'm sorry, young lady, but we have witnesses who say otherwise."

"I don't care what they say. It's not the truth."

We followed him farther down the hall until he finally turned into another darkened room. This one was slightly larger than the one before. In the corner, Daddy sat in a chair with his head down and his hands cuffed behind the back of the chair. He tried to lift his head. It bobbled back and forth until his chin rested on his chest once again.

"Daddy!" I exclaimed, running to his side. With effort, he opened his eyes. With a glassy expression, he looked down at me kneeling by his feet. It seemed he didn't even recognize me or even where he was. "What have you done to him?"

"He was getting out of sorts," one of the big men said. "We had to sedate him."

I looked from Christopher to First Officer Murdoch. "They're lying. When they took him away, his hands were cuffed behind his back. How could he possibly act out in a position like that?"

First Officer Murdoch walked up and stood beside me. He leaned down to Daddy and said, "We will gladly listen to your side of the story, sir."

Daddy lifted his head. It buoyed back and forth and then he let it drop.

Officer Murdoch looked at me. "I'm afraid we can't do anything until he tells us what happened."

"That's not fair," I said. "You're the ones that did this to him. How is he supposed to tell you what happened if he can barely hold up his head?"

"I'm afraid that's the only way. Like I've stated before, we have witnesses who say he pushed a woman. We need him to at least make a statement in favor of or against those claims."

"I was there," I told him. "I can tell you what happened myself."

"It's proper protocol," First Officer Murdoch bellowed authoritatively. "I am not at liberty to say one way or another. Your father will need to speak up in his own defense."

"I witnessed everything as well," Christopher replied. "This is a mistake. This man did nothing to warrant this treatment."

"I'm sorry. You know the rules. The man must speak up in his own defense."

"But you take the words of those so-called witnesses," I said.

Officer Murdoch stood strong with his arms crossed while shaking his head and repeating the words, "I'm sorry, miss; it's protocol."

It was like speaking to a child. Realizing Officer Murdoch wouldn't budge, I turned back to Daddy. "Can you at least take off these awful handcuffs? Look at him. He's not going anywhere."

"He needs to be restrained for safety purposes."

I cradled Daddy's wobbly head in my hands. Blood seeped from the large gash on his forehead. "He needs medical attention."

No one moved. "He needs medical attention now!" I barked.

"The only person that can make that call is the Captain," Officer Murdoch said.

"But he's not here," I pointed out.

"I'm sorry, ma'am."

"Oh, Daddy! Don't worry. Everything will be fine. I'll make sure of it." I kissed his cheek. "You've taken care of our family for so long. I respect you so much for that. Now I'll be strong for you. Can you hear me, Daddy? I love you."

Just then, Captain Smith burst in and surveyed the room. "What the hell is going on here? Murdoch?"

I glanced back at Christopher, who stood in the corner, his brow raised compassionately. "Corinne, I'm so sorry for all of this." He turned back to Captain Smith. "Uncle, please let this man go. He has done no harm. You know that. *Please*."

"But we have witnesses," Officer Murdoch called out. "This man needs to be detained."

"What this man needs," Captain Smith said, "is medical attention. Look at his face." He turned toward the large men standing over a slumped-over Daddy. "Get Doctor Wahlberg here." When the men hesitated, he barked, "Go now!"

Both men quickly exited, slamming the door behind them.

"Sir," Officer Murdoch said, "you need to understand that we have witnesses who say this man accosted a female passenger."

"Who cares about your witnesses?" I yelled. "You saw it with your own eyes, Captain. My father did not strike Sophia."

"Corinne, please," Christopher said. "My uncle will handle this."

"What is there to discuss?" I interrupted. "Look at him," I said, lifting Daddy's head. "He's been beaten and drugged."

"My men told me he was acting out," Officer Murdoch proclaimed. "They are under strict orders to keep him in control."

"Liar!" I yelled. "How much acting out could he do in such a condition?"

"Murdoch, release this man," Captain Smith said. "I am the only witness that matters. This man did not strike anyone."

"You're only doing this because he's Black," I said to Officer Murdoch. "If he were a white man, you would take no issue."

Officer Murdoch cleared his throat and stared the Captain down. "It's not that simple, sir. This has nothing to do with his color. It's proper protocol."

"William!" Captain Smith's patience was wearing thin. "I am Captain of this ship and you will do as I say. Let him go or I'll expect your resignation on my desk right away."

Officer Murdoch scowled, but eventually relented. He took a small key from the pocket of his pressed uniform and slapped it into Captain Smith's hand. "I would like to go on record as saying that I do not agree with this nor will I be held responsible for any repercussions that may occur."

Captain Smith nodded. "Understood. You may now return to your post, Murdoch." He placed a hand on Officer Murdoch's shoulder and steered him toward the door. "You are a good and loyal man." Captain Smith then lowered his voice to a whisper.

"We have been having complaints regarding missing merchandise. Please attend to that matter, if you will, and I will see to this."

"Yes, sir." First Officer Murdoch turned and walked out the door.

When Officer Murdoch was gone, Captain Smith leaned down and unlocked the restraints around Daddy's ankles and hands. He lifted Daddy's chin and inspected his eye. "Sir, did my men do this to you?"

"Of course they did," I called out. "You're the Captain. How can you not be aware of what your men are doing?"

"Young lady, if my men did this, then appropriate action will be taken against them—but understand that I would never condone violence."

Daddy's small voice called out from behind us. "I don't believe for one minute Captain Smith would allow such a thing."

The captain knelt down by Daddy's side. "My men did this to you without just cause?"

Daddy managed a small chuckle as he lazily said, "Well, sir, I sure didn't walk into no walls if that's what you're implying."

Captain Smith stood up and grabbed a towel resting on the dusty, wooden desk in the corner. He took the towel and dabbed at the gash on Daddy's forehead. "I'm sorry, sir. I had just assumed—" He trailed off. "Sir, my sincerest apologies. They will be dealt with accordingly."

Captain Smith stood up and went to the door. "What is taking Doctor Wahlberg so long?"

All of a sudden, with no warning, the ship began to shake violently. It only lasted a few seconds, but that was enough to have all four of us on the ground, grasping for refuge.

"Are you all right, Corinne?" Christopher asked, helping me to my feet.

"I think so." I reached for Daddy who had been knocked over in his chair. Christopher reached down and helped me place him back onto the chair. "Are you all right, Daddy?"

The momentary shaking must've knocked some life back into him. With clear eyes and even clearer speech, Daddy nodded as he said, "I'm fine."

Christopher looked toward the door. Captain Smith was lying on the ground. "Uncle!" He quickly helped him up to his feet. A large bump began to swell on his right side temple. "Can you stand?" Christopher asked.

With his hand to his head, Captain Smith slowly nodded. "Yes. I'm just shaken up a bit, is all."

"What was that?" Christopher asked.

Just then, Mr. Harland barged into the room. "Oh, there you are. Captain, I'm afraid we have an emergency. Please come with me." He looked past the Captain and saw Daddy and me. "Is everything all right, Edward?"

"Yes, yes, everything is fine," Captain Smith said.

Mr. Harland's chubby fingers took ahold of the Captain's arm. "Edward, you have a wallop the size of a baseball on your head."

"I'm fine," Captain Smith muttered. "What happened?"

Mr. Harland hesitated. He glanced around the room at the sea of confused faces. "It's probably best if we discuss this in private."

"Percy," Captain Smith said, "tell me what happened."

Mr. Harland hesitated for another second, but then finally blurted, "I'm afraid we've hit an iceberg."

·•❧[32]❧•·

" I received word that the inclement weather made for dire visibility," Mr. Harland said. "At approximately eleven thirty-five in the evening, our lookouts spotted a massive iceberg from the ship's bow, about a quarter of a mile ahead."

"How badly were we hit?" Captain Smith asked, poking at the large, purple bruise forming on his forehead.

"Are you sure you're all right?" Mr. Harland asked.

"Yes," Captain Smith insisted. "Now, please go on."

"Last report," Mr. Harland said, "the iceberg struck starboard bow side and brushed along the side of the ship. The impact, although jarring to the crew down in the forward area, should not have been noticed by many of the passengers on the upper decks."

"Good," Captain Smith responded. "Have Wallace and the rest of the musicians set up on deck right away. What's the total damage?"

Mr. Harland frowned. "Edward, I think you'd better come with me."

"Of course," Captain Smith said. "We'll need to locate Thomas and his apprentice in order to conduct a visual inspection. Also, locate Chief Officer Wilde and have him meet me on deck—as soon as possible!"

"Yes," Mr. Harland said.

"I should come as well," Christopher offered.

Captain Smith placed a firm hand onto his nephew's shoulder. "Retrieve your mother. I'll need you to head to the third-class dining room. Have the purser make an official announcement to have all passengers meet in the dining room in twenty minutes. Do you understand?"

Christopher nodded. "Yes, sir."

"Good," the Captain said. "Also, make sure each passenger carries his life vest with him."

"Edward!" Mr. Harland called as he headed toward the door. "We need to go."

"Yes, yes, I'm coming." Captain Smith turned to me. "Young lady, I'm sorry for your trouble. If you want to wait here for the doctor, you may. He should be along any moment now."

I nodded weakly as the two men dashed out the door.

"You should wait for Doctor Wahlberg," Christopher advised. "I'll have to leave you for a few minutes, but I'll return soon." Christopher turned to dash out the door behind them, but I grabbed his arm.

"Is this serious?" I asked.

Christopher placed his palm to my cheek. His hand was clammy and his face was flushed. He leaned down and kissed me, just like the first time, only this time, there was a slight tremble in his lips. When he pulled away, I saw fear in his eyes. "Everything is going to be fine, Corinne. Take care of your father until the doctor arrives." He turned and hurried out the door.

I turned around to tend to Daddy. He was already on his feet, brushing himself off, as if the last few hours never happened.

"Where are you going, Daddy? They said to wait for the doctor. You are in no condition to be on your feet now."

He looked up at me. "Ain't no doctor coming. Did you see the look in that boy's eyes? We need to get out of here and get your sister quick."

Daddy and I scampered through the halls. Most passengers were either casually strolling down the corridors or engaging in relaxed conversation with stateroom neighbors. With my hand on Daddy's elbow, I aided him down the hall. Each person passed, briefly glanced in our direction and then continued on with their conversation. From the deck, there was a faint but distinct melodic harmony of string instruments playing the tune, "Eternal Father, Strong to Save," a song I hadn't heard since I was young.

Daddy chuckled nervously. "They could have picked a better song, eh?"

"Should we say something to the passengers?" I whispered as we made our way down the hall.

"Not at this point. You heard the Captain. They will make an official announcement over the system. Besides," Daddy said, "we don't know the specifics yet. It may not be as bad as originally assumed." His bottom lip trembled and he avoided eye contact. "But then again you were there. You saw Mr. Harland's face when he informed the Captain of the iceberg. However, that doesn't necessarily mean it's a grim situation." Daddy abruptly stopped walking. "On second thought, maybe we could casually mention that they should go and retrieve their life jackets."

As we headed farther down the hall, we came across a group of tuxedoed gents chatting in the seating area. Two of them had fancy walking canes resting against the chairs. One sipped a glass of brandy while two others smoked big, fat stinky cigars.

Daddy limped over and gave a polite nod. "Gentlemen, an announcement is about to be made. Apparently, the ship has struck something and it would be wise to go and gather your families and life jackets as soon as possible."

The men looked from one to another. The tallest man in the group with the black coachman hat stood up and grinned. A chubby man with one of the stinky cigars dangling between his fingers stepped up. "I assure you, even if that was the case, this ship is unsinkable." He placed a firm hand on Daddy's shoulder. "But from the looks of it, you may be the one that is sinking. For goodness sake, clean yourself up." The rest of the men in the group laughed.

Daddy hobbled his way back to me. "Can't do nothing for somebody that don't want to hear nothin'."

A few others had the same reaction. It was only when we headed down to second-class did people take heed to our warning. One man standing outside his stateroom door, enjoying a cigarette, quickly went inside. Before we made it to the end of the corridor, he and his wife, along with their two children, headed to the third-class dining room safely secured in life vests.

"Are we doing the right thing?" I asked. "What if this isn't too serious? What if we're wrong and people panic?"

Daddy looked at me. "I'd rather be safe and wrong than unprepared and right. Now go get your sister. I'm going to my room to get a few things. Pack all you can in one suitcase and meet me in the dining room in ten minutes. Do you understand?"

I nodded, still in disbelief at what was happening.

"Astrid?" I called as soon as I pushed the door open.

There was no sign of her.

I stared off down the hall, wondering where she could have gone. Seconds later, the toilet flushed and Astrid exited, fully dressed. Her hair was neatly combed and she was wearing full makeup.

"It's about time," she said, heading back to her bed. "So did you tell his mother? How did they take the news that their prestigious son was marrying a little ol' colored girl?" She sat on the edge of the bed, reached under it and pulled out a pair of fancy shoes. "I would have paid any amount of money to be there when that conversation took place."

"Why are you all dressed up?"

"I can't stay in this bed any longer."

"Do you even feel up to it?" I asked, watching her fasten up her shoes. "And isn't it kind of late?"

"I feel fine and have for the past day. The best time to go out is nighttime." She glanced up. "What the hell happened to your face? Don't tell me the ol' gal done slapped the nigra one time." She chuckled as she continued lacing up her shoe.

Standing atop a large box platform at the end of the hall, a uniformed man made the announcement;

"Ladies and Gentlemen, please return to your cabins promptly. There you will find life jackets contained in a chest at the foot of the beds. Please secure each family member with one of these life jackets and head to the dining room. Thank you."

Then a second announcement came in French;

"Mesdames et messieurs, s'il vous plaît retourner à votre cabine rapidement. Gilets de sauvetage sont dans une caisse au pied des lits. S'il vous plaît mettez un gilet de sauvetage et passer à la salle à manger. Je vous remercie."

The announcement was made in four other languages—most of which I did not recognize, but one sounded German and another, Dutch.

"What is going on?" Astrid asked. "Do they know it's almost midnight? Fine time to have a drill."

"It's not a drill," I told her. "That's why I'm here." I went over to the closet and pulled out our smallest suitcase. "We need to get our life jackets and a few belongings and go to the third-class dining hall as soon as possible."

"You can't be serious. For what purpose?"

"Didn't you feel that tremble earlier?" I grabbed a few things and shoved them into the suitcase. "We'll have to share this one, so bring as little as possible—only the necessities."

"I felt it, but ships do that all the time. It happens when you hit a wave. A steward came by and told us so."

"Oh, Astrid," I said, still gathering items. "That hardly felt like a wave." I headed into the bathroom and grabbed my brush and two hand towels.

"Stop it," Astrid commanded. "You're making me nervous."

I stopped packing and walked up to her. "This is serious. We need to get our things together and get upstairs right away."

"No," she protested. "I'm not going."

"Astrid! Listen to me. Get your things. We're to meet Daddy in ten minutes."

"No!"

"Fine," I yelled. "Stay here and drown."

Astrid, who had not moved, suddenly reached over to her night-stand and grabbed her brush. For several minutes, both of us silently packed, avoiding one another's gaze.

"I didn't mean what I said," I finally told her.

"What part? About me drowning or that there's even a possibility that may happen?"

"I don't know if it's a possibility. I only know something terrible has happened and I want to make sure my family is all right."

Suddenly, there was a loud explosion that rocked the entire ship. It sounded as though it came from below.

"What was that?" Astrid asked. Her hands were shaking and she was taking deep breaths, her chest rapidly heaving up and down. "Corinne, tell me what that was."

"Everything's fine, Astrid. Keep packing and we'll go to the dining room," I said, hoping I was a better liar than both Christopher and Daddy.

I reached into the chest at the foot of my bed and pulled out a life vest. I went into hers, but aside from a few manuals, there was nothing else there.

Astrid peeked over the top of the opened chest. "Where's mine?" she asked, in a panic. "Oh, God, don't tell me I don't have a life vest."

"Calm down. Everything's fine, Astrid," I repeated. "You can have mine. I'm sure they have extras in the dining hall."

Not wanting to give her another reason to panic, I quickly placed my jacket around her and securely fastened each latch. I took a step back. "There. You're safe." At that moment, I felt like Momma when, as children, she dressed us in our rain gear before heading us off to school.

There was another smaller explosion, only this one sounded like it was coming from down the hall. When we heard the sounds of stampeding feet outside our door, we stared at one another, afraid to move.

"Corinne, wh-what are we going to do?"

With one hand, I grabbed her elbow and with the other, I snatched the leather handle of the suitcase. "We have to go." I pulled opened the door. Several people scurried about—some toward the dining hall and others in the opposite direction. Some passengers were fully clothed with life jackets on while others were barefoot and wore only night dressings. Nothing about this appeared orderly at all. Due to the chaos, people yelled to be heard. I did the same. "Make sure to keep hold of my hand! If for whatever reason we separate, meet me by the Captain's table in the dining hall. Do you understand?"

She furrowed her brow, so I wasn't sure if she heard me. I didn't have time to instruct her again. There was another explosion and the boat rocked back and forth. It wasn't as strong as the last, but it was much closer. The vibration caused passengers to topple to the ground—myself and Astrid included. Screaming ensued as electrical sparks shot out like firecrackers only a few feet away. Not wanting to be trampled, I quickly stood to my feet. I reached down to help up a few other passengers. I glanced around and realized Astrid was nowhere in sight. I yelled for her repeatedly but my voice was lost in the chaotic din.

"Astrid!" I called louder, only to be met with the sound of pounding footsteps and screaming children. I headed up to the dining room, hoping to meet her there. Water washed through, flooding the other end of the hall. The water was only about a half-inch high, but it rose rapidly.

I hurried in the opposite direction and up the steps, passing several families in the process. There, another man stood atop a second platform, fruitlessly attempting to calm passengers as they scrambled by.

I passed a woman with a small child. The frustrated woman spoke to a man in uniform, who only kept shaking his head and saying, "Speak English."

I listened closer, understanding very few of her words. She was speaking French.

"Excuse me, sir," I said. "I speak French."

"Good," the uniformed man said. "I don't understand a word

she's saying." He took off down the hall, leaving me with the crying woman and her screaming child. Immediately, she began rattling off words.

"You need to slow down, ma'am," I said. "*Vous devez ralentir, madame,*" I repeated in French.

I listened as well as I could, but with all the noise, only a few of her words were comprehensible. She pointed to the small child and then tugged at her life vest. "*Ma nièce a besoin d'un d'entre ceux-ci.*"

I understood. She was looking for a life vest for her niece. I thought a moment and then said, "*Allez à la salle à manger. Ils devraient avoir plus là.*" I pointed toward the dining room, letting her know there should be vests in her niece's size there. I tugged at my vest-less blouse and informed her that's where I was headed. "*J'ai besoin de celui aussi.*"

The young lady pushed her way past me, tugging the child up the steps and toward the dining room. "*Merci très beaucoup,*" she called back.

"Be careful," I called after her.

I watched after them until the woman's head disappeared into the crowd. I looked further and saw Daddy. He was heading for the dining room.

"Daddy!" I yelled, frantically waving my arms in the air. I tried to keep my sights on the back of his head, and did so successfully, until he dipped behind a tall man. Then he disappeared through the hall's double glass doors.

·❧{ 33 }❧·

MIDNIGHT

I was a few feet from the double doors. An even bigger crowd had gathered, pushing their way through. Neither Daddy nor Astrid were anywhere in sight and I was getting worried.

The ship rocked violently and passengers stumbled and fell onto the water-soaked carpet. Those that could, frantically scrambled to the side to avoid being trampled. Others weren't so lucky. With the last wave, a portly lady grabbed my arm, pulling me down with her. I landed on top of her and my elbow jabbed into her fleshy mid-section. She made a big *oomph* sound as she wrapped her arms around herself.

"I'm sorry, ma'am." I jumped to my feet and pulled her up before the crowd crushed us both. "Are you all right?"

Grumbling in a foreign language, she stood and shoved me out of the way so hard, I collided with another passenger. The woman may have been older, but she was extremely healthy.

The disorganized scene became even more chaotic as people continued pushing their way into the dining room. A few passengers plowed their way through, shoving me and several other passengers aside. Out of breath, I gave up and took refuge against the wall. What they failed to realize was that for every few steps taken toward the dining hall entranceway, the ship would either rock or a few of the larger passengers would shove their way through, jostling them right back right to where they had started. At least thirty minutes had passed and the faces I had scuttled up there with were the exact same faces before me now—and I wasn't moving.

"There aren't enough drills in the world that could prepare us for this," someone said.

A diminutive older lady took shelter against the wall with me. She was hunched over and leaned onto an intricately carved wooden cane. "I have no idea how they expect a crippled seventy-two-year-old woman to make it out of here alive," she said. She reached into the pocket of her coat and pulled out a soggy, wrinkled picture. It was a photo of a boy, about ten or eleven years old, sitting on the branch of an old oak tree. "I suppose it would've been nice to make it to my grandson's wedding," she continued. "But I don't think that's going to happen."

Someone grabbed my arm. It was Dr. Wahlberg dressed in a cocktail jacket. His dark, curly hair was wet and matted down. He looked at me. "Follow me in. I should be able to make it through."

I grabbed the elderly lady's free hand just as Dr. Wahlberg pulled me toward the glass doors. I held on to the lady tightly, but the crowd was too panicked and Dr. Wahlberg was pulling so hard. The ship rocked violently and my hand let go of the lady. Within seconds, she disappeared back into the crowd.

After a few accidental stepped-on toes and a couple of jabs to the ribs by panicked passengers, Dr. Wahlberg finally pulled me through the double doors. When I was in, I saw that it was just as crammed on the inside.

"Thank you," I yelled to the doctor, but he was already headed in a different direction. I stood on my toes and scanned the room for familiar faces. That was when I understood the ship's enormous size. We had been sailing for four days and most of the faces were unrecognizable.

There had to be at least eight hundred people jammed into a room that only allowed for half that, at most. I reached down and gathered up the hem of my dress, preparing to make my way toward the back. I pushed by several passengers, but then noticed the fire exits were on either side and toward the front.

I turned, preparing to head back to the front, when I felt a pull on my gathered-up hem. Figuring someone had just stepped on a piece of its dragging edge, I plodded on.

There was another tug. A tiny boy pulled at the dress' hem until several people scurried by, forcing his head to slam into my knee.

"Watch out!" I angrily shouted into the massive crowd. I bent down and scooped up the little boy. Tears flowed down his little red-streaked face. "Are you hurt?" I asked. He cried even more frantically.

"Where is your mommy?"

The word, *mommy*, made him howl even louder. "Oh, I'm sorry. Please don't cry," I said, gently nestling his face into my chest. "We'll find your mo—I mean, we'll find someone for you."

The ship viciously rocked back and forth. I struggled, but lost my footing and both the boy and I went down. A few other passengers tumbled and landed on top of us.

As I fought to stand up, I spotted a young girl my age lying on the floor a few feet away. She threw her arms over her head to keep from being trampled, but passengers stomped down on her like a roach on the living room floor. Most hadn't realized she was even down there—or if they did, they were too preoccupied to care.

With the boy still in my arms, I jumped up. "Help her!" I yelled, barely hearing my own voice. "Someone help her."

Eventually, a kind man reached down and helped the girl stand to her feet. Blood dripped from her nose and there was a quarter-sized black and blue bruise on her cheek. She glanced at me for less than a second, but it was long enough to witness the despondency in her eyes. I wondered if she saw the same thing in my face as well.

The boy screamed in my ear, "I want Mommmmmyy!" The ship tilted and this time the dining hall lights flickered as I struggled to maintain my balance with the shrieking boy in my arms. I was extra careful not to fall again. Next time I may be the one not able to get up and would need to rely on the kindness of a stranger, but at this point, kindness and compassion were personality attributes many passengers didn't have.

Somehow, I pushed my way toward one of the fire exits and stood against the wall with the boy in my arms. When the lights flickered once again, panic ensued and we were tossed back toward the center of the room.

I carried the screaming boy out the door and onto the ship's upper deck and was immediately met with a brand-new crowd of panicked passengers. I heard the clash of violins playing *"Songe d'Automne"* against the chaos. The chilled air struck me like a block of cement as the cold ocean droplets sprayed onto the deck. I grabbed onto the iron railing for stability, but still struggled to keep my footing on the drenched wood.

Out of nowhere, a short, stocky woman reached over, attempting to snatch the boy from my arms. "Give him to me!"

"What are you doing?"

"Give him to me," she demanded again.

I turned and pulled away with my feet almost slipping out from under me. "What's wrong with you? What are you doing?" I asked again.

"I don't want you touching him!" She lunged for him, but I pulled away.

When the boy saw the lady, he screamed, "Moooommmy!"

The boy struggled to reach for the woman, so I willingly handed him to her. He scrambled into her arms and went to give her a hug, but instead, she held him up like a doll and inspected every inch of him.

"Did this girl hurt you, Damien?"

He shook his head. "No. She helped me."

The lady glared and then stomped off, pulling her son alongside her. Little Damien turned and looked at me with sadness in his innocent brown eyes. He waved good-bye and then disappeared into the crowd.

I thought of Momma back in Cherbourg and how I was glad she wasn't on the ship. Being sick, I didn't believe she would have fared well in these conditions, but I would have given anything to be in her arms and have her tell me that all would be well. Watching the situation unfold as it had made me understand how much I loved my family. Everything they did was done out of love.

The surrounding bedlam suffocated me. Passengers screamed and scrambled for some assistance, but help wasn't coming fast enough. The noise was deafening. Children and women cried as men shouted over each other. I wanted to curl up in a corner right there on that cold, slippery deck and give up. *I couldn't do this. I wasn't strong enough. This ship was going to be my coffin, taking me to my watery grave. I was certain of that.*

"Corinne!"

Daddy waved at me from a distance. "Corinne!"

"Daddy!" I screamed, forcing my way toward him. When I

finally reached him, I hugged him and cried until my sides hurt. "Daddy, I couldn't find you and then I was so scared, but—"

He threw his arms around me, hugging me tightly. "It's okay, Corinne. Everything is going to be fine."

"I'm so sorry."

He raised his brow. "Sorry about what?"

"I blamed everything on you. You and Momma always wanted the best for us. Even if I didn't agree, I should've respected that."

"I understand," Daddy said with a quick nod. "You can tell me all this when we're safely ashore."

He grabbed my shoulders and pulled me toward him. In the center of all the confusion, we desperately held on to each other, not ever wanting to let go. I was afraid to, scared of what would happen if I did.

A few passengers bumped into us, but we held our embrace. When he finally pulled away, he looked down at me. "I need you to listen to me, Corinne." The fear behind his eyes sent a shudder down my spine. "I found Astrid. She's waiting for you at the end of this deck. Are you listening to me, Corinne?"

I nodded. When I did, tears formed in the corners of my eyes.

"They are putting us on lifeboats," he continued. "You and your sister will go together. Do you understand?" His chest heaved up and down as he spoke. "Do you understand me?" he repeated when I didn't answer.

I blinked through my tears and nodded. "What about you?"

"I will be taking another lifeboat."

"No, Daddy," I protested. "I want you to come with us."

He shook his head. "I can't. Women and children on one and men on another. It'll be fine. I'll be right behind you."

He took off his jacket and placed it around my shoulders. "Take care of you and your sister, okay?"

Tears began flowing down my cheeks. "What about you?"

"When you get to shore," Daddy said, "as soon as you can, you and your sister head back to Canada. Go to family and they will take care of you."

"And you?"

"I'm telling you this in case we don't meet up," he said, but then quickly added, "but I know we will."

"But, Daddy—"

"Just do it, Corinne! I'm counting on you to take care of things," he said out of breath. "Just until I get there."

He brushed his fingertips against my cold, wet cheek. "Don't worry," he told me when he saw my expression. "I'll be there." He pulled me to him and embraced me with all his strength. *"Je vous aime."*

"I love you, too, Daddy."

"Remember, don't worry," he said, pushing me away. "I will be there."

I held on to Daddy's hand, remembering the time I prayed in the chapel. Suddenly, I realized my prayers had been answered. Daddy was finally seeing me as an adult. When he let go of my hand, I turned my back to him and made my way through the chaos. After a few steps, I looked back one last time.

He was gone.

I shuffled through the crowd, dodging passengers barreling toward me. I made it as far as the dining room when I heard a thunderous, popping sound followed by a hallow crackling. The blast was earsplitting.

The lights in the dining hall blew out and in the darkness, panicked passengers stumbled over one another, pushing their way toward the exits. I scurried away from the entrance just as the glass doors broke open. Shards of glass flew in every direction as screaming, bloody-limbed passengers toppled over one another, spilling out onto the deck. A man with blood oozing from the corner of his mouth stumbled out the door, fell and disappeared beneath the mob's feet. Anyone in the near vicinity was trampled to the ground and left for dead.

I grabbed onto the railing and made my way down the deck in search of Astrid. I was halfway down the ship's decks until I made a fatal error. I tripped. I looked down at the sack I fell over, only it wasn't a sack at all—it was the body of a very large man, face-down. A few feet ahead lay the very same silver-plated governor walking stick Mr. Harland carried.

"Oh, God, no!" I screamed. "Someone please help me!"

The ship rocked back and forth, but on the last rock, it rolled Mr. Harland's body over so that he was now lying on his back. His face was a deep-purplish color and his eyes were frozen wide open.

I knelt over the lifeless body as several passengers scuttled around the both of us. I closed my eyes and prayed. That was the first time I understood my own mortality.

The combination of the rocking and the slipperiness of the deck glided his body off to the side where it lodged itself between the railings and got stuck. I went to pick up his cane, but before I could, someone snatched it and ran.

In shock, I stared down at his limp body. I had never seen a dead body. I had never even been to a funeral.

"Help me, please," I said softly. Passengers pushed through me like a bed sheet hanging from a clothesline until a lady wearing a bright-red scarf stopped.

"At this point, he's better off than we are," she said. "It's best you carry yourself to safety." She was eerily calm as she continued down the deck.

The ship rocked again and Mr. Harland's body pushed through the railings and fell headfirst.

"Corinne!" someone called from a distance.

I snapped back into the moment. I shot up from the cold, wet deck and looked around.

"Corinne! Over here, it's Christopher."

My gaze washed over the sea of frightened faces. *Where was he?* "Christopher, I don't see you," I called back. "Where are you?"

"Over here, Corinne."

Desperate, I scanned the crowd, but there was no sign of him. "I can't find you."

There was no response.

"Christopher?" I called, panicked.

One of the passengers knocked into me, causing me to smash up against the railing. From the deck above, I looked down and saw the body of Mr. Harland lying in a puddle of his own blood. People scurried about him like he wasn't even there.

"Corinne," Christopher said, grabbing my arm, "I didn't think I would ever find you."

I threw my arms around him. "God, help me. I can't do this."

"Corinne," he said, "calm down."

"There are dead bodies everywhere," I choked. "People...children...drowning."

"Look at me!" he commanded. "You have got to calm down."

"I can't do this!" I yelled, shaking my head.

"You can and you will," he said. "Have you found your father?"

I nodded weakly.

"Good," Christopher said. "But listen closely, Corinne. We've hit an iceberg. The watertight compartments are flooding and water is beginning to spill over the tops of the transverse bulkheads. We have several distress calls out and the order has been given to start loading the lifeboats with women and children first."

"What does all that mean?"

"The ship is going down. We've got to get you and your family out of here."

I lifted my sore and tired arm and pointed down the ship's deck. "But Daddy went the other way," I said weakly. I was losing touch with reality, I could feel it.

"Wake up!" Christopher commanded. "The ship is sinking. If you don't get yourself together, you will die! Do you hear me?"

I focused on the terror in his eyes and was immediately brought back to reality.

"That's impossible," I said, remembering his earlier statement.

"What's impossible?"

"The ship sinking. How can this massive ship sink?"

"Listen to me!" he yelled. "We need to get you out of here." He looked down toward the other end of the ship. "There's a rescuer down the end of this deck, but hurry, it's quickly filling up."

"What about you?"

"I'm going to make sure my mother is safe."

"I'll come with you," I said. "Then we can all get on a rescuer together, you, me, your mother and the Captain. Astrid is on one and my father will be on one as well."

His silence frightened me.

"Christopher?"

He bowed his head. "Corinne, I—"

"We'll find her and then your uncle," I said. "He's the Captain of the ship, for goodness sake. They'll have to hold a rescuer for him."

"No, Corinne. You've got to get on that lifeboat."

"It shouldn't take long to find them," I said, realizing how ridiculous that sounded. It took me fifteen minutes to walk ten feet. There was no way searching this entire ship full of panicked passengers wasn't going to take time.

"Please go," Christopher pleaded. "We don't have much time."

I raised my head and held my chin high. "Now *you* listen to *me*. We can either stand here arguing, wasting more time, or we can go look for your family." *Move forward or step to the side*, was what Granddad LaRoche had always told Daddy. As scared as I was, I was ready to move forward even if I had to force myself to do so.

"Okay," he said, relenting. "But if we don't find them in the next twenty minutes, you will be on one of those lifeboats. Agreed?"

"Agreed."

He grabbed my hand and pulled me through the side exit double doors and off we went to find his family.

·❦[34]❦·

*I*f I thought pushing ahead in a crowd was difficult, shoving your way *against* the crowd was nearly impossible. We made it as far as the second-class corridor before Christopher pulled me toward a large, rust-colored door. Outside, we heard the loud boom of the distress rocket being fired.

"This hall is for staff," he told me. "We should be able to move a little faster this way."

He pushed up against the large secured door with his shoulder, but it didn't budge. He did that several times before giving up. "I have an idea." He took a firm hold of my shoulders, then guided me to the other side of the hall. "Stand here."

He took a few steps back, standing at least twenty feet from the door. He bowed his head and stiffened up his left shoulder. "All it needs is one good shove."

"You can't be serious," I said, grabbing his wrist. "You'll surely break your arm."

"We have to get in there and I don't have a key for the lock."

"Hold on a second." I looked around for any large, strong object that would smash the door in. I saw shoes, belts and other left-behind clothing accessories but nothing strong enough to knock down a steel door.

"Why didn't I think of this in the first place?" I reached up and carefully pulled out a lone hair pin.

"What do you plan to do with that?" Christopher asked.

"You'll see." I bent down and looked at the tiny steel lock. It was dark and the light above was flickering, but I was able to see enough to stick one end of the pin into the lock's hole.

I jostled the pin around a few times and within seconds, the lock clicked, popped open and fell to the ground.

"How in the world did you know how to do something like that?" he asked.

"My sister…"

He shook his head. "Say no more."

With little resistance, he pushed open the door with his shoulder. The darkness rushed in, leaving us scrambling about. He reached into his jacket pocket and pulled out a mini-light. The tiny light only illuminated a few feet ahead of us. However, we didn't need light to realize that we were wading through at least a foot of ice-cold water.

"Is this safe?" I asked.

"I don't know."

We trudged on through in the darkness. Several objects, like hair brushes, eating utensils and various articles of clothing, floated past us. I held on to Christopher's hand and followed , shivering from the freezing waters.

"Where is your uncle?" I asked.

"Mr. Harland said he came down here to get the crew out safely."

The mention of Mr. Harland's name sent shivers down my spine. Suddenly I couldn't breathe. "I saw him, Christopher. Mr. Harland is dead."

He stopped walking. "Oh God." He took several deep breaths and then continued on, with me following. "You sure you can do this?"

I nodded.

Something slimy floated by, scraping against my dress. "Christopher, I'm scared."

"We're almost there."

I heard scraping. The noise happened several times, followed by tiny squeaks. "What is that?"

"Fleeing rats."

I wished I hadn't asked.

We turned down another corridor where the rushing water was waist-deep. Christopher flashed the light down the hall. I couldn't see around him, but when he turned back to me, his face was ghost white. He quickly grabbed my hand and headed down the other direction. "We need to go this way."

"What is it?"

"Let's go," he said, forcefully pulling me down the hall.

We turned down another hall and were met with frantic staff rushing toward us through several feet of foaming ice water. Most of them were empty-handed, but others carried drenched suit-cases or small children.

One of the staff shouted at us. "No, no, other way! Water coming!"

Christopher let go of my hand and caught the man by the arm as he tried to rush by. "Gaston," Christopher said, "have you seen Mrs. Smith or Sophia?"

Gaston shook his head and said in broken English, "No, this way. Must be safe."

"Where are they?" Christopher yelled. "Listen to me, Gaston, I need to know where they are. Tell me."

"I don't think he speaks English very well," I told Christopher, recognizing the accent. "Let me try."

Christopher reluctantly let go of Gaston, who immediately tried fleeing with the rest of the crew, but Christopher caught his arm.

"Have you seen them?" he yelled. "Tell me!"

I stepped up. "*Gaston, Gaston, où est Madame Smith?*"

Gaston shook his head. "*Madame Smith est au point.*"

"Are you sure?" I asked. "*Est-ce que vous êtes positifs qu'elle est au point?*"

"*Oui. Madame Smith et Sophia a quitté il ya quelque temps. Capitaine Smith retourna à ses quartiers.*" Gaston pointed down the hall. "*Capitaine Smith est allé de cette façon.*"

Christopher let go of Gaston's arm and he and the rest of the crew fled down the hall.

"What did he say?" Christopher asked. "Where is Mother?"

"She's fine. Your mother and Sophia headed for the deck some time ago."

Christopher let out a sigh of relief. "Good. That means they are on a rescuer."

"But according to Gaston," I continued, "Captain Smith headed back to his quarters."

Christopher dropped his head. He closed his eyes and took in a deep breath.

"Why would he do such a thing?" I asked. "Where are his quarters? We can find him and take him above, then get on a rescuer." I looked down the hall. "Is it this way?"

Christopher grabbed my arm. "Corinne," he said softly, "we have to get you back on deck."

"We don't have time," I said. "Now which way do we go?"

"Corinne!" he exclaimed. "I am taking you back to the ship's deck where you will get on a rescuer. Do not argue with me, *please*." He grabbed my elbow, pulling me back in the direction from which we had come. "We'll go this way."

As we headed down the hall, the cold waters began to rise and had reached waist-level.

"We can't go back this way," he said. "We'll have to find another exit."

We turned down another hall, but the waters rushed in way too quickly. Suddenly, he stopped. "No, wait, Corinne. We can't go that way either. The doors are locked. We have to go back this way." He nodded toward the hall from which we had just come.

"Are you sure?" I asked. Since the freezing waters had risen another few feet, there was no way we could make it down that hall without having to swim.

A terrifying chill ran down my spine. The day I knew I would regret not learning how to swim was here.

"You can't swim," Christopher said. "I had forgotten."

"There's got to be another way," I said, panicked. "What about this hall?" I looked down the hall to the right. Sparks from loose electrical wiring shot out in all directions, making the hall look like a mini-firework show, however, the water was only about two inches deep. "We can go this way."

"Are you mad?" Christopher asked. "We'll be electrocuted before reaching halfway down the hall."

I looked down the flooded hall once again. "Are you sure?"

"Let me present it another way. Would you rather *most certainly* be electrocuted, or take your chances swimming down the hall?"

"I'd rather neither, thank you."

"Trust me," he said, "this is the only way. Take my hand and we'll do this together."

I shook my head. "If I take your hand, I'll likely drown us both."

"You can do it, Corinne. Just kick and flail your arms until you're at the surface," he said. "That's it, nothing fancy."

He was a fool for believing that, if he really did. Regardless, I nodded. "I trust you."

We counted to three and then dunked our heads under the

rising waters. As I struggled to press forward, the iciness sucked the oxygen from my lungs. Christopher stayed behind me, pushing my backside all the way toward the exit while I flailed in the waters like a broken-winged duck. The door looked so far away, I thought I would never make it, but that was when he pushed my backside even harder. When we reached the door, he swam past me and took the lead. He pulled at the knob. It opened immediately and washed us into another corridor. Once we were both through, he quickly shut and sealed the door.

"Are you all right?" he asked, out of breath.

Unable to catch mine, I managed a weak nod.

Once again, he took my hand and led me down a much-drier hall. We continued on until we found ourselves back on the deck amidst the chaos. He zigzagged his way through the crowds and to one of the lifeboats. Cramped in the boat were mothers holding small babies, mothers holding children and quite a few ladies holding on to tiny dogs dressed in fancy diamond collars. Nowhere in that crowd did we spot his mother.

Christopher grabbed the arm of one of the seamen who had an elderly lady by the elbow and was lifting her onto the boat. "Dodson, where is my mother?"

At first Dodson appeared annoyed, but when he turned around and saw it was Christopher, his expression immediately changed. "Oh, Mr. Smith, I'm glad you're here. I received word about your uncle. I'm so very sorry. He was a great man, your uncle. He will truly be missed."

"Thank you, Officer."

"What's he talking about, Christopher?" I asked, confused. "Your uncle isn't dead."

Dodson turned and reached for the rope of one the davits that was securing the boat. "His legacy will most certainly live on."

Christopher's gaze dropped to the ground as he struggled to find the right words. "I aspire to be half the man he was," he told the seaman. For the first time since this voyage began I glimpsed a chink in Christopher's armor, but he quickly recovered. "Have you seen my mother? She's supposed to be on one of the boats, yes?"

"That she is, sir, but I haven't seen her."

"Are you sure?" Christopher asked.

Dodson nodded. "I would have definitely made sure she was on one of these rescuers. Hold for one second, sir," he said, turning to another seaman. "McKissick, have you seen Mrs. Smith?"

The man nodded as he continued to lower a lifeboat down into the water. "She was put onto one of the first rescuers on the western wing."

Christopher leaned over the ship's rail to make sure the lifeboat made it down safely. "Thank you, gentlemen." Then he turned back to me. "We need to get you onto a lifeboat before they're filled. What about your sister?"

"Daddy told me Astrid's already gone. She'll be fine. And if I know my sister, she would kick an old lady in the neck to get at a spot in one of those lifeboats. Perhaps it'd be best if we go now, Christopher."

"You need to get on one of those rescuers." His expression glassed over and his voice cracked. He grabbed my hand, practically dragging me down to the ship's bow and toward the lifeboat. With me in tow, he plowed his way through several people and dashed on with desperate determination.

"Christopher?" I asked. "What did that man mean about your uncle?"

"Please, Corinne. We don't have much time." he said, continuing to pull me down the deck.

"Christopher?"

"No more questions!"

"Don't you yell at me like that!"

He stopped short on the deck. "Corinne, *please*," he pleaded. "Do you not understand the seriousness of this? We don't have time to question. We need to get you out of here before it's too late."

"Christopher, please," I begged. "We *both* need to go. What about us being together and getting married?"

There was a long pause. He squared off his shoulders and lifted his head. "I'm not coming."

My heart crept up to my throat. I tried to swallow as the tears stung my eyes. I could barely breathe but still I managed a meek protest. "What do you mean you're not coming? Of course you are. Your family is fine. Your uncle is probably fine. Now we've got to go."

"My uncle is not fine, Corinne."

I shook my head. "Stop it, Christopher, *please*."

I looked into his eyes, pleading for him to come with me and at the same time, trying to figure out why it was that he wouldn't. Then I understood. "Christopher, *no!*" Blood rushed to my head and I stumbled backward.

He grabbed my shoulders to steady me. My nails dug into his flesh as I hung on to his arm. "Listen to me, Corinne. I am the Captain now. You will get on that rescuer or I will have one of my men put you on one."

"I won't hear this. If I let go, I'll lose you forever."

"Listen to me!" he yelled. "There's not much time."

"Christopher," I said, feeling defeated, "please, let's go. We need to go. We need to get off this ship and get married. What about our children? What about growing old together?"

This time he shook his head. "Stop it, Corinne," he said, barely above a whisper.

"No, Christopher. I'm not leaving without you."

"Please, Corinne. This is my duty. I have to try to help in any way possible. Please understand that. Like my uncle, I am not coming off of this ship until every person has been saved."

"We both know that's never going to happen."

He looked at me and I felt him taking in my soul. I felt him seeing our children, what would have been our lives, through my eyes. "Take care of your family, Corinne. I will see you again. That I promise."

"Christopher, please don't do this," I begged. "You have your whole life before you. *We* have our lives before us."

He wrapped his arms around me and held on tightly. There was so much love in his embrace. At the same time, he hugged me so tightly, I felt his heart pounding through his chest. He was scared, but he was sad too. I melted in his arms, holding him close. I wanted him to never let go.

But he did.

"We will meet again," he said. "I promise. Do you believe that, Corinne? Do you believe that we will see each other again someday?"

I searched in his eyes. Although he may not have been deeply religious either, I understood. He believed we would meet again and that made me believe.

"I do."

"I do, too," he said. "It will happen. I love you."

The bittersweet words pierced my heart like a sword. That was the first time Christopher had told me he loved me. The words came from his heart, but I felt it within his soul. He truly meant it. Unlike Sébastien, I wasn't shocked by Christopher's proclamation, nor should I have been. There was never any doubt in my heart that Christopher loved me.

He kissed my cheek before darting off in the opposite direction. I tried to follow, but couldn't keep his furious pace. "Christopher, wait!"

Within seconds, he disappeared into the crowd and into the midst of all the panic and chaos. I had never felt so alone.

·◦[35]◦·

"The ship is sinking!" someone yelled. Waters came rushing in from all directions. The level of panic rose when the ship fiercely rocked from side to side. Passengers scrambled, toppling over one another. I watched helplessly as a man flipped over the rails and plunged to his death.

The full moon had suddenly disappeared behind a billowy storm cloud, making visibility almost non-existent. The ship rocked once again and several more passengers went down, sliding about in darkness.

When the moon peeked from behind the cloud, giving some light, I reached out and grabbed onto the rail. I clamped down and hung on for dear life. Icy waters splashed up from the ocean over the railing and soaked me from top to bottom. When I thought I could not hold on any longer, I wrapped my arm around the top of the railing. Whenever the ship shifted, the rail bashed into my forearm. With the last turbulent rock, the crook of my arm slammed into the railing so hard, I let go. I fell to the deck, landing on my arm with a hard thud. There was a loud crack immediately followed by intense throbbing. Wracked with immeasurable pain, I reached up with my good hand and desperately clutched onto the railing before the ship rocked again.

A man a few feet from me, hanging onto the railing, flipped over its side. The sound of his horrid howl as he plummeted to his imminent death would be etched into my brain forever. With each sway, others plunged into the salty freezing cold waters below. When the shifting ceased, I scurried toward the lifeboat at the end of the deck.

The deck was sopping wet and each time I took a step forward, the heel of my boot slipped. I winced as I tucked my right arm across my chest. The pain was intense, I nearly blacked out. But I had to hold on, remain conscious. Slowly, I bent down, unlaced my shoes and slipped them off. The deck beneath my stocking feet was cold and wet.

"Give me that!" a man next to me yelled. Two men were in a shoving match for a life vest. I made my way to the other side of the ship, but one of the men pushed into me and I fell to the ground. Tears stung my eyes as I gritted my teeth, attempting to bear the sharp pain in my arm.

"He's got a gun!"

Two shots fired into the air. Most of the crowd pushed forward while others ducked.

There was another shot.

A woman screamed, "He shot him! He shot that man to his death!"

I stood up and shoved my way forward through the stunned crowd. A man lay on the ground with blood spurting from his neck. There was so much blood everywhere.

A man from the back of the crowd bent down over the wounded man. "I need a tourniquet!"

"You killed him," a woman said to the uniformed seaman.

The man turned around. I recognized him as First Officer Murdoch, the officer who had detained my father.

"He came at me," Murdoch said, dumbfounded. "I...I didn't mean to. I'm sorry." For several seconds, he stared down at the body, but when he looked up, he saw me.

Our eyes locked.

As the crowd scrambled on, First Officer Murdoch reached for the rope of one of the dangling rescuers and attempted to cut it. He turned back around and stoically watched the surrounding chaos for a few moments. He appeared to have been in shock.

He then reached into his pocket and produced a shiny black object. The panicked crowd was oblivious, as he raised the gun to his temple and pulled the trigger. There was a loud pop and then Officer Murdoch's body toppled overboard. No one really noticed. The few that did, looked at First Officer Murdoch's suicide as a footnote to this ongoing tragedy and kept moving.

I did the same. I had to.

Up ahead a lifeboat dangled from the davit's rope like it was hanging from a piece of thread. My toes felt numb and my arm seared with pain, but I pressed forward.

"Corinne!" Astrid called. "I'm here."

Astrid sat toward the back of the rescuer, frantically waving her arms in the air. As the men were about to lower the lifeboat, she yelled, "Stop! My sister is coming."

The men continued to slowly lower the boat.

"Do you not hear me?" she questioned. "I told you my sister is coming."

"Ma'am," one of the seamen said, "we've got to lower these. Now please sit down before we eject you from the boat."

"Eject me and I'll eject your lips from your face."

The guy looked toward the other seamen, who only shrugged.

Astrid reached over one of the other women, knocking into her head. When the woman sneered, Astrid sneered right back, only her look was ten times more frightening.

"She's right here," she said, reaching her hand out to me. I grabbed it with my left hand and she pulled me on. I slammed into sneer lady, knocking my hurt arm into the side of her jaw. My unbearable pain intensified to new levels.

"Now you may lower the stupid boat," Astrid said.

Who was in charge here?

I looked around at the faces of the frightened passengers, stopping on one particularly jarring one.

"She is not supposed to be in first-class," Sophia said from the other end of the rescuer. "They both shouldn't be here."

"Excuse me?" Astrid said defiantly. "At this point, there is no first-class, but you're more than welcome to get off and wait for an untainted lifeboat if you so choose."

"You really shouldn't be here." A woman with a tiny dog sitting in her lap glared over at Astrid. "There isn't enough room."

Most of the passengers—who were non-first-class—glanced up in surprise at the audacity of the two first-class women, who only shot back at them with disgusted looks.

Astrid made a fist and stared both of them right in the eyes. "There definitely won't be enough room if I reach over and give you both a fat lip. And how is it that this mangy mutt was rescued before people?"

Dog lady gasped at my sister's challenge. "Did you just threaten me with physical violence?"

"I wasn't speaking to the dog," Astrid said.

"She's right, you know," Molly Brown said from the back of the rescuer. "That dog should not be on this lifeboat."

"Maybe you shouldn't be on this rescuer either," dog lady said.

Molly narrowed her eyes. "How about I second that fat-lip motion." She stood up and looked at the other passengers. "Do I have a third?"

"Ladies," the seaman said. "Please control yourselves."

"Astrid?" I called softly, but she didn't hear me. She was too busy engaging in a heated conversation with dog lady. My head started wobbling back and forth and I felt a nauseous churn in the pit of my stomach. I was about to vomit.

I swallowed down the queasiness. "Astrid?"

"Is it just me," she said, "or are these women insane?" She looked down at me. When she saw my face, she asked, "Corinne, what's wrong?"

I sat on the rescuer, staring straight ahead. "He's gone, Astrid."

"Who's gone?"

"He's gone. He's not leaving the ship."

"Who are you talking about?" she asked. "Is it Christopher?"

When she said his name, I began bawling uncontrollably. Immediately, Astrid plopped down next to me and wrapped her arms around me.

"I'm so sorry, Corinne. But—"

But what? How could that sentence possibly end? My mind raced back to one of the last conversations I'd had with Momma. In the kitchen, she had told me that the man after the cheater was to be my true love. Was that true? Had Christopher been my one true love and now he was lost forever?

The rescuer tipped back and forth, jostling the passengers on board. One of the seamen reached into his pocket and brandished a knife. He grabbed the rope tied to one end of the rescuer and attempted to slice it in half, but the rope was too thick and the knife, too dull. Eventually, the violent rocking calmed.

"Astrid?"

"Yes, Corinne?"

"I didn't mean it when I said maybe we would be better apart," I told her. "Remember? In the cabin the other night?"

"I know you didn't," she told me. "And Corinne?"

"Yes?"

"I do believe in God."

"Why are you telling me this?"

She looked at me and shrugged. "I don't know."

"*Wait!*" a woman yelled. The mother of the little boy, Damien, I had found in the dining room earlier was stumbling toward the lifeboat. In one hand, she carried her son while hanging on to a small tattered suitcase with the other. She slid from side to side on the wet deck and at one point almost dropped the little boy. "Wait, please!"

"Didn't you hear her?" Astrid called to the seaman who had started lowering our lifeboat. "She's coming and she has a little boy in her arms."

This time, the seaman spoke up. "We have no more room. She'll have to wait for the next one."

"What next one are you referring to?" Molly challenged. "In case you haven't noticed, this may be one of the last. If she misses this, she and that little boy are probably as good as dead. Besides, this boat is hardly full. There's room for plenty more people. Why is it that these rescuers are only half-full?

The seaman, looking quite irritated, stared down both Molly and Astrid. He had no idea what he was up against. Astrid folded her arms across her chest and narrowed her eyes right back at him.

"Do you want their blood on your hands?" Molly asked. When he hesitated, she shouted across the boat at the seaman. "You got seaweed in them ears? I asked if you wanted their blood on your hands."

The seaman kept silent. He looked up at the woman and the boy. It appeared he was relenting and going to allow them onto the rescuer. Just then, one the ropes holding up the lifeboat snapped and the rescuer cocked to the side. Frightened passengers scrambled about, trying to hold on to anything within their reach. The boat plummeted several feet before coming to an abrupt stop. When it did, passengers attempted to gather their bearings.

Astrid reached up for the woman. "Give me the little boy," she called out.

The woman looked frightened but obliged. Carefully, she lifted Damien over the railing, preparing to hand him down to my sister. Once again, the ship rocked and she and Damien tumbled backward.

Astrid reached up for the railing and struggled to heave herself over it. She fell over onto the ship's slick deck and quickly pulled herself up.

"Be careful, honey," Molly yelled. "If I wasn't so portly, I'd come up there and help you."

Astrid grabbed Damien and handed him down toward me. "Corinne, can you reach him?"

I scooted over to the far right side of the rescuer, as far as I could go. With Damien in her arms, Astrid stretched, but the lifeboat dangled too far down to reach him.

"I'll have to drop him in your lap," Astrid said.

"No!" the mother behind her screamed. "She'll miss."

"Lady, if you don't, he'll die," Astrid told her.

The woman took a step back. "Will she catch him?"

From over her shoulder, Astrid said, "She will." She turned back to me and mouthed, "You will catch him, won't you?"

My heart pounded through my chest as I reached up as far as I could. At this point, my right arm felt like it was on fire so I had to rely on my left hand. "I'll catch him."

Astrid closed her eyes and at first I thought she was second guessing herself but then I saw her lips move. She was praying. She opened her eyes and let go. Damien plummeted toward the dangling rescuer.

By the grace of God, I caught him, but when I did, the lifeboat tilted to the side and both Damien and I came dangerously close to falling overboard.

"Don't worry, I have you." Molly grabbed the back of my dress and pulled. She reached around me and hoisted up Damien, who was dangling over the rescuer's edge. There was a collective sigh of relief when he plopped onto my lap and started bawling.

We had done it! I wanted to laugh and cry at the same time.

I looked up toward Astrid to tell her the boy was safe. Before I could, there was an earsplitting explosion. Fire engulfed the entire deck, starting from the middle where the blast occurred and making its way toward the front...toward Astrid.

I looked up at Astrid and our eyes connected.

"Corinne!" she called before another thunderous explosion. She leaned over the railing, reaching down for me. I ignored the piercing pain extending from my shoulder to my wrist and reached up toward the ship.

It was too late.

The remaining thread of the rope snapped and I fell back into the rescuer. I was forced to watch the horror in my sister's eyes as I plunged toward the deep ocean waters.

❦❦ 36 ❧❧

2:24 A.M.

*W*e hurtled down into the waters and landed with a huge splash, jostling the passengers about. The woman who had been seated next to me had bounced all the way to the other end of the rescuer and hung lifelessly over its edge. I glanced up toward the ship, frantically searching for Astrid. She was nowhere in sight. The place where she stood moments ago was swallowed up in flames. Burning embers hurtled down at the rescuer like meteorites. I crouched down and used my arms to cover my head for protection, but I still felt tiny burning sensations on my arms and legs.

"Astrid!" I called up toward the ship. "Astriiiiiiiiiid!"

"Please, ladies," the seaman said in a panic, "you have to sit down."

"This is your fault!" Sophia said, pointing her finger at me. "You and your sister."

"I didn't see you trying to help anyone but yourself," I yelled back angrily. "At least my sister saved the little boy's life."

"And you see where that got us," Sophia said. "She almost killed us all."

"Oh, shut up," Molly said to Sophia. "You have been a right

pain in my rear since the beginning of this trip. The girl is right. Her sister gave her life to save another."

Molly's words echoed in my ears like a church bell. *She gave her life, she gave her life.*

Astrid was gone.

Molly looked at me apologetically. "I'm sorry, I didn't mean it like that."

"You are upsetting Lord Vargas," dog lady said over the noise. "Poor poochie."

Molly lunged at Lord Vargas, who had begun yapping loudly. "If I get ahold of that mutt, I'll toss him in the waters," she said.

"You wouldn't," dog lady said.

"And you'd be next," Molly warned.

"Ladies!" the seaman rowing the rescuer exclaimed. He turned toward Molly and pleaded, "Ms. Brown, please sit down and remain calm."

"And why are these damn boats only half-full?" Molly questioned again. "Don't you hear the screams of the people?"

"Margaret," the seaman said, with an exasperated sigh, "we simply cannot go back there. It's too dangerous."

Between the waves and the antics, the lifeboat rocked unsteadily, but no one seemed to notice.

"Ladies!" the seaman yelled over the shouting. "I won't tell you again. Please sit down."

Sophia stood to her feet. "This is ridiculous! I demand you get me to shore, or I will have you fired," she spat.

The lifeboat shook as the icy waters splashed onto the passengers. The seaman grabbed both oars, attempting to secure it.

Sophia glared at me. "This is your fault!"

One of the other women shot up out of her seat. "The sinking of the ship is her fault?" she asked incredulously. "That's absurd."

"Mind your own business," Sophia said. "You have no idea what her kind is capable of." The look she flashed in my direction was so hateful, so angry, she frightened me. I had never personally known anyone to have so much hatred in their heart that they were willing to kill someone, take another life without so much as a second thought.

Sophia had that look.

Without warning, she lunged toward me. The already unstable lifeboat rocked back and forth uncontrollably causing the passengers to stumble back and forth, including Sophia. She lost her footing and slipped, knocking her head on the rescuer's edge and plunging into the shadowy waters in a big splash.

She was gone.

Passengers screamed as they dipped their heads over the edge of the lifeboat. "Where is she?" Molly yelled. "I don't see her."

The seaman shone the flashlight over the rocky waters, but there was no sign of her. I stood up and peered over the lifeboat's edge, attempting to catch a glimpse of her.

"Please sit down!" the seaman yelled. "The entire lifeboat is about to flip."

I looked back in time to witness the ship that was deemed unsinkable tilting to a forty-five-degree angle as the steel upper structure disintegrated right before our eyes. As the ship's bow submerged into the ocean, the colossal propellers lifted out of the water. She was going down.

A large piece of the stern broke off and plummeted to the water. The impact created a rippling effect of mini-tidal-wave proportions that engulfed our little boat. Before we knew it, the lifeboat capsized and we were all dumped into the freezing waters.

As I struggled to push my way back to the surface, my lungs contracted in the below-freezing waters. The more I thrashed about, the worse it became. The darkness quickly surrounded me and I slipped even deeper. I thought about what Christopher had told me earlier and began kicking both feet while flailing my good arm in hopes that I was making some sort of headway back to the surface. My entire surroundings were black. At one point, I assumed I was flailing in the wrong direction and toward my watery grave. Even with darkness all about, my eyes fixated on a small shiny object.

The cigar band around my finger that Christopher had given me radiated in the darkness. My lungs felt as though they were about to collapse inside my chest. Out of reflex I took a deep breath, expecting to inhale more water, but instead, my lungs filled with air. I had made it to the surface.

But how long could I stay there?

My collar tightened around my neck, stifling the little bit of air I had left in my lungs. Someone had grabbed the collar of my dress and was pulling me into another rescuer. As I life-lessly lay on my back, I looked up at the pitch-black sky and saw tiny bright speckles. I struggled to maintain consciousness by listening to background noise. My body shivered violently. In my head I told myself that more rescue boats would come, and that no, we were not going to drown, and no, we were not going to freeze to our deaths.

With the cigar band clutched in my hand, I drifted in and out of consciousness. *Home,* I thought. Home as I knew it was a place I would never set foot in again, yet still I couldn't help but refer to it as my home. I thought about all the animals on the farm back in Cherbourg, but mostly I thought about Momma. We had left so quickly, I never said a proper good-bye to her and now it was too late.

When my eyes opened again, the sun was high in the sky. The

warmth of its rays felt so good against my cold cheeks. When I focused, I saw a huge sailing vessel with *SS Carpathia* printed on the side in white lettering. I figured it to be a dream, so I took one shallow breath and let my heavy eyelids close once again. That's when I saw God standing before me.

·•❧[37]❧•·

Dusk was my favorite time of day, so no matter what I was doing, I made a point to sit in the fields and bask in the last remaining rays before they disappeared for the evening. The only noise came from the faint engines of the cars pulling up into the driveway and a grumbling Aunt Carolina, who was plucking weeds from the garden she spent years growing.

"*Geneviève!*" she yelled. "So many of my beautiful flowers are bug-eaten. I spent forever trying to get these things to grow and these pesky critters munch on them like a holiday feast." Unaware that I was lying in the grass only a few feet away, Aunt Carolina grunted obscenities. Quickly, I bowed my head and said a silent prayer for her.

She bent down to scoop up a few more weeds and then yelled, "*Geneviève*, send Malcolm out here to help with these darned things!" She stood up and placed her hand on her lower back. "And make sure he brings my pills."

Her eleven-year-old son, Malcolm, dashed out the back door and toward the garden.

"Boy, get down here and start picking. The guests are arriving. And where is your cousin Corinne?"

Seconds later, Momma emerged in her creaky wheelchair with a cherry-pie-soiled apron fastened around her diminutive waist and a sour look on her face. "I've told you already, we have enough flowers," she said in a wearisome tone.

"*Geneviève*, you know you can never have enough flowers or food for colored folk," Aunt Carolina said, with a hearty laugh.

With her hands on her wide hips, Aunt Carolina straightened up and pointed her thick, stubby finger at the ground. "Malcolm, be sure to pick them azaleas from the roots, so they don't die right away."

Malcolm bent down and pulled up a flower by its stem. Aunt Carolina smacked the back of his head. "I said from the roots. You kids sure don't know how to listen, d'ya?"

"Leave him alone," Momma said. "He's trying." She paused to take in a deep breath and then wiped her forehead with the back of her hand and looked toward the fields. When she did, she spotted me idly resting in the grass.

"Corinne," she said, surprised. "Why are you lying in the grass? You'll dirty yourself up." She glanced down at the book by my side. "And leisurely reading of all things? Shouldn't you be ready-ing yourself for our guests? Time is drawing nearer."

"I'm lying on a blanket. See?" I told her. "Besides, it's so beautiful out this evening and I had to finish the last chapter. After today, who knows when I'm going to get a chance to relax and read again, let alone finish an entire book?"

Momma nodded weakly as she gazed up toward the sky. She was tired and rundown. "I must say, Winnipeg is as splendid as Cherbourg. But you have more important things to do. Why do you suppose your aunt is stressing herself with all those flowers… and the food," she said, shaking her head. "There's enough in there to feed an army."

"Are you sad Daddy and Astrid aren't here?" I asked.

"I said pick them right!" Aunt Carolina exclaimed in the background. "If I have to tell you again, I will burn your hide, boy." She raised her hand to smack the back of Malcolm's head but he ducked and she missed.

Momma sighed. "Of course I miss Astrid and your father, but I know they're looking down on us right now."

"And Astrid is probably saying she hates my hair."

We both laughed.

"People are arriving," Momma said, looking at the cars approaching the driveway. "I'd better go see to them."

I stood up from the grass, picked up the blanket and neatly folded it. As I took the handles of her chair and helped her back inside, I inhaled deeply, taking in the intoxicating smell of the combination of Momma's sweet perfume and the blooming azaleas. Momma had been so weak these past few months. Every week, it seemed the doctors gave her only another few months to live. Every time she outlasted those doctors' expectations, but with each month, her health deteriorated. It was only a matter of time. She and I both knew it.

I peeked inside the tiny house and through the opened front door. Hordes of people socialized on the freshly cut front lawn. "I'll be in soon," I told her.

Once Momma was inside, I returned to my spot in the pasture. I rested my head on my arms and stared up at the sky that had fallen a shade darker.

After the sinking, as per Daddy's wishes, I contacted Aunt Carolina, who had taken me in without question. "If it was my brother's wishes," she had said with a warm smile when she opened the door to greet me, "then I shall abide." Then she had hugged me and asked if I remembered her. I politely smiled and told her yes. The truth was, if not for Daddy's stories describing his youngest sister's distinct appearance, I wouldn't have known her from a stranger on the street.

Daddy had described Aunt Carolina perfectly, right down to her potato frame and short cropped 'do that had a tiny bald spot in the back from when, as kids, he had chucked a rock at her. The one thing he neglected to mention was her Southern-American ways that included cooking everything in animal fat and smothering it in gravy.

"Look what I found," Malcolm said. He plopped down into the grass next to me. He opened his cupped hand and revealed a tiny green grasshopper. "I think I'm going to keep it as a pet."

"What'll you call him?"

He inspected the tiny green insect for a minute. "It's a her and I think I'll name her Skeech."

I wrapped my arms around my stomach and laughed. Skeech was the nickname Daddy had given Aunt Carolina when she was five. Malcolm laughed, and when he did, the gap from his two missing front teeth was in full view. The way the cricket chirped, it did remind me of Aunt Carolina every time she asked us to do something. "Get the broom, *chirp*." "Clean the floors, *chirp*." "Go pick the vegetables, *chirp, chirp*."

Every time the cricket chirped, Malcolm would say, "Quiet down, Skeech." And that would make us hoot for another ten minutes.

"Maaaaaaalcooooooooooom!"

With her hands on her hips—her trademark stance—Aunt Carolina bellowed for her young son. "Didn't I tell you to tend to these folks?"

"*Vous feriez mieux de laisser*," I whispered.

"What does that mean?" With the single blade of grass dangling between his lips, Malcolm reminded me of Daddy, who used to have that same habit with his cigars.

"It means you'd better get inside before Skeech runs your little hide. And I'm not talking about the grasshopper."

He hopped up and darted toward the house. "Aren't you coming?" he asked.

"Be there in a minute."

I closed my eyes and thought of Christopher—something I did every evening at dusk. He had said we would see each other again some day and to this day, I believed it. I couldn't say how my relationship with Astrid would've been if she had lived, but right here, right now, she died being the bravest, most compassionate human I had ever known.

I thought about Daddy often, too. The last thing he told me was that he'd be there for me. On this evening, I honestly felt it. Daddy was here.

"Corinne!" Momma called. "Hurry. We're running late."

I jumped up and dashed off toward the house. When Momma saw the grass on my dress, she frowned. "Oh, Corinne, you've messed up your beautiful dress." She began furiously picking away loose blades. "The truth is," Momma said, still brushing, "as strange as this may sound, things are exactly as they should be. God makes no mistakes. You and I are here for a reason and under that same faith, Astrid and Daddy aren't. Years ago when the doctors told me I would probably pass in a month or two, God had other plans. He knew you would need me." She reached up and tugged at the sleeves of my dress, making sure they were perfectly aligned. "And you know what else?" she whispered. "Your father would have been so proud to see his youngest daughter graduate from the famous Daytona Educational and Industrial Training School for Negro Girls. That's a rare thing. Do you know when he had promised you to Byron years ago; he was so excited to tell me about how he had found someone who was from a good family and how he was to attend college that fall?

He also boasted about this wonderful boy that was a devout Christian who respected his mother immensely."

I smiled. "And what a coincidence it was that Byron and I accidentally met while overseas in the U.S. two years ago."

"A coincidence? No," Momma said. "God makes no mistakes."

I reached down and gave her a hug. She kissed my cheek and said, "Now go finish brushing off that grass from your beautiful wedding dress. Byron is waiting at the end of that aisle to make you his wife." She placed the palms of her delicate hands on my cheeks and kissed my forehead. *"Tout est comme il devrait être."*

I nodded. "Everything is as it should be."

About the Author

Nicole Bradshaw was born and raised outside of Philadelphia, Pennsylvania in a quaint little town called Malvern. She currently resides in Freeport, Bahamas, with her husband and three children. During her college years, she needed funds for books, so she came up with the bright idea of starting an on-campus advice column. She charged students $7 for her witty advice on dating and relationships. That year she made $14.

This is Nicole's first novel. She is currently working on a second historical piece. Her e-book prequel to *Unsinkable* is *A Bond Broken*. Her next novel is *Champagne Life* and its e-book prequel is *Caviar Dreams*.

Discussion Questions

1. What was the social atmosphere like in the early 1900s? How does it differ from today?

2. In the early 1900s, people were judged according to what class they were in. Socially and economically, what class do you think Corinne and her family were in?

3. What struggles did the LaRoche family face? How do their struggles relate to the struggles African Americans face today?

4. As a fifteen-year-old girl in the 1900s, Corinne has peer pressures. Name some of the peer pressures she faced and how are they different from the pressure teens face today. How are they the same?

5. Christopher, the Captain's nephew, is clearly attracted to Corinne as she steps onto the ship. How do you feel others would perceive this attraction? Why?

6. Astrid, Corinne's older sister, has big, somewhat unrealistic dreams. Give reasons as to why she might have such immense goals.

7. Joseph, Corinne's father, feels as though he's been discriminated against. Give some examples of the kinds of discrimination he experienced on and off the ship.

8. Why do you think Christopher's family wanted him to marry Sophia? Why didn't they want him to be with Corinne?

9. For what reasons do you believe Christopher asked Corinne to marry him? Why do you think she accepted his proposal?

10. Discuss Joseph's feelings regarding Christopher's proposal to his youngest daughter.

11. Why did Joseph try to help Christopher's family as the ship sank, despite their earlier treatment of him?

12. In the end, Corinne made a choice. Who do you believe she chose—Christopher or her family?

13. How does religion play a part in the novel?

14. Do you believe Christopher and Corinne were ever really in love or was it simply a situation of convenience? Give reasons.

15. Do you believe Corinne was a strong or weak protagonist? Give reasons.

Champagne Life

BY NICOLE BRADSHAW
COMING SOON FROM STREBOR BOOKS

SEVEN MONTHS EARLIER

He scrunched up his face and narrowed his eyes. The tiny, protruding purple vein in his forehead began pounding. Slowly, he balled up his fists. "Nah, man," he said between clenched teeth. "I don't believe I heard you properly."

"Stop it," I begged, but it was too late. He didn't even glance in my direction. His eyes were fixated on his mortal enemy, the man who had just told him that I was having his baby.

I grabbed his arm, but he snatched it away, never once looking in my direction. "Please, let me explain!" I yelled.

The pulsating vein on his forehead was joined by another in his right temple. His breathing was heavy, like a wild beast on the hunt. I had never seen him like this before.

He took another step toward his enemy. The two men were standing toe-to-toe. Neither was ready to back down.

"Just go!" I demanded. All he had to do was turn and head for the door, that was it, but it was too late. With his left hand, he snatched up the guy by the collar of his white shirt. He balled up his hand and, with his massive fist, he punched the guy square in the jaw. I heard a crack as blood gushed from the corner of the guy's mouth. He crumpled to the ground and landed with a hard thud. The fight was practically over before it began.

"Oh, God, please!" I screamed. "Stop it! You're going to kill him."

I saw him raise his fist again and down it went, crashing against the side of his face.

"Go!!!" I yelled. "Please!"

The scene may have been chaotic, but for a brief second, he looked up at me and our eyes connected. His eyes glassed over, almost as if an evil force had taken over.

I thought the fight was over when he stumbled backward, but he still had the guy's collar in his grasp, causing the guy to fall back with him. They tussled on the floor for several minutes. The tables had turned; he was now the one on the bottom and the guy was pummeling him in the face with fists of fury.

I grabbed the guy by his shoulders and tried pulling him off. "Stop it!" It was no use. I felt a sharp, burning sensation on my right side. I had been accidentally elbowed in the right side of my gut. Seconds later, his left elbow came back and struck me in the face. The blow didn't quite knock me out, but disoriented, I fell back. I reached up and held on to the wall to steady myself. Through blurred vision, I glanced over in the direction of the two men, who were still wrestling about on the floor. This time he was back on top and pounding the guy with iron fists. Blood was everywhere.

I scrambled over to my purse and rifled through it, looking for my cell. When I looked up again, I could only make out the silhouette of two bodies rolling about on the floor.

When I located my cell, I immediately tried to dial, but my vision was so blurred, I couldn't make out the numbers.

Clumsily, I punched in 9-1-1.

"This is 9-1-1 emergency," the operator said. "What is your emergency?"

"I need help!" I screamed into the phone. "They're going to kill each other."

"Please, ma'am, slow down. I can't understand what you're saying."

"I need help!"

One of the guys was standing over the other while holding a round, light-colored object in his hands. There was a huge crash and pieces of my opaque wedding vase scattered everywhere.

Disoriented and with blood gushing from every orifice on his face, the guy on the floor grabbed a long, sharp sliver of the broken vase. He extended his arm and held out the jagged edge like a sword in a bullfight.

Like a bull, the other guy stood up and charged, right toward the sharpened edge.

My legs buckled from underneath me and I fell to the ground. In the background, I heard the faint sound of the approaching sirens and then everything went black.

Before the night was through, someone would be dead.